THE QUEEN

Kit Scarlett Mysteries
Book Five

Adele Jordan

SAPERE BOOKS

Also in the Kit Scarlett Series
The Gentlewoman Spy
The Royal Assassin
A Spy at Hampton Court
The Lost Highlander

THE TRAITOR QUEEN

Published by Sapere Books.

24 Trafalgar Road, Ilkley, LS29 8HH

saperebooks.com

Copyright © Adele Jordan, 2023

Adele Jordan has asserted her right to be identified as the author of this work.
All rights reserved.

No part of this publication may be reproduced, stored in any retrieval system, or transmitted, in any form, or by any means, electronic, mechanical, photocopying, recording, or otherwise, without the prior written permission of the publishers.
This book is a work of fiction. Names, characters, businesses, organisations, places and events, other than those clearly in the public domain, are either the product of the author's imagination, or are used fictitiously.
Any resemblances to actual persons, living or dead, events or locales are purely coincidental.

ISBN: 978-0-85495-025-6

CHAPTER 1

Chartley, Staffordshire, 1586

"Nothing to be afraid of, eh?" Kit Scarlett huffed and lowered herself into the water. It was shallow in these parts, barely deep enough to be called a babbling brook. Her clothes were soon soaked, the heavy hose and jerkin weighing her down. Taking off her cap and ruffling her short auburn locks, Kit took a deep breath before plunging under the water.

The view of the green riverbank disappeared, along with the reeds and the overhanging oak trees. The sweltering heat of the summer's day vanished too as the cool water lapped over her. Holding onto the bedrock of the river, Kit pulled herself along the brook, keeping her body close to the shingle. She glanced up at the glistening surface, wary of just how far she had to travel before she could take a breath.

The water was an old fear, one she had faced many times now. Though this was still no easy task. Her fingers pulled so much at the shingle that she stirred up the sediment, making her view through the water cloudy.

Once she reached a point in the river where the reeds grew thicker, Kit pushed her head above the water and took a grateful breath. Here she was hidden from the riverbank, but only just. It gave her the perfect view of a large barn on the bank.

Francis Walsingham, spymaster to Queen Elizabeth, had set Kit this commission with one goal in mind: to catch Mary, Queen of Scots committing treason.

"She will have to take the bait first," Kit murmured now, as she peered out from the reeds.

The barn — home to the local brewery — was so isolated that anyone approaching it by road would easily be seen, but not from the river. There were too many reeds for any boat to pass, so no man who walked this land would suspect they'd have a visitor come this way. Kit was safe from discovery, for now. She kept low in the water, feeling the reeds slide against her skin as fish darted past her legs.

"Where are you?" Kit whispered, staring at the barn.

Chartley Brewery was tasked with supplying Chartley Castle with its beer. Kit had already spoken to the brewer.

He strode out of the barn now, scuffing stones beneath his heavy leather boots. He was no great actor, and, uncertain what to do with his arms, he repeatedly folded them then let them hang loose at his sides. Kit sighed deeply, fearing that the brewer could be the one loose link in their chain.

She didn't have to wait long until the visitor arrived. Cloaked in deep red silk, the rider was clearly no ordinary messenger. His coiffed hat was pulled low over his brow and fixed to his temple with a golden cord. When he saw the brewer, he stiffened in his saddle, reining his grey horse to a sharp stop.

"You have the message?" the brewer asked, with no words of greeting.

The rider looked down at the plump brewer with clear disdain. "How can I be certain this will reach her?" The man did not deign to step down from his horse. He kept a good distance between himself and the brewer, apparently fearing what would happen if he came too close.

Kit could smell the scent of hops competing with the river water. The rider clearly smelt the same thing as he pressed a herb-soaked linen to his nose and lifted his chin an inch higher.

"Any letter that has come through me has been seen by her," the brewer said sharply, shifting his arms restlessly once again. "You don't want your message delivered, then fine. I'll take the beer without it." He turned to walk away, back toward the barn.

Angered that he was giving up so easily, Kit veered forward in the reeds. It was her task to keep an eye on the brewer, Mackintosh, and make sure he kept to the plan. At her movement, a fish moved beneath her foot and, startled, she splashed in the water.

The rider looked sharply in her direction and Kit ducked down, masking her body with the reeds. She didn't dare move or look again, in case it gave away her location.

"Are you alone here?" the rider called to the brewer. Judging by the sound of wheels on the track road, Kit guessed he was readying his cart with the barrels of beer.

"I have my workers," the brewer answered in a calm tone.

"And the river?" The rider's voice grew nearer as he edged his horse toward the reeds.

Kit sank further into the water, until her chin was just above the surface. Reaching down, she took hold of one of the two daggers she carried on her belt. Her fingers tightening around the carved hilt, she waited to see if the rider would find her.

"We have some big fish," the brewer said with a chuckle. "I don't have long. Do you want your message sent to her or not?"

"I do." The rider's voice retreated. Kit raised her head enough to peer through the reeds.

The brewer had stopped by the cart and was holding out the palm of his hand, which was worn from years of work. The rider wrinkled his nose as he stared down at it. Reaching into his doublet, he pulled out a letter, which he placed in Mackintosh's hand with some hesitation.

"How will you get it to her?"

"Same as I send them all." Mackintosh turned to the nearest barrel on the cart and reached up. With thick arms, he laid the heavy barrel on its side and stopped it from rolling away with a stone. Taking the wooden cork out of the barrel, he raised it high to reveal that it was hollowed out. The letter was rolled up in a hurry and stuffed into the cork. The cork was then sealed with a lid and returned to the barrel.

Kit shook her head with a smile. The first time she had caught the brewer doing such a thing, he'd quivered in his boots to find her standing behind him, a dagger in her hand. Now, he was working with her and Walsingham's other intelligencers.

Of course, had Walsingham not threatened to take the brewery away from Mackintosh, he might have refused to help them. He was a man who thought of the money in his coffers, and little more.

Mackintosh returned the barrel to its upright position and slid it to stand alongside the others on the cart.

"How do you know?" the rider asked with a quick flick of his hands at the other barrels. "How do you know which one it is in?"

The brewer grunted and took out a small blade from his belt. He carved a small cross on the side of the barrel. "Only me ever sees it."

Kit smiled, knowing it was not the truth. Gilbert Gifford, a double agent who had once been loyal to Mary, Queen of Scots and now worked for Walsingham, had been the first to notice such notches. It hadn't taken many questions to work out what the beer barrels were really being used for.

"She'll get your letter," Mackintosh said and walked around the cart, heading toward the horses.

"And her reply?"

"It could come tomorrow. It could come in a month." Mackintosh smiled as he took his place in the driver's seat of the cart. "From what I've seen, she is in no hurry to answer her letters. You got a name? Somewhere I can find you to let you know when she replies?"

"No," the rider answered sharply. "I will come back myself for her answer." Neglecting to thank the brewer for his part in what could be a treasonous affair, the rider turned his horse and took off at a fast gallop away from the brewery.

Kit pushed back the reeds completely, revealing her face. The brewer looked toward her with an uneasy expression.

"I pray you are right about this," he called to her. "I don't want trouble."

"You found trouble, Mackintosh, when you let their coins grace your palm. Now, go. Deliver your letter." She waved a hand at him to continue on. He grumbled something she couldn't hear and then flicked the reins, the cart setting off along the track.

Despite the cold water making her shiver, Kit didn't hesitate to return the way she had come. Diving once more under the river's surface, she pulled herself along the riverbed, just as she had done before, to prevent any passers-by spotting her. When she reached the place where she had entered the river, she broke through the surface.

A horse nearby whinnied in recognition. Pushing her wet red locks back across her head, she clambered out of the river and ran toward the horse.

"No time to waste, boy," she urged the horse. "We'll have to be fast if we're going to catch up with him." Pulling herself up into the saddle, Kit flicked the reins and took off. They galloped onto a track that was parallel to the one the rider would have taken away from the brewery.

As she reached the main track, Kit halted, turning her head back and forth in the hope of seeing the rider. She caught a glimpse of dark red silk disappearing around an oak tree and urged the horse after him.

Slowing to a trot, Kit prayed the horse would make as little noise as possible, so she would not be discovered, but the man in front didn't once look back. For now, she was safe.

They rode as far as Uttoxeter. When they passed into town, Kit wound a confusing path through the streets, passing other individual riders and carts, so she never once looked like she was following the grandly dressed rider.

Passing an inn in one of the first streets of the town, Kit hesitated for just a moment. She had stayed at that inn during the recent winter with her old spy partner, Iomhar Blackwood and his family whilst on a mission to deliver a letter from Queen Elizabeth of England to Mary, Queen of Scots.

That meeting had not ended the way she had hoped. Mary Stuart had cast her out of the room, with no wish to accept the offer of renewed friendship from her cousin. For her trouble, Kit had been taken by one of Mary Stuart's most loyal supporters, Lord Ruskin, and tossed from a cliff in misplaced revenge for the death of his wife. Had it not been for Iomhar, she might have died that day.

Shivering at the memory, Kit returned her focus to following the rider through the town. Suddenly, he picked up speed. A small group of children who had been playing in the street all jumped back, startled. A man yelled at the rider, saying he should not ride so fast through the town, for it was dangerous.

Kit increased her pace and followed him. It was clear that the rider had realised she was there, for now he glanced back at her, repeatedly. He was so busy looking over his shoulder that he almost knocked a lady down in the street. She barely managed to jump out of his path in time.

Darting over a bridge, he pushed a small man out of the way. The man staggered against the side of the bridge, dangerously close to falling in.

Kit rode on after him, with just as many people shouting at her as the rider in front.

"What do you think you're doing, lad?" the man on the bridge barked after her.

The rider of the grey horse was stretching ahead now. The road had been busy and the buildings densely packed, but suddenly the obstacles began to thin out.

They passed a decrepit church, the old stone building almost collapsing. The rider rode through the graveyard, narrowly missing a mourner dressed in black who had come to pay their respects. Kit followed, but at a safer distance.

"My apologies!" Kit shouted as she passed, giving them a wide berth.

The town's streets fell away, and they met an area of woodland. Where there had been cobbled roads before, there were now dirt tracks that had been scored by years of use from carriages, carts and horses.

"Stop!" Kit called out to the rider up ahead. Her horse would tire soon, and she needed to find out who he was, or at least, who he was reporting to. The rider glanced back, but he didn't slow down. His horse galloped away and then took a sharp turn up a steep bank.

Kit couldn't turn in time and came to an ungainly halt on the track, peering up at where the rider had gone. He'd clearly known about this lesser-trodden path in advance, for it was well hidden. With the rider no longer in sight, Kit hastened to follow, urging her steed up the bank.

It was a steep climb and Kit's horse grunted at the effort, but they eventually came out onto a flat road. Hearing the sound of galloping hooves and harnesses being flicked, Kit turned in the saddle to see a carriage led by four horses charging toward her.

"God's wounds!" she cried, pulling her horse to the side of the track and barely escaping their path. The carriage flew past. A glimpse through the window revealed that her quarry was now inside, and there was another with him. Glancing back along the track at the rider's abandoned horse, Kit spurred her own horse into a gallop.

She tried to keep up with the carriage, but the four horses pulling it had the advantage. They took up most of the road and Kit was forced to ride along the grassy bank at the side of the track, but her horse was tiring fast and she could not draw level with the carriage.

A curtain was pulled back from the gap in the door. Kit turned to it, desperate to see just who was inside, but a vast hat covered the person's face. A hand reached through the window, bearing a pistol.

"No!" Kit cried out in panic. She pulled sharply on the reins of her horse as the shot went off.

Crows took to the air at the noise, cawing loudly as the shot landed in a fir tree, splintering the bark. Kit turned her horse and backed up, letting the carriage escape before the person inside could reload and fire again. She glanced back over her shoulder. There had been something familiar about that pistol and the hand that held it.

"It could be him," Kit murmured to herself as she turned back toward Uttoxeter.

Whoever was sending messages to Mary Stuart at Chartley Castle, they were making use of other men to send the letters, as well as men they had paid off such as Mackintosh. The rider worked for another.

"It could be him," Kit whispered to herself again as she rode away down the road. "It could be Lord Ruskin."

CHAPTER 2

"What does it say?" Kit asked as she sat down by the fire. Thomas Phelippes didn't answer at first. He was bent over in his stool, his small brown eyes dancing across the page that was lit by the firelight. "Phelippes?" she said impatiently, her tone sharp.

Walsingham's man looked up at her and blinked. "I didn't notice you were back."

"Always a pleasure to see you too," Kit said tartly and leaned toward the fire, keen to warm up after her dip in the river. "You're not exactly the most talkative of spies to work with. Any of your other partners ever told you that?"

"No. I do as I'm told by Walsingham. Everything else is just…" He waved a hand in the air, unable to find the right word, and returned his focus to the paper before him.

"Frippery?" she offered, and he nodded. "It is frippery to chase down the man who sent Mary Stuart a letter, is it?"

It was one of the tasks Kit had been given by Walsingham once they had set up the watch on Mary Stuart's communications. Any man seen to be corresponding with her had to be followed, and their identity discovered.

Kit thought of the hand she had seen grasping the pistol out of the carriage window. It was just possible that she had known that hand, that it belonged to Lord Ruskin, but it could just as easily have been her imagination. The Scottish lord was on her mind these days, not just because he had tried to kill her on that clifftop, but because back in London he was the topic of most conversations between the members of the Blackwood family. They spoke of the man who had betrayed and murdered their beloved husband and father constantly.

"Did you get him? The man who sent this?" Phelippes asked.

"No."

"Then to answer your question, yes, it is frippery."

Kit leaned her head on the stone hearth and sighed deeply. Phelippes was no great friend to her. They'd frequently argued in the past when they had come across one another, for they were both considered fine codebreakers for Walsingham.

"I don't want to argue with you today," Phelippes said eventually as he made notes, decoding the letter.

"At least an argument would be a conversation." Kit's words were met with a glower from Phelippes, who scratched the scruffy beard on his chin. He returned his focus to the letter, disregarding her. She would have infinitely rather worked with her last spy partner, but at the moment, she was one of the few who knew he was still alive. "I miss him," she whispered to herself, so quietly that Phelippes did not hear her.

Iomhar was at his house in London with his mother and siblings. They were all hiding there, far away from Scotland and, hopefully, they were safe from the clutches of Lord Ruskin. He'd already attempted to see Iomhar dead once, and with the rest of the family at risk, he had moved them all to the relative safety of the capital.

Kit tried to shift Iomhar from her mind. He had occupied her thoughts a lot as of late, ever since she had helped him escape from Urquhart Castle, where he had been imprisoned for a year. She raised a hand to the neck of her doublet and pulled out the gold necklace he had given her to wear, clutching the pendant — a Celtic shield knot said to protect the wearer. Quickly tucking it away again beneath her shirt, she shifted her focus back to Phelippes and the letter he was decoding.

"Any ideas?" she asked.

"A few. We're lucky that brewer didn't drop this one in the beer like he did the last." Phelippes cursed under his breath, making it clear what he thought of Mackintosh.

Shortly after the brewer had been given the letter by the red-cloaked rider, he had driven the cart to their agreed meeting point, where Phelippes had been waiting. It was a small, cobbled house outside Uttoxeter, well hidden from the roads and on the edge of the Chartley Castle estate. Once it had been decoded by Phelippes, it would be sent on to its original recipient at Chartley Castle, Mary Stuart.

"There." Phelippes drew a line under a fresh piece of paper. "Oh..." He slumped down as he read the letter in full.

"Phelippes? What does it say?" Standing up from her place at the hearth, Kit reached for the letter.

It was signed by an Anthony Babington.

"Babington? Who is he?" Kit asked, her voice quiet.

"Derbyshire gentry," Phelippes explained with a wave of his hand. "Walsingham calls him a recusant."

Kit read the letter with growing shock. It spelled out a plot to put Mary on the throne of England. It was clear from the letter that Babington was a fierce Catholic. He viewed Queen Elizabeth as a heretic leader, and one that could legitimately be assassinated, as the Pope had excommunicated her.

Reading his words sent a shiver down Kit's spine, despite the warmth of the fire in the room.

Myself with ten gentlemen and a hundred of our followers will undertake the delivery of your royal person from the hands of your enemies. For the dispatch of the usurper, from the obedience of whom we are by the excommunication of her made free, there be six noble gentlemen, all my private friends, who for the zeal they bear to the Catholic cause and your Majesty's service will undertake that tragical execution.

"He speaks as if religious zeal makes murder forgivable," said Kit. Phelippes remained silent. Had Iomhar been there, his reaction would have been a lot stronger than that of a man who just tapped his fingers on the table, lifted a quill, then replaced it. Phelippes was as mild-mannered as a mouse.

Babington presented a plot to Mary that would see her on the throne of England. By assassinating Elizabeth and encouraging a long-term occupation by Spanish and French forces, Babington hoped to build a stronger England with Mary as their leader.

"He wishes to make us a puppet state," Kit said sharply.

"Hmm." Phelippes still had little to add.

"Is this not enough?" she asked, holding the letter high. "There is another plot. This is the proof of it. Is it not enough to take this to Walsingham as it is? Babington would be arrested. His co-conspirators' names I do not doubt Walsingham would prise from him."

"Yet it is not enough proof against Mary Stuart, is it?"

Kit thought back to the lady she had met in the winter. Tall, with a formidable presence, Mary Stuart could leave no one in doubt of what she thought of her own position. That same need for reverence was matched by her disregard for others. She had ordered Lord Ruskin to kill Kit as if she were nothing more than a fly dancing around her marchpane.

"Walsingham will need more if he is to accuse her of treason," Kit said.

Phelippes folded up the original letter then replaced the red wax seal he had initially broken by simply melting the wax and letting it drip off. He burnt a fresh red wax stick, ready to seal the letter again.

"Wait." Kit held out a hand to stop him.

"What for?"

When he made no effort to pause his movements, she took his wrist and pulled his hand away from the paper, so the wax dropped on the floor between them. He glared at her.

"What are you doing?"

"We both wish for this to be over, yes? For Walsingham to at last have proof that Mary Stuart is involved in a plot against the queen." She didn't need to wait for his answer, for he was already nodding. "Then we goad her." She released Phelippes' wrist.

"How?"

"She may not reply to this letter." Kit waved the translation in the air. "She could easily let Babington's plot go ahead without her confirmation. Let's add something to it."

"Add what? How?"

"Are you not an expert forger as well as a codebreaker?" Kit asked with a smile. "What if Babington were to ask for Mary's encouragement?"

"Perhaps." Despite his uncertain words, Phelippes was already opening the original letter again. Using the code he had deciphered, he added a single line to the letter that requested Mary's approval of the plot, should she wish for her escape.

I most humbly beseech your approval. My friends and I will then seek to free you from your prison.

"Do you think she will respond?" asked Phelippes.

"We have to hope she will." Kit folded the letter and returned it to the table.

As Phelippes prepared the red wax seal, ready to fix it in place once again, Kit left the room. She walked out of the cottage and into the grounds. Beside a narrow lane stood Mackintosh. His cart of beer barrels was behind him, with jackdaws landing on the edge, clearly curious about his cargo and the strong stench of ale. He waited patiently for the return of the letter, murmuring to the horses beside him.

"How long, ma'am?" the brewer called to her.

"Until what?" she asked.

"Until she's taken to the Tower. Can't be long now." Mackintosh shook his head, causing his heavy jowls to tremble. "Not with all these letters passing back and forth."

"We'll see." Kit folded her arms, waiting for Phelippes to be done with the letter.

That morning she had received another letter from Walsingham. He was growing impatient at their lack of progress. He wanted answers and longed to see Mary Stuart's arrest warrant.

"Here it is." Phelippes appeared beside Kit. He was much shorter and crept around her to deliver the letter into Mackintosh's hand. Mackintosh returned the letter to the trick cork, then placed it in the barrel. They stepped back and waited for him to ride away. Once he was gone, Kit held up a hand to Phelippes, preventing him from going back inside just yet.

"Walsingham wrote today. He's tired of delays," she said. "He's restless."

"For the queen's sake or his own?" Phelippes asked, and Kit managed a smile.

"Both, I think." The last few months had not been easy on Walsingham. Not only did he feel guilt, a debt to the queen that he had to pay by keeping her safe, but his health was worsening with every day that passed and it soured his mood further.

"When we do see him, I pray we have good news," Phelippes said with a sigh and stepped into the cottage.

"As do I." Kit thought of the news she had withheld from Walsingham. Iomhar had begged her not to tell the spymaster he was alive and back in London just yet. The longer the deception went on, the more the guilt weighed on Kit.

A few months ago she'd had no qualms about keeping the secret, for she'd felt Walsingham had betrayed her by not telling her where he had sent Iomhar. Now, he was ageing, and his health was deteriorating, and she was concealing important information from the man who considered himself her guardian.

"He must be told soon," she resolved quietly.

CHAPTER 3

"He's here." Kit stepped back from the cottage window and hurried to the door, flinging it open. It had only been a few days, but now Mackintosh had returned. He was sweating profusely in the sweltering heat, wiping his brow as he stopped his cart and jumped down.

"Well?" she called to him.

The brewer nodded and walked around the cart, reaching for one of the barrels on the back.

"Phelippes?" Kit called to the codebreaker. She strode out of the cottage as Phelippes appeared in the doorway and peered out into the bright sunshine.

She helped Mackintosh pull a barrel down from the back of the cart and roll it onto its side. They levered out the wooden cork before Mackintosh popped the lid. Inside was a curled-up piece of white paper. Kit took it from the brewer's fingers, noting the red wax seal. She expected it to be blank, in an effort to hide the sender, but it seemed Mary Stuart had been so certain that her message was secret, she had allowed the seal to be marked. It bore the symbol of two unicorns, facing one another.

Kit smiled at the sight of it. "It's from her," she called to Phelippes in the doorway, who showed no sign of stepping out into the heat. Kit took the letter to the codebreaker, who snatched it from her fingers and hurried indoors.

Despite the bright sunshine, the cottage had so few windows that there was little light inside. Phelippes moved to the nearest window and flattened out the paper against the pane.

Kit restlessly tapped the toe of her boot as she watched Phelippes work. He drew a copy of the unicorns in the seal first, so he could replicate it later, then took a candle and melted the wax, tipping the letter so that it dripped into a small brass bowl. When it was thin enough, he unfurled the paper. Applying the same code he had used to decipher Babington's letter, Phelippes decoded this one much faster.

Kit moved to his shoulder, craning her neck for a closer look. The smell of burning wax hung in the air, mixed with ink. She wrinkled her nose at the scent as she read the message that emerged.

It was a long letter. Mary Stuart expressed her gratitude to Babington and his friends in their bid to free her from imprisonment, and she approved the assassination of her cousin, Queen Elizabeth.

A hard knot formed in Kit's stomach.

"It's the proof Walsingham has been after," she whispered. "The very words."

"It is not enough," Phelippes muttered, continuing to decode the letter. With each deciphered line, the heavy feeling in Kit's stomach grew. Mary Stuart encouraged Babington to befriend the Puritans, for that way he would then garner the support of both the Catholics and Protestants, which would be needed after Elizabeth's death in order to make Mary the Queen of England.

"It is enough!" Kit hissed. "What more do you need?"

Phelippes stepped back from the window and sighed, wiping a hand across his sweaty brow. "We need the names of the conspirators. There's no guarantee that Babington would give them up."

"Mary does not know them." Kit shook her head. "Babington came to Mary with the plot to assassinate Elizabeth. That is what we know."

"We still need more," Phelippes insisted.

Kit turned away and marched across the cottage, her boots thudding upon the flagstone floor. She had to duck under low timber beams to avoid hitting her head, and only narrowly missed one as an idea occurred to her. She turned back to Phelippes.

"What if Mary were to ask for the conspirators' names?"

At Phelippes' frown, Kit continued.

"You added a line to Babington's letter, did you not? Why not do the same now? Add another part to the letter."

"Make Mary Stuart ask for the names of those involved in the plot, so that she may know who she will be indebted to." Phelippes' thin lips curled into a smile. "It's bold, a risk. It might not work."

"Do you doubt your forgery skills, Phelippes?"

"Mary Stuart's writing is much more difficult to copy. I shall write a new version, so they will detect no difference between her lettering and my own. It will take time."

"Then use the time." She waved a hand at him, urging him to begin. "If we can get a letter to Babington, asking for those names, then he may well reply with the evidence that we need."

"It is worth a try." Phelippes sat down at the small table and set to work composing a new letter. He worked slowly, painstakingly redrawing every part of the code, with all its symbols and figures, on a clean sheet of parchment. When he came to the end, he and Kit composed a fresh paragraph.

I would be glad to know the names and qualities of the six gentlemen which are to accomplish the assignment, for it may be, I shall be able upon knowledge of the parties to give you some further advice necessary to be followed therein; and even so do I wish to be made acquainted with the names of all such principal persons, as also from time to time particularly how you proceed, and as soon as you may, for the same purpose who be already and how far every one privy hereunto.

Kit stepped back from the parchment and watched as Phelippes sealed it. He dripped fresh wax onto the folded letter and then carved the shapes of the two unicorns with a small knife. As he worked, the blade scattered red flecks across the table.

"There it is." Phelippes held the letter up when he was done. "I pray you are right about this, Kit."

She took the letter from him and returned it to Mackintosh.

Kit urged her horse into a gallop as she entered London. It had been a day since she had left the Chartley Castle estate, and she couldn't afford to lose any more time. Tucked into the pocket of her doublet were two letters. One was the fateful letter Mary herself had signed, betraying her treason. The other was Babington's reply. Just as she had hoped, he'd fallen for the trap Phelippes had set. He had provided Mary with the details of all those involved in the plot, only she would never receive that letter.

Night was growing thick over the city. Lanterns and candles were pressed to the windows, like fallen stars scattered through the street. At times they did little to aid her progress, merely offering a soft glow on cobbled roads or dirt tracks marred by cart wheels. As she galloped past one of the nightwatchmen, he called out, trying to stop her.

"You're out too late, sir!" he bellowed, mistaking her for a man in her hose and doublet, with her black hat pulled low and a deep red cloak wrapped around her body. "You'll miss the night bell."

"I'll make it home!" she called, deepening her voice to deceive him, though she had no intention of heading home. There was another she had to see.

The horse abided by her wishes, darting down streets and narrow lanes that were barely wide enough for them to fit through. A young couple, out late together, were spooked by her arrival and darted into a nearby doorway. A dog yelped and ran away too, fearful of being caught under the horse's hooves.

Kit didn't once let up her pace, for she couldn't afford to do so. The sooner Walsingham and the privy council read the letters, the safer Queen Elizabeth would be.

When she reached Seething Lane, Kit slowed her pace at last. Lifting her head, she passed under the archway that led into the courtyard in front of the spymaster's building. It was even darker here — there was just one lonely lantern that appeared to have been abandoned in the middle of the square casting an orange glow into the dark corners of the street.

Kit pulled the horse to a halt. The animal complained with short snorts until she patted his neck, calming him. Her eyes darted from the single lantern to the cobbles around it. There was no sign of the person who had left the lantern.

"Something is wrong," Kit whispered to herself. Slowly, she stepped down from the saddle, trying to make as little noise as possible. The horse hung his nose down to the cobbles, tired after their long ride, and she gently patted his neck again. She then reached for the lantern in the middle of the courtyard. The black iron case was marred by years of use and its edges had been knocked. Kit took hold of the handle and lifted it high, using the light to look around the courtyard.

Empty. Not a soul or shadow moved in the corners.

"Who left this here?" Kit murmured, fixing her gaze on the lantern. The candle inside still had plenty of tallow wax left. Whoever had left it behind clearly intended to return and collect it.

She returned the lantern to its place, her uneasiness growing. She jumped as her horse snorted. She waved a hand, pleading with him to be silent. Slowly, she approached the hidden door of Walsingham's house. She raised a hand to knock on the wood, hoping the housekeeper, Doris, would let her in, when her hand froze in mid-air.

The door was ajar, the false plaster wall not quite flush with the timber surrounds. Curling her gloved fingers around the edge of the door, Kit pushed it open and poked her head through. Resisting the temptation to call out Doris's name, she stepped inside.

The usual candles were lit, though some had burned down quite low. Those fastened to the corridor wall in sconces had bold flames, and Kit could see a candle through the doorway to the kitchen resting on the table, wax dripping onto the plain brass holder. It had been discarded amongst the unwashed supper pots. Kit stepped closer to the door of the kitchen, turning her head back and forth for any sign of Doris.

There was no one inside, not even the maid that Doris had been having so much trouble with as of late, though there were signs that someone had been there. A bucket of water stood at the side of the kitchen, still clean, ready for washing the pewter trenchers.

"Doris?" Kit whispered into the darkness.

A muffled sound came from deep inside the house. Kit jerked back her head, listening hard. Floorboards creaked overhead, and the sound came again — a woman's voice, protesting, though Kit could not discern the words.

Grasping one of the daggers from her belt, Kit held it at her side, the blade pointed a little forward. She crept along the corridor, inching closer to the stairs that led up to Walsingham's rooms.

She had played in this old house as a child, and had learned how to sneak around without drawing Walsingham's attention. She knew which floorboards and which stairs creaked, and therefore which to avoid. She mapped that path now, moving slowly on the balls of her feet, not wishing to put the heels of her boots down and draw attention to her presence.

As she reached the top of the stairs, the light grew dimmer, for there were less candles on this landing. There was just one pinned to the wall outside of the closed door leading to Walsingham's study. Kit put her head against the door, straining to hear some of what was going on inside.

Doris's voice was as plain as day, pleading with someone.

"I beg you, do not do this. He is a good man. Do not hurt him!" The sound of a slap followed, and the housekeeper cried out.

Kit flinched, fearing someone had hurt Doris.

"Quiet. Ye will not make another sound. Understood?" The voice bore a strong Scottish accent. Kit knew she had heard that voice before, but her heart was thumping too hard for her to immediately place it.

"Goodbye, old man."

The simple words had Kit launching herself at the door. She thrust it open and leapt into the room. Her eyes quickly took in the scene in the dim candlelight.

Doris was tied to the mantelpiece, hunkered down on her knees with her wrists bound together. There were tears on the old woman's wrinkled cheeks. Across the room, Walsingham was tied to his chair, which had been dragged out in front of his desk and the shelves of scrolls that stood behind it.

The man standing before Walsingham was cloaked in black, his face hidden by a dark cloth that covered the lower half. He held a basilard high in the air, which glinted in the candlelight as it hovered over Walsingham's temple.

CHAPTER 4

The crash of the door bouncing off the adjoining wall was enough to make the assassin freeze. He jerked his chin toward Kit, the eyes above the mask as black as night. His hand froze in the air as it clutched the basilard.

"Kit." Walsingham murmured her name. The word angered the man. He bolted forward, no longer interested in Walsingham, but aiming for Kit.

She lashed out with her foot and kicked a nearby Savonarola chair. The wide seat tipped over, knocking into the assassin's knees and causing him to stumble. The valuable few seconds gave Kit enough time to dart to Doris's side. She cut through the rope that bound the housekeeper's wrists with her dagger before pushing the old woman behind her, backing up across the room.

"Who is he?" Kit called to Walsingham.

"An assassin! What more do you need, Kit?" Walsingham barked, pulling at the ropes that bound him to the chair and groaning in pain. No doubt the back problems from which he suffered were causing him agony at this moment.

"How about a name?" Kit growled.

"He knocked on the door, as if he were any other visitor," Doris whispered in panic behind her, as they collided with the wall.

The assassin picked up the chair and snapped off one of the legs. Now he had two weapons. In his right hand he clutched the basilard, and in his left he wielded the chair leg as a club. Angling his face toward Kit, he strode forward. There was no mistaking his intent.

"Time to part, Doris." Kit thrust the housekeeper toward the open door and leapt aside just as the assassin was about to bring the club down on her head. She avoided the blow, but another one was quickly coming. Bringing up the basilard, he aimed for her chest, but she knocked his hand away with her dagger, slicing the blade across his knuckles. He cried out in pain, the sound muffled slightly by the black cloth over his mouth.

Doris hastened through the doorway and down the stairs.

"Call the constable, the nightwatchmen, anyone!" Kit shouted after her. Doris nodded as she clung to the banister with her bony hands.

The assassin shifted his focus to the doorway, through which Doris had left. Clearly fearful of being caught, he moved toward it, intent on going after her. Kit blocked his path.

"Not another step," she warned. Standing so close to the assassin, she was certain she had seen him before. It wasn't only his voice she recognised, but those eyes too. "It can't be," she muttered. Yet she had no further time to debate who she thought the man was.

He struck out at her with the club. She dodged the blow, then captured his wrist under her arm and applied pressure, bending his wrist back at an unnatural angle. The bone snapped audibly, and he dropped the wooden chair leg, flicking back his head as he grunted in pain.

She released his hand as he brought down the basilard, aiming it toward her chest. As before, she knocked it away, but was unprepared for his next action. He hurled the basilard toward her.

"Kit!" Walsingham cried out. She barely managed to move out of the way in time, flattening herself to the wall as the basilard embedded itself into the doorframe beside her. It wobbled, the metal ringing in the air. The blade was an inch from Kit's eye.

She now had the upper hand. The assassin had no weapon, and she blocked his path to the door. Smiling, she advanced on him. He backed up, his black boots moving fast. He then turned and ran across the room, heading straight for Walsingham.

Reaching for the spymaster, he called out, "Goodbye, Walsingham!"

"No!" Kit ran forward, but she was not fast enough. The man placed one hand on Walsingham's temple, the other at the back of his neck, intending to break it.

Kit copied the assassin's own action and tossed her dagger through the air. The assassin tipped his body weight to the side, to avoid being struck, and took Walsingham with him, tipping over the chair.

Kit ran forward and slid her body across the floor, just as Walsingham came down on top of her.

"Argh!" She grunted at the pain of the heavy weight. Walsingham had fallen on her legs, but the act had narrowly prevented him from hitting his temple on the floor. He lay limply in the chair, staring at her with wide eyes.

A shadow moved behind him. The assassin was running.

"Stop!" Kit called out to him, though it was futile. She tried to shift Walsingham from her legs.

"I cannot move, Kit," he protested. She reached forward and shifted the chair, heaving him around to flick him onto his back. Her muscles objected at the strain, but it worked to release her legs.

There was no time to speak as Kit ran from the room, following the path the assassin had taken. He was already far ahead of her, darting down the stairs. She jumped over the

31

banister to get ahead. It was bold, and she did it without thinking of the great distance she was leaping down. But she had a soft landing, for she fell on the masked man.

Together they clattered to the bottom of the stairs, landing in an undignified heap. The man moved to his knees, trying to flee as Kit reached up and tore the cloth from his face.

"You!" Despite the gloom, she could plainly see his face. It was the same face that had stared at her in York in the winter, the one that had been sent to hunt her down by Lord Ruskin.

Stunned, Kit stared at him for a beat too long. He thrust an elbow into her stomach, winding her. She rolled onto her back, gasping to catch her breath. The sound of his running footsteps echoed along the corridor. She scrambled to her feet, but she was too far behind. She loped to the doorway, clutching her stomach and the fresh bruise she now had.

In the courtyard, the assassin snatched up the lantern before pulling himself into the saddle of Kit's horse. The candlelight lit up Doris's panic-stricken face, and as he galloped off, he knocked her to the ground.

"Doris!" Kit cried out, running toward her. Taking the old lady's hands, she pulled Doris to her feet and supported her weight. "Are you hurt?"

"I pray not. These old bones of mine are brittle enough as it is." The housekeeper clung tight to Kit, her bottom lip trembling. "Merely bruised, Kitty. Merely bruised."

"Let's get you inside."

"But the man…" Doris waved a bony hand in the direction the man had gone. "Kitty, he's gone."

"For now," Kit murmured. "But I have no doubt we will meet again. Come on, let's get you inside."

Around the courtyard there was a commotion. People thrust their heads out of windows, asking what all the noise and shouting was about. Kit didn't answer them. By now, the assassin would be far away on her horse. The nightwatchmen worked on foot and could not pursue a man like him easily. They would not catch him tonight.

Kit led Doris inside and took her into the kitchen.

"Where's your maid?" Kit asked.

"She has the night off." Doris's hands trembled.

Kit stirred the flames in the grate to life, then put a pot of water on the fire. "I'll make you something to drink. Rest yourself here. I must go and release Walsingham from his bindings." She made to leave, but the old woman lifted her hand and caught her palm.

"Thank God for you, Kitty. Thank God."

"There's no need to thank me," Kit replied, scarcely daring to imagine how the night could have ended had she not been there in time. She squeezed Doris's fingers and then released them, leaving the woman with wet eyes and trembling hands.

In the hallway, Kit locked the door built into the wall and fastened it tight by pushing one of her daggers between the doorframe and the lock. No one else would be able to barge their way in that night. Hurrying up the stairs, she returned to Walsingham's room, where she found him wriggling against his bindings, desperate to escape.

"Get me out of this," he pleaded. "I'm in such pain." His eyes repeatedly darted to the door.

"The assassin is gone," Kit said as she knelt down and released him. "Doris is shaken, but not hurt. What of you?"

Walsingham turned to her, his entire body trembling. "I nearly died! He had that knife, and was ready to plunge it into me." He paled, his gaunt cheeks seeming hollower than normal. "What did he want?"

"He wanted to end your operations." Kit righted the chair and guided him into it, treating him like a child rather than one of the most powerful men in England. "Walsingham? Walsingham, look at me." He was staring past her, breathing fast and hard. "How did he know about your lodgings here? Few people know of it."

"What do you mean? Who was that?" the spymaster asked, his words running into one another.

"Graham Fraser." The words fell uneasily from Kit's lips. Turning her back on Walsingham, she began to tidy the room. She took the rope that had tied Doris's wrists together and piled it with the rope that had bound Walsingham. Then she took hold of the basilard, which was still embedded in the doorframe. "We have met him more than once before."

She had first seen Graham Fraser in a back street of London, passing letters between Mary Stuart's supporters. His brother had been arrested for being part of such a plot to put Mary on the throne. She had seen him again last year in York, when he had tried to kill her on the orders of Lord Ruskin. The last time she had seen him was on that clifftop where Lord Ruskin had tried to do the deed himself.

"They want the end of us — the end of me," Walsingham mumbled in a rush. He leaned forward, resting his elbows on his knees and holding his head in his hands. The once formidable man was a shadow of his former self. His grey hair matched his grey clothes, and the pallor of his skin. It was as if he was fading with age. "Kill me and they think they can end our espionage. Pff! Ridiculous. If I was to go tomorrow, it would be Lord Burghley's task to work out the details of what I do. He would do it easily enough."

Kit was not so convinced. As Lord Treasurer and Chief Advisor to the queen, Lord Burghley certainly kept an eye on the spy network, and was a part of it, but she didn't know any other man who knew as much about it as Walsingham did. If Lord Ruskin and his co-conspirators, along with Fraser, wished to help clear the path for Babington's plot to put Mary Stuart on the throne, then making sure Walsingham didn't interfere would certainly be a good way to begin their task.

Kit walked toward the fireplace and laid the basilard on the mantelpiece. There were no identifying marks, nothing to ascertain who the dagger belonged to. It had a long blade with a wooden handle, but all she could discern from it was that the weapon had been recently sharpened. It was lethal.

"I need to change lodgings at once." Walsingham stood and returned to his usual place behind the desk. He appeared to have regained some of his composure and was no longer trembling. "I won't have them coming after me again."

"We'll see," Kit murmured. "I have a feeling that they'll find a way to discover where you are, whether it's here or anywhere else, even your grand home in Richmond."

Walsingham cursed at her words and sank down into another chair. This one creaked so loudly beneath him that she thought it was a wonder it didn't snap.

"Why are you here, Kit?" he asked abruptly. "I thought I told you not to return from Chartley until you had what we need. I cannot keep the queen safe until we are certain of Mary Stuart's guilt."

"You could have just thanked me for rescuing you," Kit said wryly.

"Kit!"

She reached into her doublet and pulled out the two letters. Crossing to Walsingham's desk, she laid them down in front of him. He stared at them.

"I have what you asked for," Kit whispered. "You have Mary's own words in that letter, confessing her wish for a certain Thomas Babington to go ahead with a plot to kill Queen Elizabeth, and to encourage an invasion from the Spanish and the French." She paused. Walsingham had become quite still, his expression unreadable. "She took three days to reply, but she encourages Babington to go ahead with the plot. This is her own letter —" Kit gestured to the documents on the desk — "along with a copy of Babington's original letter and the reply that came with it. Phelippes copied Mary's correspondence and added a short addendum. He asked for the names of the conspirators in her name."

Walsingham snatched up the letters. He shifted between them, barely scanning one before he was onto the next. He even waved Kit away so he could read them in peace.

She retreated downstairs to check on Doris. She made the housekeeper a hot drink infused with spices, said to calm the spirit and any excess yellow bile, for a nasty shock was sure to result in an imbalance of the humours. The scent of cloves filled the air as Kit returned upstairs. She took a small cup with her and a second one for Walsingham, though when she placed it down beside him, he ignored it.

When he finally sat back, a muscle twitched in his jaw.

"This is what we have been waiting for!" he said eventually, his excitement betrayed. He thrust a fist down onto the desktop and then moved to his feet. Kit could have sworn he had grown an inch, for he stood taller with his back straight. "We have what we need to urge the queen to sign Mary's death warrant. It must happen. Tomorrow, Kit, tomorrow we will see the queen. You must be there. You must see her with me."

"As you wish," said Kit. "You are not done with me on this commission, then?"

"Far from it."

Kit peered at him over the rim of her cup, taking in the scent of orange and cloves. He stared back at her, that gaze unyielding.

"The path between accusing Mary Stuart and seeing her walk to her death will not be an easy one, Kit. Our commission to keep the Queen of England safe from her cousin — it truly begins now."

CHAPTER 5

"It's time to come out of hiding." Kit shrugged off her cloak and her hat. Rolling up the sleeves of her shirt, she pulled open the tight collar of her waistcoated jerkin, trying to free some of the heat from her skin, and turned to face Iomhar.

He stared at her from his seat beside the unlit fireplace. In his hand was a goblet of clove-scented wine. If Kit listened hard, she could hear the voices of his family elsewhere in his London house. The dulcet tones of his mother Moira, Lady Ross, carried from a distant room. She was talking to her two daughters, Abigail and Rhona, whose voices were slightly shriller.

Iomhar said nothing, but lifted his goblet of wine to his lips and took a sip.

"You and I have had this argument before," Kit said tiredly, undoing the last lace around her neck to loosen the doublet completely. A breath of cool air passed through the open window, softening the heat of the summer night.

"Aye, and we will have it again, it seems." Iomhar sat forward in his chair, his features no longer in shadow.

Her former spy partner was much recovered from his year-long imprisonment in Urquhart Castle, from which Kit had rescued him the previous winter. His face was no longer gaunt and the black beard on his chin was not as wild. Thanks to the administrations of both his mother and his cook, Elspeth, Iomhar's figure was not so thin, and he had regained the strength he'd had before. Yet there were scars upon his skin, in addition to the two on his cheek that he'd earned from Lord

Ruskin's sword. They marked the torture he had faced in the castle's dungeon.

"Ye ken I have nay wish to come out of hiding." Iomhar shook his head. "If Walsingham cannot even find out that I am alive and living in his own city, then he's not quite the excellent spy I thought he was."

"He's the queen's spymaster."

"Aye, it's the same thing," Iomhar protested and sat back again. "I cannot come out of hiding, Kit."

"You must." She perched on the edge of a table, pausing as she heard the voices of the Blackwood family growing louder. "Something is wrong."

"My sisters are restless, my mother too," Iomhar agreed slowly. "We have received a letter to say the house in Scotland is being watched, constantly. The staff do not feel safe. Mother intends to write to them and send them home." He shook his head sadly.

"You think Lord Ruskin and his men are watching the house?"

"Who else would it be, after our last meeting with him?"

The blunt question made Kit shift uncomfortably on the table. If Lord Ruskin had had his way, Iomhar would have still been locked in a dungeon, and she would have lain at the bottom of the cliff he'd pushed her from.

"Mother longs for home," Iomhar said now, his voice deep. "Nay, she may not say it, but I can see it. It's plain to read on her face."

"I know." Kit had seen it often enough these last few months. When they had returned to Iomhar's house in London, she had attempted to move back to her own attic lodgings in Vine Street, but Iomhar had refused to let it happen. Her rooms had been ransacked not long ago, and he argued she could easily have been attacked had she been there at the time. In the end, she'd given in to his request to remain at his house, but she claimed she'd only done so for a quiet life.

The truth was she had done it for another reason entirely. After spending a year apart from Iomhar, she was comforted by his presence and did not wish to be apart from him again so soon.

"There is something you must know." Kit told Iomhar about the letters that Mary Stuart had sent and the attack that evening on Walsingham. To her surprise, Iomhar chuckled.

"You find it amusing to hear that Walsingham nearly lost his life?" she asked.

"In the name of the wee man, what do ye think of me?" he asked, still laughing as he sipped his wine.

"I hoped you had a little more honour in you than that."

"So do I," he protested with a smile. "Maybe I just find it amusing to think that Walsingham now knows what it's like to fear for your life." The smile disappeared and a darkness returned to his gaze; a look Kit had often seen since Iomhar had escaped the dungeons of Urquhart Castle. She didn't doubt he was thinking of what he had suffered there.

"Iomhar, you need to come out of hiding," she pleaded. "Tell Walsingham you are alive and begin your work again."

"What for? So I can help ye protect that man? Pah! I will not do that, Kit. Ye may look at the man as a father to ye —"

"I do not!" She matched his tone in firmness.

"Well, a guardian of sorts, then. Ye certainly trust him more than I do."

"I'm not sure how much that trust stretches anymore," she grumbled. There were many things she could lay at Walsingham's door. She had been furious when he had refused to tell her where Iomhar had gone when he'd left London the previous year, and there was still a lingering suspicion... "Remember what our informer said, in Northumberland? There is a spy who works for Mary Stuart on the privy council."

"The Rose." Iomhar repeated the codename they'd learned.

"Were you not the one who said that could be Walsingham himself?"

"I thought it possible. Ye did not, though, did ye?"

"Maybe I do not know what to think anymore." Kit shook her head. For some time there had been a seed of doubt growing in her mind, but it wasn't one she wished to sustain. Walsingham was still the man that had raised her, and, if her earliest memory was true, then he was also the man who had prevented her from drowning when she was little more than a baby. He had pulled her from the water and saved her life.

"If Walsingham works for Mary Stuart, then why would one of her supporters try to kill him this evening?"

"Aye, that does not make sense." Iomhar lifted his goblet and took a sip of wine. "There's something ye should know too, since ye have been gallivanting around Chartley with that fool of a man, Phelippes."

"Ah! You do not like the man?" Kit teased, folding her arms.

"He is hardly your favourite person either, is he?" Iomhar retorted, casting his eyes to the ceiling, apparently pleading with the heavens for patience.

"He's a good codebreaker," Kit said reluctantly. As much as she wished to praise her own ability, after seeing Phelippes at work she had to admit that he had a skill she did not possess. "Maybe he has proved himself useful now."

"Ye sound as if ye admire him." Iomhar sat forward in his chair abruptly, his spine stiff.

"Jealous?" Kit asked playfully, watching as Iomhar smiled at her before his face turned serious again.

"What's that?" he asked.

Iomhar heard the sound before she did. She was too busy staring at him, enjoying goading him about Phelippes.

There was another heavy knock at the door and a voice from outside.

Iomhar was on his feet as Kit leapt off the table. They both hurried out of the room and ran for the front door. Kit snatched up a candle and held it high in the air.

"Who's out there?" Iomhar called darkly.

"Ye must make your visitors quake in their boots," a voice replied from the other side. "Ye going to let me in or not?"

Kit exchanged an easy smile with Iomhar as he opened the door wide so that his younger brother Niall could step inside. He used his brown cloth hat to wipe his brow free of sweat as Iomhar closed the door behind him.

"Hard day?" Iomhar teased. "Nice to see ye working up a sweat for a change."

"This from the man who hides in his own home, in case his employer realises he's still alive."

"I'd like to see what ye would do after spending months in Urquhart Castle."

"I'd do better," Niall argued.

"Would ye? Ye fell in the well on the estate when ye were ten and hid in your room for a week."

"It was not a week. It was six days."

"Aye, that makes the world of difference," Iomhar mocked.

Kit cleared her throat and they broke off their argument. She had noticed over the last few months that the easy laughter that had always been between the two brothers was becoming strained. They had spent too long under the same roof, talking of the same things, over and over again. "Where have you been?" Kit asked Niall.

"Did Iomhar not tell ye?" Niall raised his eyebrows. "I've been following the man that was watching the house today."

"What man?" Kit turned to Iomhar as they all walked back into the room. When Niall took Iomhar's seat and his goblet of wine too, Iomhar perched beside Kit on the table and poured them out two fresh cups. "Who was this man?"

"He was watching the house from the shadows across the street." Iomhar pointed to the nearest window with his goblet. "I went out to talk to him and he scarpered, as if hounds were at his heels. Niall ran after him."

"Followed him as far as the Thames and the wherry men," Niall went on. "Paid my toll to cross, but by the time I had got to the other side, he'd gone." He shook his head and sighed, looking down into his wine. "I have a fair guess who it was, though."

"One of Lord Ruskin's men," Kit surmised. It took no great leap of the imagination. Lord Ruskin feared retribution from Iomhar's family now they knew it was he who had murdered their father, on Mary Stuart's orders. He wanted them isolated and watched until they were no longer a threat to him. "If Graham Fraser is in London, then I don't see why Lord Ruskin wouldn't be as well."

"Aye, it's possible," Iomhar growled.

"You wish to find him?" Kit turned and fixed Iomhar with a stern glare. "You wish to end this battle between you so your family can go home to the lives they miss?"

"Kit, of course I wish it to end. Nothing would please me more than to see Lord Ruskin standing in a court to face punishment for his crimes and what he did to our father, but it isn't that easy, is it? Even if Niall and I could find him tomorrow, he would escape, like sand through our fingers. He's done it many times before."

Niall shook his head and downed what was left in his goblet. "Any more of this wine?"

Iomhar purposefully filled up Kit's and his own glass, so there was none left for his brother.

"Oi!"

"Ye stole my seat," Iomhar said, by way of explanation.

Niall sighed deeply and tipped his head back in the chair. "Ye are right, Kit. We do need to find a way home again. This is not what our father would want, is it? All of us dreaming of revenge, only to live life in the shadows of London."

"That is what you are doing, isn't it?" Kit appealed to Iomhar. She pulled on the sleeve of his doublet and he looked at her, his green eyes narrowing. "You wish to live in the shadows forever?"

"Nay." His answer was simple this time. "Yet I ken what ye want, Kit. Ye want me to work for Walsingham again. How can I do that? He sent me to Oswyn Ingleby knowing full well it was a trap."

"You do not know he knew that for certain."

"If I suspected it, he did too, and when I did not return, he sat behind his desk and did nothing to help me. What does that remind ye of, eh?" Iomhar arched a dark eyebrow. "Ye remember the day we met, Kit?"

She stared at him, her goblet frozen halfway to her lips. She could remember the day clearly. They had broken into Edinburgh Castle to collect a message for Walsingham from a prisoner. The prisoner was a spy who had worked for Walsingham, but Kit had only been asked to get the message out of the castle's walls, not the man.

"Walsingham was going to help that man. Eventually."

"Ye see?" Iomhar stood up, his tone suddenly sharp. "Ye still cling to a wish. A wish to believe the best of Walsingham, even when the proof is before your eyes. He never got that man out of Edinburgh Castle, just as he sent nay one for me, either. *Ye* are the only reason I escaped, Kit. *Ye*. Not him. I'm enjoying being free of him." His rant over, Iomhar walked across the room to the window, staring out at the dark street with his goblet thudding down onto the wooden surround.

Silence prevailed for a minute and nothing disturbed it but the sound of a muffled argument between Moira, Abigail and Rhona in a distant room. Niall raised an eyebrow at Kit, clearly hoping she would say something.

"What?" she mouthed to him.

"Well, we both know ye are more likely to improve his mood than I am," Niall teased her, loud enough for Iomhar to hear him.

"Stop causing trouble, Niall," Iomhar ordered.

"Me? Trouble?" Niall said with mock-innocence. "Never!"

"Let the birds fall from the sky before ye cause trouble, eh?" Iomhar said wryly.

"Aye, just so." Niall laughed, then he looked between Iomhar and Kit, clearly noticing the distance between them. "If I am not permitted to make any jests, then I will say something serious instead."

"Hurrah." Iomhar's tone was deadpan.

"Brother, Kit is right." Niall's words had both Kit and Iomhar snapping their heads in his direction. "If we are going to get back the lives we once had, free of the threat of Lord Ruskin hanging over our heads, then we have to find him. Ye and I have not found him in the months we've been here. Even our friends and the informers I have in the armies of

Scotland have not heard any news of him. We are making nay progress."

Iomhar turned to face his brother and folded his arms across his chest. "If I work for Walsingham again, then maybe I will be able to find Lord Ruskin's trail."

"See? Always knew ye had special powers, Iomhar. Seems ye can read my mind." Niall tapped his temple. "If we wish to find him, then maybe there truly is only one way to do it. Join with Walsingham again."

Niall didn't wait for his brother's answer. He moved to his feet and walked in the direction of the oak door that led to the back rooms. "I'll go find our brother and ask for how much longer he can put up with our mother and sisters arguing so much." He closed the heavy door behind him.

Kit faced Iomhar and offered a weary smile. "Your sisters argue because they enjoy doing so. Has he not noticed that?" Her question had Iomhar chuckling softly, but it didn't last long. He hung his head forward a little.

"I cannot trust him, Kit. Walsingham."

"You never did before, not completely."

"Yet I cannot do it at all now."

She walked toward him, slowly, and stopped when she reached his side. He turned to look at her, so they were staring at one another in the warm orange candlelight.

"I'm not asking you to trust him," she whispered. "If anything, I'm asking you to use him to get what you and your family want."

"I wish to be free of men like Walsingham. I told ye that before." Iomhar's voice was deep as he bent a little toward her. "I told ye what I wish for in my future. I will return home to Scotland, with my family."

Kit swallowed a lump in her throat and blinked quickly. She wanted to hide from him just how much it hurt to think of him returning home. He'd asked her to go with him to Scotland, but it was not a question she had yet been able to answer. All she knew for certain was that if he left, she would be heartbroken.

"Then you need to use Walsingham," she said with vigour. "We have the letters that prove Mary Stuart is guilty of treason. Do you not wish to see her punished, Iomhar? Is she not the one who ... who..."

"Who ordered my father's death? Aye," Iomhar finished the sentence tartly and looked away. Kit nudged his shoulder, trying to get his attention. He nudged her back, but didn't quite turn to look at her.

"You do not have to trust Walsingham. You just have to work with him," Kit pleaded. "I'll be there too, and you know you can trust me."

Iomhar's lips curled into a soft smile. "Nay one else in this world would sneak their way into Urquhart Castle to get me out, would they? Ye do not need to ask me if I trust ye, Kit. I always will." They stared at one another for a second before the argument in the back of the house grew louder and they both looked away. "Ye are right, as is Niall." He paused and brushed a hand through his dark hair, pulling on the loose locks in frustration before he sighed and stood straight, his mind made up. "It does not seem wise to my own mind. Yet it may be the only way."

"Does that mean you agree?" Kit asked. "You will come out of hiding and show Walsingham you are alive?"

"I will." He held her gaze. "Let's pray the wee man above keeps us safe for this foolish decision."

CHAPTER 6

"It's not possible." Doris's voice trembled as Iomhar stepped into the house in Seething Lane. Kit hastily shut the door behind her. She felt eyes on the back of her neck, and she turned around, seeking out whose they were.

The young and inept maid hired last year by Walsingham to help Doris was standing in the doorway of the kitchen. Her small blue eyes were fixed on Kit. Her dark brown hair was gathered into a small bun at the back of her head. When she realised that she had been caught staring, she half hid herself behind the doorframe. She was as quiet as a mouse, and made a squeak too, completing the illusion. Slight of figure and wearing a white apron with a light green smock beneath, she must have found it easy to hide in corners.

"Mr Blackwood." Doris was tearful as she leaned toward Iomhar, stretching out her arms. Kit tore her gaze from the maid and watched as Iomhar took Doris's hands in greeting, smiling fully.

"How are ye, Doris?"

"How am I?" She laughed, a tear trickling down her cheek. "Oh, what folly. How can you ask me that after you have been gone so long? I feared you were…" She broke off and covered her mouth with her hand.

"Fear not for me, Doris. Aye, I'm safe." Iomhar glanced quickly at Kit. There was a silent meaning in that look, though she turned away from him swiftly enough. These last few months, he had thanked her more times than she cared to hear. As she turned, the maid retreated into the kitchen and knocked over a pot so loudly that it echoed around the house.

"Oh, Joan. You are becoming worse every day, I swear it!" Doris hurriedly released Iomhar's hand and stepped into the kitchen, waving in disapproval at the maid. "How will you look after this house if you are constantly knocking things over?"

Joan didn't murmur an apology but hung her head and returned the pot to the table. Those keen blue eyes glanced Kit's way, but not for long.

"I'm so glad to see you are back in London, Mr Blackwood." Doris grasped his hand again. She was caught between two humours, elated at seeing Iomhar and furious at her maid. "So thrilled indeed."

"Thank ye, Doris."

"Is he in, Doris?" Kit asked, gesturing toward the stairs.

"He is. Though be wary of the storm that will fall when you go up there. I have never seen him so fearful. He's ordered spies to guard the house so nothing like what happened here last night can happen again. They arrive later today. All this protection, yet he's ordered a horse too, saying he must see the queen. Whatever news you brought to him last night, Kitty, it has him in a tither."

"I thought it might," Kit said and took Iomhar's arm, trying to steer him further down the corridor. He shared one last smile with Doris before they hastened to the stairs. "That maid," Kit said when they reached the staircase. "She's not getting any better at her job."

"She's still young."

"Hmm." Kit had taken no notice of the maid before. Yet there was something off about the way young Joan had stared at her with such fixed attention.

When they reached Walsingham's door, she knocked hurriedly.

"Kit? Kit? Come in." Walsingham's voice was full of taut excitement. She opened the door and led the way inside.

The room still displayed the scars of the attack from the night before. The doorframe was splintered and the ropes that had been used to bind Walsingham and Doris were slung across the hearth beside the fire. Walsingham took no notice of these things, nor of Kit's presence. He was hurrying back and forth behind his desk.

He had discarded the grey robes she had seen him wearing the night before. Today, he wore a black jerkin with a high white collar around his throat. He had to be hot wearing it, given the heat of the day, but he didn't seem to notice. There were beads of sweat high on his temple and dripping across his receding hairline.

"Much to do, much to do," he muttered to himself, or to Kit, she wasn't really sure at first. "We must go at once to see the queen, Kit. I've already sent word to Lord Burghley this morning. He will meet us at the palace to discuss all with Her Majesty. His message. Oh, his reply! He is quick to anger. There's too much yellow bile in him." Walsingham turned and reached for his desk, popping a gleaming silver pill into his mouth. "We will prepare the death warrant at once. It must happen. Mary Stuart will be formally arrested, along with her conspirators, then the threat over our queen's head will be at an end at last."

Kit winced at the sight of those pills. He'd taken those *stones of immortality* for years, yet his health seemed to be steadily declining. He spent most of his time in the privy these days, and complaining of an ache in his lower back.

"Before we depart for the palace... Pray, Walsingham, look up," Kit said, just as Iomhar stepped into the room. His heavy boots on the floorboards seemed to capture Walsingham's attention as much as her words did.

He pushed the box of pills across his desk and looked up. His jaw slackened and the pill he'd taken nearly fell from his lips as he stared at Iomhar. His eyes danced up and down his body before they came to rest on his face.

"It's not possible." His words were feeble. Stumbling out from behind his desk, Walsingham moved to the middle of the room with a quickness to his step, then he fell still and his manner changed abruptly. He smiled, laughed, then covered his mouth with his hands, muffling the sound as he stared at Iomhar. He walked forward. Slowly, he lowered one hand from his mouth and reached for Iomhar's shoulder. Iomhar was much taller than Walsingham, so he had to reach up, his crooked back straightening as he did so. "You are alive, Iomhar," he whispered. "I can scarcely believe it. You are here before me. It is not my imagination."

"Aye, what ye see before ye is real." Iomhar spoke with coldness, but he didn't shift his shoulder out of Walsingham's grasp. Kit could see he was holding back his true thoughts, for a muscle twitched in his jaw, as if the words longed to escape.

"You are alive!" Walsingham said again with glee. Then he raised his hand from Iomhar's shoulder as if he had been burned, and turned to look at Kit. "How long have you known?"

"Since the winter," Kit answered succinctly. The shadow that clouded his features was so sudden that she shifted her weight between her feet.

"You knew he was alive, all this time, and you did not tell me. You left me to grieve him, Kit."

"Ye grieved?" Iomhar's eyebrows were raised, his voice pitched high in disbelief. "I find that hard to imagine."

"I did," Walsingham insisted, looking between the two of them. "I thought you were dead. Why did you not come here? Have you been at home all this time?"

"Aye." Iomhar turned to Kit, waiting for her to say more. Walsingham did the same.

"What do you wish me to say?" she asked Walsingham. "He had no wish to come out of hiding."

"You did not?" Walsingham jerked his chin toward Iomhar.

"It might have had something to do with being sent to my death." Iomhar turned cool green eyes on Walsingham.

Walsingham flinched, his black cloth shoes inching back a little on the floorboards. "I ... I did not send you to your death. How could you think that?"

"Ye must have feared it was a trap. A letter from Oswyn, a man we know works for Lord Ruskin, yet ye sent me alone regardless."

"What else was I supposed to do?" Walsingham asked with sudden ferocity, no longer the weak and ailing man. His chin lifted high, and he barked his next words. "If there was a chance that Oswyn truly wanted his pardon, *you* were the man to go and meet him. You knew him, knew the way he worked, and you would be wary of him. That was what was needed. You were the best man for the commission. You must see that, Iomhar. For all that you wish to think ill of me for my decisions, you *must* see why I made that one."

Iomhar said nothing. He stood as still as marble, his face turned toward Walsingham. Kit stepped away from the two of them, longing to be far from the coldness that had descended. Moving to the window, she felt the sunshine streaming through the glass. It was another hot day, and she pulled at the collar of her jerkin to loosen it.

"Are you hiding from me, Kit?" Walsingham's voice was just as cool as it had been when he'd spoken to Iomhar. She turned away from the window, facing the spymaster across the room. "You have known Iomhar was home since the winter, and yet you told me nothing of it. You kept secrets."

"What of it? You keep secrets from me." Her sharp retort had him moving to his desk, hurrying to put himself behind it. His dark eyes flicked between Kit and Iomhar.

"I am glad you have returned, Iomhar, but I will not atone for the decision I made a year and a half ago. It was the right one, and you must see that."

"Fortunately, Kit did not see it the same way." Iomhar shifted, folding his arms across his chest.

"What did you say?" Walsingham asked, his voice low. "Do you mean to suggest... Kit, did you go looking for Iomhar?"

She breathed heavily, but she could not hide from this moment. She had gone searching for Iomhar without hesitation, well aware that Walsingham would be furious if he ever discovered she had disobeyed his orders. She had done so regardless, knowing she had to bring Iomhar home.

"Kit!" Walsingham snapped at her. His voice made the glass inkwell resting beside him on the table ring momentarily.

"Yes, I found him." Kit turned to Walsingham. "When the queen asked me to deliver her letter to Mary Stuart, I took advantage of the time to search for Iomhar."

"Aye, and I am grateful ye did." Iomhar sat down in the nearest chair and flicked his ankles onto a nearby stool, looking as relaxed as if he made this room his home every day. "Or I might still be in the dungeons of Urquhart Castle."

"Urquhart." Walsingham repeated the word with quiet trepidation, then shook his head sharply. "Kit! How can you disobey my orders so?"

"Were you not the one who said you were glad to see him again?" Kit motioned toward Iomhar. "He was a loyal intelligencer for you. You know that."

"I would never dispute that. Nor would I argue against his skill." Walsingham turned his back on Iomhar. "Yet this has nothing to do with him. I am asking you, Kit, *you*. You hid this from me for so long. You disobeyed me more than once, did you not? I told you to leave the matter alone for your own safety. Do you not remember those words? I pleaded with you in this very room!" Walsingham stepped out from behind the desk and moved toward her, his heels thudding against the floorboards. His pale features had turned an unnatural shade of red, almost puce. "It was for your own good. You not only hid what you did from me then, but for the last few months too."

"Yes, I did." Kit felt as if she was a child again. She'd stood in this same room once while he had reprimanded her for escaping her lessons, and racing across the nearby rooftops in the hose and jerkin she'd taken from one of the serving boys. Walsingham had glared at her with the same ferocity that day. "And I do not regret it."

Walsingham stepped back and shook his head. "How can I trust you anymore, Kit? There was a time when you never would have lied to me. Never."

"There was a time when I thought you wouldn't lie to me." Kit held his gaze.

Walsingham sighed deeply. "I cannot trust you, Kit. Not after this. No." He shook his head, lost in his anger.

"What more would ye have her do?" Iomhar's voice broke into their conversation. "Ye were happy to see me alive a minute ago, now ye blame her for it."

"I blame her for keeping secrets from me. How can I trust my intelligencers if they do that?"

"And a spymaster has nay secrets of his own, of course."

A grunt escaped Walsingham's lips. He turned away and retreated toward his desk. He leaned on it heavily with both hands planted on the wood, making it creak ominously.

"Would you dismiss me for this?" Kit's question hung in the air.

Walsingham started down at his desk before reaching for his box of pills. He tried to take another one out, but Kit moved quickly toward him and snatched them from his grasp. He stared at her, his eyes narrowing accusingly. "You have taken them already." She opened a drawer and stuffed the box inside. "They do not help."

"They certainly will not help this." His voice was grave. Lifting a bony hand, he brushed back the little hair that remained on his temple. "What to do with you, Kit? What to do? Any other intelligencer I would dismiss in a moment for lying to me for so long."

Iomhar leaned forward out of his chair, planting his boots on the floorboards. Kit held her breath, waiting to hear what Walsingham would say next.

"With you, I cannot." Walsingham sat down heavily on his chair and then groaned, reaching a hand around his body to clutch at his back. "I cannot dismiss you."

"Because you need me?" Kit asked.

"The queen certainly relies on you too much for me to oust you from my service."

"Ye would never send Kit away." Iomhar's deep voice disturbed the two of them. "She has been your pet for too long."

"Iomhar!" Kit said sharply, but he simply shrugged, showing he did not care if she was angry at him for it.

"I do not believe he would get rid of ye, Kit."

"In a way, he is right." Walsingham nodded slowly before turning his dark eyes on Kit. "You have been part of my life for too long to see you go now." He reached out, as if he would take her hand, but he let it fall quickly. "But I cannot trust you as I did before. You have damaged that trust, Kit."

"You did that of your own accord." Until the day Walsingham told her the truth about how he'd found her, there would be this lingering doubt in her mind. "Yet you need me, for now. I suggest you need Iomhar too." She nodded at the Scotsman. "You need him, for he knows Lord Ruskin's ways better than any other. If we are to arrest Mary Stuart and all of her supporters, you need us both."

Walsingham looked silently between the two of them. Slowly, he raised his bony white fingers and steepled them in front of his face. "You are right. I need you both."

CHAPTER 7

"Tell me again, I pray you, Walsingham, for I long to hear it." Lord Burghley was beside himself with excitement. Standing in the garden of Richmond Palace, he clutched his cane tightly as he hopped from one foot to the other, his thin lips stretching into a smile that caused his long, wispy white beard to quiver. "She has been caught, yes?"

"Yes." Walsingham stepped forward, his voice solemn, hiding his own excitement that had been so apparent back in his rooms. "By her own hand, she has been found to have approved of a plot against Her Majesty."

The two men spoke as if the Queen of England was not beside them. Queen Elizabeth stood a short distance away. Her ladies-in-waiting had retreated across the garden, though Kit could see that they intermittently glanced the queen's way, wary of what was happening. She faced the open lawn, her back to Kit and the men. Her shoulders rose and fell with each deep breath she took.

"The conspirators are to be arrested," Walsingham continued. "Babington has been found and is being pressured now for the names of the other conspirators."

"Pressured?" Iomhar repeated the word from where he stood by Kit's shoulder. It was the first word he had yet uttered in that meeting, and he earned a dark glare from both Walsingham and Lord Burghley for his interruption.

"He means tortured," Kit explained in a wary tone. The queen's shoulders shook, but she said nothing.

"This is good news, is it not?" Lord Burghley's cane struck the paved cobbles beneath his feet excitedly and a laugh escaped his lips. "Your Majesty, will you say nothing?" He turned to the queen at last. "Is it not what we have been hoping for?"

"It is the end you hoped for, Lord Burghley, but do not pretend it was my wish," the queen answered. Her voice was deep.

Slowly, she turned around, her vast white gown crinkling with the movement. Kit thought she was looking older. The lines of her face were more pronounced than before, and there was a gauntness that hadn't always been there, with her cheeks hollowing out like concave moons. Her skin was plastered with some sort of white powder, and her lips were rouged an unnatural shade, contrasting with the ginger locks of her wispy hair. Those lips were pressed together in a harsh line.

"Tell me, how would you feel to be told that thanks to your cousin's treason, you must see your own blood, your own flesh, executed?" Her gaze burrowed into Lord Burghley. When the councillor had no answer to give her, she shifted her pointed chin in Walsingham's direction. "Well?" she said impatiently.

"No one would relish the task, Your Majesty. It does not mean it must not be done."

She uttered no words and turned away again, to look down the lawn.

Kit shifted, watching the conversation as if it was some performance in a sweltering theatre. The heat didn't seem to affect the queen, for she didn't fidget or pull at her gown, but it did bother the two gentlemen who constantly shifted in their black robes and exchanged uncertain looks.

"It must be done," Walsingham said again. "The conspirators will all be arrested, and Mary Stuart must be moved from Chartley Castle."

"What of Fotheringhay Castle?" asked Lord Burghley. "It would make a fine prison."

"A fine prison indeed," the queen retorted, her voice full of scorn. "A queen, now a prisoner."

"She is no queen, Your Majesty. She has not been for many years," Walsingham reminded her.

"Do not talk to me as if I am a child," the queen snapped over her shoulder.

Kit exchanged a glance with Iomhar, seeing his dark eyebrows raised in a questioning look. She rather thought that, like her, he was wondering why they were here for this meeting. It was a discussion Walsingham could have had alone with the queen and Lord Burghley.

"I cannot deal with these thoughts now. They plague me, like some disease that clings to my bones, and to my…" The queen paused and turned around. Her hand was resting on her chest, over the place where her heart was. "You have told me what you needed to. Make your arrests and leave me with my dreads." She delivered the swift order to Walsingham and Lord Burghley before her dark eyes turned in Kit's direction. "I see you have brought Miss Scarlett with you again, Walsingham."

"She helped to intercept the messages," Walsingham explained. "I wished for you to hear it from her lips, as well as my own, so you could be certain of what I told you."

"No, you did not." The queen tilted her chin a little higher. It was a formidable look, one that rather belonged on a kestrel, with the eyes keen and unblinking, looking down on what its next meal would be. "You brought more people to your side to persuade me that this is the right course of action, that I must authorise my cousin's death."

Walsingham didn't dare to argue; he merely held her gaze.

The queen shifted her focus to Kit. "I thank you, Miss Scarlett, for the interception you have made. I may have been facing death were it not for your actions, but I have no wish to hear what you read."

Kit curtsied in acknowledgment, assuring the queen she would not go into such details.

"Pray, leave me now." The queen's final order was delivered with vigour as she stepped away, heading in the direction of her ladies-in-waiting.

"Your Majesty?" Lord Burghley called, moving after her and striking the cobbled path with his cane. "There is more we must discuss, much more."

"Then it can wait," she snapped at him. "Leave me be." She left so swiftly that her farthingale and the large sleeves of her white gown knocked the heads off the blooming red roses beside her. The crimson petals fell to the path like drops of blood.

"She will hear no more today," Walsingham said in a low tone to Burghley. "She is ruled by her heart."

"We should not speak of the queen so," Burghley muttered, yet he didn't refute the words.

Kit stared after the ghostly figure of the queen as she fled through the garden. Taking hold of her skirt with her long fingers, she raised it around her ankles to aid her progress. Her farthingale swung with the movement and her sleeves rippled.

"We must act, even if the queen does not wish to hear it," Walsingham said to Burghley. "Have the warrant drawn up and ready for her seal."

Burghley nodded. "I have already begun such orders. You must find all of her conspirators."

"I will."

"And take Mary Stuart to Fotheringhay too. She cannot stay at Chartley anymore."

"Of course." Walsingham nodded in agreement then stepped away, leaving Lord Burghley staring after the queen through the garden. Walsingham moved toward Kit and Iomhar, his voice low. "You must go to Chartley. Arrest Mary Stuart and take her to Fotheringhay Castle. I will arrange for other intelligencers to accompany you both."

"To accompany us?" Kit's eyebrows rose in surprise.

"Did you think I would trust you to go alone after what has passed?" Walsingham waved a dismissive hand. "Come to me tomorrow morning for your final orders, then I'll send you on your way. Do not disobey me, Kit. The arrest of Mary Stuart could be the single thing that prevents a Spanish and French invasion. I pray you understand that."

"I would never risk the queen's safety," Kit said. "You know that."

Walsingham raised an eyebrow, as if in doubt, then walked off.

"Ye two have changed since I last saw ye together," Iomhar murmured at her side. "Ye are not what ye once were to each other."

Kit nodded sadly. "I fear you are right."

"Ye must go," Niall urged from where he stood in Iomhar's doorway.

"I ken that." Iomhar lifted a bag and threaded it around his shoulder, though the darkness in his expression showed he took no pleasure in agreeing to go.

Kit stood beside Niall, leaning on the doorframe with her eyes on Iomhar. Since they had returned from their meeting with the queen the day before, he had been restless. Each time she'd asked what was bothering him, he would mutter the same words: *Lord Ruskin.*

"Do you think he will be there?" Kit asked, knowing that Iomhar wouldn't need to ask who she meant.

"Aye. He will be hiding somewhere. From the lengths he has already gone to for his queen, I doubt he will let us take her now without putting up a fight. Perhaps it is a good thing Walsingham intends to send us with other intelligencers. There will be more protection if Lord Ruskin sees us coming." His eyes lingered on Kit, and she shifted uneasily. The last time she had seen Lord Ruskin was on that cliff.

"He will not hurt us."

"Aye, I bet ye thought the same shortly before he threw ye off a cliff." Iomhar's wry tone made Niall laugh beside her. She tapped him sharply on the arm.

"Ow," he said, rubbing the sore spot. "Ye do that harsher than anyone else."

"I told ye, she's trained to fight," Iomhar said and pulled on his boots.

It was the early hours of the morning, and the rest of the house had not yet risen. The sun streamed in through the window and the day already promised to be warm.

"Our mother, is she still asleep?"

"Aye." Niall answered swiftly. "Nay one else is yet awake. I'll wave ye off on your journey."

"Ye only do that for ye wish to come with us."

"I do." Niall sighed deeply and rubbed his palms together. "What I would give to be there when Mary Stuart is arrested. Aye, I'd probably dance for joy. When was the last time she saw a volta performed? I'd perform one alone before her, to revel in her misery."

Kit could not blame him for it. The discovery that Mary Stuart was responsible for ordering the murder of his father was enough to darken anyone's thoughts.

"I might just do that myself," Iomhar said with a small smile. That smile quickly fell from his lips. "Once I ask her why she ordered our father's death in the first place."

"We have to reach Chartley first," Kit reminded him. "Are you ready?"

"As ready as the sun is today." He glanced out of the window with a grudging look at the bright sky. "Let us depart."

Niall left the room abruptly. Kit waited until Iomhar drew level and lowered her voice, casting a glance back into the hallway to ensure Niall wasn't near enough to hear the last thing she had to say on this matter.

"When we find Lord Ruskin again, what do you intend to do?" she asked. Her question made Iomhar pause, and his brows knitted together.

"Ye ask me that?"

"He will face a judge, will he not?" Kit's voice was firm. "You will not take justice into your own hands, tell me that, Iomhar."

"An eye for an eye. That's what they say, aye?" He stepped away from her, moving into the hallway and leaving Kit staring after him.

"You wish to end up in prison?" She chased after him but gained no answer to her question.

Chartley Castle grew in the distance, the grey turrets peeking between the trees as if they were great rabbit's ears poking out through long grass. Kit squinted at the castle, seeing the grey stone shimmer in the sunlight.

"Something is wrong," she murmured.

"How can you know that when we are so far away?" The intelligencer who rode on one side of her scoffed and shook his head. Boris Laidlaw was thickly set and grunted as he spoke, as a pig might when it rolled around in mud.

"I know it." Kit didn't look away from the castle. She had watched the building enough times as of late with Phelippes at her side to know where the guards should stand and when they should be visible. Usually, two stood at the top of the east wing tower, their heads visible as small dark dots in the distance. "The guards are not in their place."

"Ye are certain?" Iomhar drew level on her other side, pulling on the reins of his stallion.

"I am. The guards are gone."

Kit glanced at the men Walsingham had gathered for the arrest. Along with Laidlaw, there were other intelligencers she had not worked with before. Somers was a wide-set man, who liked to throw insults around as if it were a sport. At the back of the group was another face, one that seemed too young to Kit's eyes to be amongst the intelligencers. His name was Marlowe and he was closer to being a boy than a man, with his fair hair curling around his ears. He'd attempted to grow a moustache, but it looked more like fallen horsehair that he had stuck to his upper lip.

Behind the intelligencers rode a small group of Her Majesty's soldiers, numbering fifteen. They kept in line and jerked their chins forward, all ready to follow the orders that Laidlaw set out for them. He'd been given seniority by Walsingham the morning before as they had set off on their journey.

"Perhaps they are having a piss." Laidlaw's words made the other intelligencers snigger. "They're men. They're not made of stone. You worry too much. Ahead!" he barked at the soldiers behind them.

Kit tightened her grasp on her reins and exchanged an uneasy look with Iomhar. His jaw was tense as he turned his horse toward the castle.

As they approached, Laidlaw delivered quick orders. Somers and Marlowe were to take half the group of soldiers and approach the castle entrance.

"Iomhar, Kit, you two stay with the rest of the soldiers in the forest."

"Ye are leaving us behind?" Iomhar demanded, incredulous.

"Someone needs to stay here in case the queen makes her bid for freedom." With these final words, Laidlaw rode on toward the castle.

Kit jumped down from her horse and wrapped the reins around a nearby tree branch. Taking up position at the treeline, she trained her eyes on the castle battlements. Iomhar joined her.

"He is not very fond of us, is he?" Kit whispered.

"Aye, he hates us as much as ye adore marchpane." Iomhar's tone was wry but he didn't manage a smile. He glanced at the few soldiers with them, then turned to watch the others as they approached the castle door. Laidlaw rapped loudly on the wood and tutted when there was no quick answer. He had to knock a second time. "Ye are right. Something is wrong," Iomhar said to Kit.

"The guards are missing." Kit nodded at the empty battlements.

"Hallo there!" Laidlaw called out and rapped for a third time.

The door finally opened and a familiar face poked through the gap.

"It's Phelippes!" Kit cried out and ran forward. She crossed the distance to the others and hastened past the soldiers, Iomhar at her side.

Phelippes was bleeding. He had a head wound and staggered against the side of the wall. Laidlaw stepped out of the way, as if the mere thought of helping another man disgusted him. Phelippes slumped against the stonework just as Kit reached his side. He fell into her arms, and she held him.

"What is this?" Laidlaw barked impatiently. "Phelippes? What are you doing here?"

"They sent a messenger for me first thing, but I was too late." Phelippes breathed heavily as Iomhar offered him a handkerchief. He pressed the cloth to his head, though it did little to stop the bleeding. "Men attacked at dawn. They did not hold back. The guards are injured; even the master of the house hid in his chamber under the bed out of fear."

"Stop blithering, man!" Laidlaw snapped. "Where is Mary Stuart?"

"Gone." Phelippes lifted his head, and his dark eyes found Kit's own. "They took her this morning."

"Who?" Kit asked. "Who took her?"

"Her own men, supporters clothed in black and red, carrying enough weapons to support an army. They must have known you were coming."

CHAPTER 8

"Someone must know something." Kit marched through the curtain wall of Chartley Castle.

"Kit, wait!" shouted Iomhar. "Ye think traipsing around here is going to solve anything?"

"It just might." She continued to stride forward, with one destination in mind. "Let Laidlaw question the guards. They are not the men who see everything there is to see."

"Ye realise how mad that sounds when guards are literally paid to watch?" Iomhar chuckled as he followed her. "Aye, sounds mad indeed."

"Laidlaw is wasting his time." Kit reached a corridor she recognised and came to a sudden stop, her boots stilling on the fine rug beneath her. The cloth was inlaid with gold and crimson thread. "Some prison Mary was kept in, eh?" At her side, Iomhar was admiring the fine paintings on the walls and the tapestries that covered the cold grey stone, giving it warmth.

"This is nay prison," he muttered under his breath.

Kit followed the route she had taken in the winter, when she had crept into the castle to deliver a letter from Queen Elizabeth to Mary Stuart. She turned left, past a privy where she had hidden the footman who had come to deliver a drink to Mary, then reached for the door to the former queen's chambers. Taking hold of the iron handle, she turned it and strode inside.

"Ah!" came a scared yelp.

"My apologies. I did not mean to make you jump." Kit held out a hand to the young maid whom she had made leap in fright. The young woman clutched her hands to her chest as her blue eyes darted between Kit and Iomhar.

"Have you come for us too now? The guards are already bleeding to death. Have you not done enough?"

Before Kit could speak again, the maid dashed into the adjoining chamber. Kit smiled at Iomhar, who sighed.

"She's frightened."

"I can see that," Kit hissed. She stepped further into the room, her pace slowing as she recalled her previous meeting here with the Queen of Scots. When Mary had attempted to hurt her, she'd found herself flattened to the table by Kit, with a dagger over her face. The recognition in Mary Stuart's eyes, as if she had seen Kit before, still haunted her memories.

Kit shook her head to clear it and walked into the adjoining bedchamber that had been Mary Stuart's. The young maid was attempting to hide behind one of the bedposts.

"Miss? You need not fear us. We work for Queen Elizabeth." At Kit's words, the maid poked her head out from behind the bedpost. "Can you tell us what happened here?"

"You do not know?" The maid quivered, pressing her lips together and opening them again. "They came first thing, the men. Dressed in dark and tartan colours. They spoke like him." She pointed an accusing finger in Iomhar's direction.

"Aye, Scottish then." Iomhar nodded and started circling the room, examining the bedchamber. The maid watched him with wary eyes and shrunk against the bedpost.

"How many men were there?" Kit asked.

"I do not know!" the maid said, throwing her arms in the air. "They attacked at dawn. I came to see Her Majesty."

"She is no queen." Kit's words were low. "You know that, do you not?"

"She insisted I address her as such." The maid hung her head. Kit shook her head, letting her eyes follow Iomhar across the room. He had hesitated by a table where there was a small carved mahogany box, and lifted the lid to reveal toilette bottles. Mary Stuart had clearly left in a rush, since she hadn't had time to take them.

"What happened to Mary Stuart?" Kit asked, taking a step toward the maid. The young woman moved from one bedpost to the next, still fearful. Kit raised a hand, as if calming a wild animal. "I merely wish to know what happened."

"I saw her," the maid said in a low voice. "I saw her! She did not look like her, but it was her. I am certain of it. They don't believe me." She cast a glance at the door, as if looking at the person she spoke of.

"Who does not believe you?" Kit took another step forward and this time, the maid did not back away.

"The master thinks I see nothing," she hissed. "He thinks me blind just because I'm a maid. Yet I saw it all! It was her. She wore clothes like this." She stepped out and held her skirt wide. "Pale blue woollen cloth — poor, cheap. She must have taken the clothes from somewhere, but I do not know where. She no longer looked like a queen. She looked like a maid."

Iomhar hesitated beside a vast coffer. He cursed under his breath as he opened it and gestured to the fine clothes inside.

"Aye, if she escaped dressed as a maid, the guards would not look at her twice, especially if they were fighting her men."

"Yes, yes, that is what happened," the maid added hurriedly. "The guards fought her men. They tried to hold them back. What they did not realise was that she was already sneaking out of the castle. I followed her and her lady's maid. They went all the way to the kitchens, then I lost them." She shrugged helplessly, then pointed at one of the windows. "I came back here and saw a brewery cart leaving. Two maids were sitting in the back. I did not see her face, but I'm certain it was Her Majesty."

"The men who came for her left soon after, I'm guessing?" Kit asked, and the maid nodded.

"The guards thought they had won. They only realised later when they came up here that she was gone." The maid sat down on the edge of the bed before jumping back to her feet and straightening the covers behind her. It seemed that even with Mary gone, she was still too afraid to sit on a queen's bed.

"Thank you." Kit nodded at the young maid, glad of her help.

As Iomhar continued to circle the room, the maid followed him, wringing her hands.

"Should you be doing this?" she asked. "These are the Queen of Scots' things."

Iomhar dropped the lid of a coffer. It fell so loudly that the young woman jumped back.

"She is nay queen of mine," he growled and returned to his searching. "We have a king on the throne. King James."

"She insisted she was queen," the maid muttered, but with less vigour in her tone.

"What are you looking for?" Kit asked Iomhar.

"Anything that could help us discover where she has gone." Iomhar moved to a table in the corner and searched underneath.

"She is long gone now." Kit moved to the window, staring out at the landscape. "They were prepared. She must have taken the maid's clothes in advance."

"I agree with ye. Therefore, she must have communicated with her followers another way — one that we don't know about." At Iomhar's words, Kit spun around to face him.

"You are right. God's blood, she cannot have only communicated with her supporters through the brewer." Kit cursed, realising that the trap they had set to intercept Mary's letters had not been enough. She must have been communicating another way in order to have set up this escape.

"Where would she hide her correspondence?" Iomhar asked, turning toward the fireplace and passing his fingers over the mantelpiece, searching for a secret compartment.

"She might have burned them." Kit turned to the maid, who was still wringing her hands. "Did your former mistress ever hide papers from you, somewhere she thought you would not see them?"

"I…" The maid trailed off. She chewed her lip before turning to one of the coffers that Iomhar had already searched.

"In here?" Kit asked, and the maid nodded.

Kit raised the lid and searched the contents. Inside was a selection of fine gowns, including the dark gown she had seen Mary Stuart wear in the winter, when she had dismissed Kit with a wave of her hand. Lord Ruskin had taken hold of Kit, ready to march her from the room. She still remembered his words: *I cannot have blood spilled here.* Kit had then been thrown into the back of a cart and taken to the clifftop.

"Kit? Anything?" Iomhar's words brought Kit back to the present. She was about to close the lid of the coffer when something caught her eye. At the edge of the lid, there was a small scrap of paper. She pulled at the corner, and the paper slid out.

"It's a false lid. There's another compartment inside it."

Iomhar reached her side and grasped the lid. Bracing one hand against the wood, he bent it backward. It snapped loudly, making the maid yelp. Papers dropped out, flying to the floor and into the coffer like feathers drifting in the wind. Kit gathered them up.

"God only knows how long she has been communicating beyond the castle walls," she murmured, shuffling them together.

"Aye. Look." Iomhar lifted one scrap of paper and raised it high. On the paper was an emblem they had both seen many times before: the Scottish unicorn, scrawled in black ink. "She has been speaking to Lord Ruskin."

"We need to get these to Phelippes. He will decipher them quicker than I can. We need to tell Walsingham what has happened, too." Kit thanked the maid for her help before hurrying out of the room. She only hesitated once to glance at the table where she had pinned Mary Stuart. For one haunting moment, she'd had the former queen at her mercy.

Iomhar raced after her, following her into the dark corridor. When they reached the tapestry-clad walls, he cut her off, stopping abruptly in front of her on the staircase. She dropped some of the letters and they both hurried to collect them again. "Think on it some more before ye run off to speak to Walsingham."

"What do you mean?"

"I mean that so few men knew we were coming here. Lord Burghley and Walsingham knew, aye. Yesterday morning, we gathered with Laidlaw, Somers and Marlowe in Walsingham's room, and he told us to come here. That is three more men. Yet even the soldiers were not told who we had come to arrest."

Kit paused with her task, a sudden chill on her skin.

"Few in this world knew who we were here for," Iomhar went on. "Laidlaw, Somers and Marlowe did not have time to send a message. It could not be one of them. So, how did Mary Stuart discover she was to be arrested? Who told her?"

"Someone else must have known." Yet even as Kit said the words, she doubted it. "No. Walsingham was careful. He swore us all to secrecy. He insisted the name of our target was not to leave the walls of Seething Lane."

"Aye, just so." Iomhar stood straight, as did Kit. She stuffed the letters into her doublet so she could not drop them again. "So, with so few who knew where we were going, how could anyone else warn Mary Stuart we were coming? The only men who could have sent a message in warning were Burghley and Walsingham. It was Burghley's idea to move Mary Stuart. It cannot have been him. But…"

"Not this again." Kit narrowed her eyes. "Walsingham is loyal to the Crown. He is loyal to Elizabeth."

"Aye, so ye keep saying." Iomhar nodded slowly. "And yet ye and I know that there is a spy on the privy council."

"The Rose." Kit whispered the codename of the traitor, looking away from Iomhar and toward the tapestry on the wall beside her. It depicted devils dancing around a woman who was burning in flames. Kit swallowed uncomfortably as she stared at the gargoyle-like faces, recreated in gold and red thread. "Walsingham is not the Rose."

"Ye cannot be certain of that anymore, can ye? Not now. Not after this." Iomhar started down the staircase.

"What of Laidlaw and the others? They knew," Kit called after him. "How can you be so certain that none of them sent a message?"

"They have not been out of our sight since they were told. Who else could have warned Mary Stuart's men?" Iomhar asked. "Ye cannot deny this anymore."

"Walsingham is loyal to our queen!" Kit insisted through gritted teeth.

They had reached the bottom of the staircase. Iomhar halted and turned to face Kit, who was a couple of steps up, so their faces were level.

"Can ye swear to me now, on the lives of everyone ye hold dear, that ye are completely confident of Walsingham's innocence?" Iomhar's green eyes did not blink as he waited for an answer.

Kit swallowed and tried to summon the words, but in the end, none came.

"Nay, I thought not."

CHAPTER 9

"Where is he, Doris?" Kit called out as she burst through the door of Seething Lane.

"Oh, heavens!" Flinging both hands to her chest, Doris stumbled back, leaning against the doorway to the kitchen. "In his rooms, upstairs. Kitty, what is wrong? What has happened?"

"I have to see him. Now." Kit marched down the corridor, with Iomhar at her heels.

"Kitty? He has someone with him. He will not appreciate you barging in."

"Then he will have to bear with it." Kit was in no mood to dally. She and Iomhar had ridden through the night to reach London as soon as they could, changing horses on their route so they could keep up the pace. She was exhausted. Stuffed into her doublet were the letters she had taken from Mary Stuart's rooms. Phelippes had been too badly injured to look at them when they had left Chartley.

"I cannot remember ever seeing you so angry," Iomhar said as they reached the stairs.

"It is time we had answers." Kit took the steps two at a time. "He's kept secrets from us for too long." She tripped on the stairs in her eagerness to reach the landing, but Iomhar's hand found the small of her back and kept her standing. As she glanced back at him, their eyes met.

"I'm hardly going to let ye fall down the stairs, am I?" he teased.

Kit couldn't summon a smile; her stomach was knotted too tight, and her palms were clammy. She took the last few steps and reached for the door, opening it without knocking.

"Kit! What do you think you are doing?" Walsingham's voice boomed. "Have you no respect? None at all? I see you no longer knock at doors."

"We must speak. Now." Kit's voice was strangely calm compared to his own. She walked toward his desk, marching past a man she did not recognise. He jumped back from her, his eyes darting down to the daggers in her belt. "Depart." She rested a hand on the hilt of one of those daggers and the man ran. He was so eager to leave the room that he nearly ran straight into Iomhar, who stood in the doorway, a smile on his lips.

"I think ye frightened him."

"Close the door," Kit urged, and Iomhar obeyed.

"What is the meaning of this?" Walsingham moved to his feet. "You cannot demand entry here, Kit. No matter what. You are my intelligencer, may I remind you. You work for me."

"Aye, I think ye have given her that lesson since she was four years old." Iomhar's sharp tone could have knocked Kit over. She turned to see his piercing gaze fixed on Walsingham. It was true. It was the only life she had ever known, being told she worked for Walsingham. Hearing the words muttered so accusingly left her feeling strangely lightheaded.

"What is this?" Walsingham demanded. "Why are you two here? You should be at Chartley."

"We were." Kit circled the desk, coming to stand at Walsingham's side. His pointed chin was turned in her direction. "We thought you would like to know as soon as possible that the pheasant you hunt has flown the nest."

"I beg your pardon?" His voice quietened.

"She's gone," Iomhar answered, leaning against the door and turning the key in the lock. "Mary Stuart fled Chartley Castle in the early hours of yesterday morning."

"No. No." Walsingham shook his head. He stood and turned to the shelves of scrolls behind him. He caught some of the papers with his fingers. "She can't be gone. She cannot. We were so close ... so close indeed."

"Yes, very close." Kit turned toward the shelves. "Only you and a few others knew where we were going, Walsingham." He didn't face her. His back was hunched and his arms shook beneath his black doublet. "Laidlaw, Somers and Marlowe knew where we were going, but the soldiers did not. The intelligencers did not leave our sight all day and night." Kit spoke quickly, barely taking a breath between sentences. "They did not have time to send a message to anyone, and we rode so fast, it would have been difficult for a messenger to arrive ahead of us. Someone must have warned Mary Stuart. Someone must have warned her followers." Kit raised her eyebrows, staring at Walsingham. "That leaves you and Lord Burghley."

"You think that *I*..." Walsingham trailed off. He stepped away from the shelves and made an effort to stand straight, but his back was so crooked these days that he failed. He was no taller than Kit now, and the wrinkles on his face trembled with his rage. "You accuse me of treason?" Walsingham's voice echoed off the walls. "Me? I would lay down my life for my queen. I have done everything I could these twenty or so years to protect her, to protect her kingdom. Do you not know me at all, Kit? Why would I turn on Her Majesty now? Why?"

"Who is the Rose, then?" Kit asked, her voice almost as loud as his own. "Lord Burghley issued the order to move her. It's unlikely to be him. It must have been someone else — another who knew of her movements. We already know there is a spy on the privy council."

"Well, then it must be me, for I am on the privy council."

"This is no time for wryness."

"How else am I supposed to respond to such madness?" Walsingham took her shoulder and shook her, but she brushed him off. "I have a good mind to send you away for such insolence. Your commission would be at an end, Kit. You would not work for me anymore. This life you know would be gone." He turned back to his desk, planting his palms on the surface.

Kit stilled, a strange coldness taking over her body despite the heat of the day. She knew no other life. None. The only world she had ever known was the one with Walsingham hovering at her shoulder, whispering in her ear, telling her what to do. The prospect of being sent away from him frightened her. What would she do for money? Where would she go? She could hardly take up a maid's position, for she did not have the skills.

In the silence, Walsingham reached for his drawer and pulled out his box of pills.

"No. No more of those." Kit strode toward him and snapped the box out of his hand.

"I need those, Kit!" Walsingham tried to snatch them back from her, but she held them far out of reach.

"You cling to these pills as a thirsty man does water."

When Walsingham leaned toward her, trying to take the box, she tossed it across the room. Iomhar caught the box easily enough and turned it over, reading the label.

"Stones of immortality?" he said. "What is this, witchcraft?"

"Medicine." Walsingham's answer was sharp. "I need them."

As if demonstrating how much he needed the pills, Walsingham reached for his lower back, grimacing in pain.

Kit reached out and guided him into his chair behind the desk. These last few years, the pain he suffered had grown worse. The physicians had no good explanation, though they wondered if his increased visits to the privy may have had something to do with it.

"You puzzle me." Walsingham gasped with the pain and looked up at her. "You accuse me in one breath of betraying our queen, everything that matters to me." He stretched his hand out toward her, in some sort of pleading gesture. "Yet you then put me in a chair as if I am an elderly man in need of care."

"Was there a question in there?" Kit asked, having no wish to answer him, even if there was. She could hardly tell him that she feared living a life without him. He may not have been her father, but he had watched over her. She both trusted him and suspected him in that moment, and it left her heart feeling as dry and shrivelled as some of the oldest scrolls on his shelves.

"I do not understand you," Walsingham whispered.

"As I do not understand you." Kit gestured for Iomhar to hand over the pills.

"What are these? Quicksilver?" Iomhar asked, taking out one of the pills and holding it up to the light.

Kit took the box and the pill, stuffing them into her doublet to hide them away. She would not let Walsingham take them again. "Walsingham does not see they make him worse."

"They do not," Walsingham argued, then he shook his head. "Enough talk of medicines. I can scarcely stomach the accusation you have just left at my door, Kit. I might expect such accusations from Iomhar." He paused, as if waiting for Iomhar to argue, then continued. "Yet you, Kit? Have I not proved to you where my loyalty lies?"

"You might have done," said Kit, "had you not been a man who keeps secrets from me." She stared at him, and he stilled in his seat. He knew what she was talking about, without her having to say the words. If he just told her the truth of how they had first met, then perhaps she could begin to trust him again.

"Where is that girl?" A sudden shout erupted from downstairs. "Joan? Joan!"

"That's Doris." Kit murmured, never once taking her eyes from Walsingham, who stared back at her. "Joan must be causing trouble again. She may have broken another pot."

"Joan!" The next shout was so loud that they all jumped.

"Something is wrong," Walsingham said. He slowly stood and held his hand out to Kit. "The pills."

"No." She shook her head and marched for the door, unlocking it and stepping out. "You reach for them every time we argue. What do you expect them to do? Calm your yellow bile?"

Walsingham muttered something inaudible as he followed her out of the door. They hastened down the stairs together as Doris's shouts became more panicked. Kit walked in front with Walsingham behind her, Iomhar bringing up the rear.

"Doris? What is all this shouting?" Walsingham called as they reached the kitchen.

Doris appeared in the doorway, red in the face and her hair damp with sweat. "Oh, Master! I am in uproar! What a mess she has left me in now."

"What do you mean?"

"I mean she has gone." Doris waved a hand at the empty kitchen. "I have checked the whole house, and she is not here. A bag of hers is missing. She has disappeared!"

"Are her clothes gone?" Iomhar asked, peering around the housekeeper into the empty kitchen.

"Some are, some are not. It's as though she left in a rush and did not have time to take everything with her." Doris shook her head and clasped her hands together. "I told you, Master, I told you she was no good. We needed a maid with experience."

"She is an intelligencer's daughter," Walsingham explained, reaching for the back of a chair by the fireplace and clinging to it. "She can be trusted. That was more important than her skill."

"Was it?" Kit asked. Her words cast a silence across the room as an idea occurred to her. "In Chartley, the maid saw everything." Her eyes settled on Iomhar, who nodded slowly in agreement. "As a servant, practically invisible, she saw where Mary Stuart had hidden her letters, and she saw too how the Queen of Scots escaped."

"What? How?" Walsingham demanded.

"She was dressed as a maid," said Kit. She turned to the housekeeper. "Which room is Joan's, Doris?"

"First door on your left, up the stairs."

Kit led the way up the servants' stairwell, with Iomhar behind her. Walsingham and Doris followed at a slower pace, still bickering.

"She is an intelligencer's daughter," Walsingham muttered once again.

"And useless. I would have been better served had you given me a pup. At least a dog can fetch and carry things well enough. Joan was idle, always standing in doorways with a dreamy look on her face. She was no good, Master. No good at all."

Kit reached for Joan's chamber door and thrust it open. Inside, the heat was stifling, as the room faced full west and had been basking in the sunlight all morning. Kit crossed to the window to find it was open far enough for someone to slip out.

"Surely she could not have climbed out," Walsingham said as he entered the room. "We are a floor up."

Kit smiled knowingly as she peered through the lead-lined glass. "It would be easy to climb down from here, especially for someone of Joan's slight size. The timber beams offer toeholds. I did it a number of times from my own room in the loft when I was young," she said, ignoring the heavy sigh from Walsingham behind her. "Trust me, if she can climb, it would have been easy for her to do."

"But why? Did she detest this job so much she could not stand it anymore?" Doris asked, her voice shrill. "The girl will die on the street. Does she wish to spend her days in hunger?"

"Maids see everything," Iomhar said darkly. "As ye say, what if she saw and heard *everything*?"

"Maybe that would explain how Mary Stuart's men knew we were coming." Kit glanced at Walsingham. "Doris, two days ago we were gathered in Walsingham's room with Laidlaw, Somers, and Marlowe. Where was Joan then?"

"She..." Doris paused, her brows knitted and her head tilted to one side as she thought. "I could not find her. She was supposed to be helping me dust the rooms, but I couldn't find her."

"She was listening in," Kit said succinctly. "If you did not warn Mary Stuart's men, Walsingham —"

"Of course I did not!"

"Someone did. What if it was Joan? What if you had a Stuart spy in your house, and did not even know it?"

CHAPTER 10

"A spy? In my own house? No, it is not possible. Surely not." Walsingham had not stopped muttering to himself since Kit had made the accusation. She and Iomhar were turning over Joan's small room, trying to find anything that could be of use to them. The truckle bed was upside down, with the straw pillows pulled apart so madly that Doris was picking up the strands off the floor, tearful and not saying much.

"It can't be true, it cannot," Walsingham said again, leaning against a nearby wall and thrusting his hands through what remained of his hair. "You are certain she was missing, Doris, when I met with the intelligencers?"

Doris stopped picking up straw momentarily. "There is no doubt in my mind, Master. I was calling her, wishing she would come and help with the dusting. When I eventually found her, everyone had left." She nodded at Kit and Iomhar. "When I asked where she had been, she said she'd been in the privy, but I had just been there myself and did not believe her."

Kit was busy searching through the coffer. Pulling out the few chemises, she soon emptied the box. She searched every crevice, but there was no secret compartment as there had been in Mary Stuart's coffer. As she returned the chemises, the last one she collected made a crackling sound, as if the cloth was made of paper.

"It cannot be possible, it cannot be," Walsingham was muttering quietly.

"How else can ye explain information leaking out of this building?" Iomhar asked, running his hands around the lead-lined window, looking for any secret hiding places. "Last year when ye and the queen sent Kit to Chartley, Lord Ruskin's men discovered the truth. Ye said only ye, the queen and Kit knew she had left London to deliver a letter to Mary Stuart. Supposedly, no other knew she had gone. Yet they did, and they tracked Kit, attacking her in York. How did they learn of her task?"

"Yes, yes, I know." Walsingham was tense as he rested a fist on the wall beside him. "Joan could have heard, but she would have to have been listening at doors to hear Kit and I talking together."

"She did keep appearing in odd places," Kit murmured as she held up the last chemise. She ran her fingers along the tightly sewn hem. "She could have heard what we spoke of."

"A spy!" Doris wailed and picked up the last of the straw. "How can this be?"

Walsingham laid a hand on her shoulder, a silent but comforting action. "Where was Joan the other night? When Fraser broke in and tried to..." He raised a shaky hand to his own throat.

"It was her night off," Doris muttered.

"How convenient," Kit said wryly. She found a part of the chemise that crackled more than any other. Here, the hem was sewn untidily. "How were Joan's sewing skills, Doris?"

"Poor. Poor indeed!" Doris huffed. "She tore one of the master's tapestries."

"She did?" Walsingham stared at the housekeeper, but Doris didn't return the look.

"It was only the very corner. I told her she had to fix it, but she fixed it so poorly that it was worse than it had been before."

"How come I never knew this?" Walsingham asked, placing his hands on his hips.

"I moved one of your trestle tables in front of it."

Kit took out one of her daggers and slid it into the hem of the chemise, slicing the poor stitching open. Iomhar appeared at her shoulder, crouching down for a better look at what she was doing.

"She had her hiding place, but she kept it very close indeed." Kit opened up the material, revealing that the chemise had a double skirt — the inside acting as a secret compartment. Two letters fell out.

"Why didn't she take these with her?" Iomhar asked, reaching for one of the letters.

"She may have run out of time." Kit picked up the other letter and unfolded the parchment. When the image of the unicorn appeared on the page, Iomhar cursed.

"In the name of the wee man above and all the devils on earth." He snatched the parchment from Kit's grasp, stood, and turned the paper for Walsingham to see. "Ye want an answer to your question, Walsingham? Ye have it. Ye had a spy under your roof."

Walsingham took the paper with a trembling hand. His lips were pale and grey, pressed firmly together. Eventually, the silence was broken, but his voice shook. "Everything I have done this last year has been overheard by Mary Stuart's spy. No wonder you suspected me." He didn't raise his gaze but kept it firmly on the letter. "We have to find her. Joan could be the link we need to find Mary Stuart."

Kit lay on her stomach by the open grate of the fire. A cool breeze passed down the chimney, offering some relief from the heat of the day. Dabbing her temple with the sleeve of her shirt, she studied the two letters in front of her. They were the letters she had taken from Joan's chemise. Before she'd left

Seething Lane, Walsingham had ordered her to decode them and find out who Joan was working for before Mary Stuart could flee from England.

Phelippes was still in Chartley and, judging by the message that had arrived that afternoon at Seething Lane, he would be struggling with his health for some time. He was certainly in no fit state to ride back to London. It was down to Kit alone to decipher what was in these two letters.

In the meantime, Walsingham had gone to see Joan's father, a trusted intelligencer, and a message had arrived shortly after at Kit's door. The intelligencer had not known of his daughter's actions, though he had confessed that there had been some secretive behaviour on her part. She kept to herself these days and avoided him.

"Katherine? Will ye come and eat?" Moira's voice made Kit look up from her task. The soft evening light filtered through the window and bathed Moira's face in a gentle hue. She wore a small smile. "Dinner has been prepared. I doubt I can hold Rhona back from eating for long. Will ye not come and join us?"

"I need to do this. Thank you, but..." Kit hesitated, looking back down at her work. "I need to get this done." She was determined to crack the code, both to clear Walsingham's name and to find a hint as to where Mary Stuart could be now.

"Ye must eat, Katherine." Moira walked into the room and sat in a nearby chair, looking down at her. "Were ye nae taught we do our best work with a full belly?"

"Someone may have said that once." Kit thought Doris might have muttered it to her on occasion.

"Aye, so come and eat. The family is waiting for ye." Moira stood and held out her hand. Kit stared, tempted to take it and leave the papers behind, yet the mention of the family urged her to stay where she was.

They were Iomhar's family, not her own. It didn't matter how close she felt to Moira these days, nor to Iomhar's sisters. They were his kin. Their presence was a harsh reminder of the emptiness she had felt when Walsingham had threatened to send her away. Working for him was her life. She had no other to turn to.

"I should work," Kit said with a small smile. "Thank you. I shall come and find something to eat later, but for now, I must stay."

"As ye wish." Moira walked to the door. Kit felt eyes on her for a minute or two, and she rather suspected Moira hovered in the doorway, watching her.

Kit returned her focus to the letters. Try as she might, she could not find a key to get into the code. She assigned letters to the most common symbols that appeared, in the hope it would open up the code to her, but each attempt failed. It was plain this code was a layered one, with not only letters swapped for others, but also entire words and perhaps names having their own substitutions. As an intelligencer's daughter, it was possible that like Kit, Joan had been taught such codes at a young age.

"My mother has sent me to fetch ye." Iomhar's deep voice from the doorway made Kit smile. "Though I doubt I could persuade ye to eat if she cannot."

"You are correct." She waved a hand at him. "You return to your food. I must work."

"We are still waiting for my brothers to return regardless." Iomhar shrugged and walked into the room, taking the seat that Moira had vacated a few minutes ago.

"The earl and Niall?" Kit lowered the quill in her hand, the soft feathers tickling her wrist. "Where are they?"

"Niall was given some information this morning that suggested someone knew something about Lord Ruskin's whereabouts." Iomhar didn't look convinced as he sat back in the chair. "They have gone to a tavern to see what a drunkard knows. Sounds promising, does it not?"

"Aye!" She mimicked his Scottish accent, prompting him to smile. "I cannot eat now," she added, raising the quill again. "Joan has cast a shadow over Seething Lane for this last year. If she is the reason we have been followed, and why Lord Ruskin seems to be one step ahead of us so often, then I have to find her."

"For Walsingham's sake? Or to find Mary Stuart?"

"Both," Kit answered simply as she lifted the quill and tried assigning a number to each coded symbol.

"I thought today your loyalty to him had wavered. Seems I was wrong."

Kit hesitated. An ink blot bled out from the tip of the quill and marred her work.

"Even if Walsingham is not the Rose, he is a flawed man," said Iomhar.

"I never said he wasn't. I still owe him my life."

"Aye, a controlled life."

"What else do I have?" Kit asked suddenly. She dropped the quill and moved to her knees, facing Iomhar. "You have another life aside from being an intelligencer, Iomhar. You have your family." She waved a hand at the door, beyond which the soft murmur of voices could be heard in the dining room. "You have another life to turn to, but I do not. You speak of Walsingham as if I should cast him away."

"Why not? He shackles your life."

"Does he? Or has he given me one when I had none?"

"I am not looking to argue with ye," Iomhar said, his voice deep. "I am telling ye something ye already ken. He controls ye."

"It's the only life I know." Kit snatched up the quill, ready to work again.

"It does not have to be."

They stared at one another, the silence stretching out between them.

"Are they home yet?" Abigail's voice could be heard in the corridor. It was so near that Kit and Iomhar looked away from one another. Iomhar sat back in his chair and Kit shuffled on the hearth rug.

"Aye! I can see them," Rhona called from nearby. "They are riding down the road now."

"They are back." Iomhar stood and left the room. Kit shuffled the papers together, frustrated that she had made no headway with the code. Now she couldn't concentrate at all.

A soft sound reached her ears and Kit stilled. Someone was humming a tune. It was gentle, nothing loud or lively. The hum grew closer and Kit turned her head toward it, thinking there was something familiar about the tune.

Moira's voice became recognisable as she hovered in the hallway by the front door. Abigail ran out ahead of her, with Iomhar at her side, ready to greet their brothers.

Drawn by the sound of Moira's humming, Kit moved to her feet and left the letters behind. Standing in the doorway to the hall, she listened as Moira sang a few words from the gentle ditty.

"In a garden so green, in a May morning,
Heard I my Lady pleen of paramours.
Said she, my love so sweet,

Come you not yet, not yet;
Heght you not me to meet amongst the flowers?"

She hummed the tune again before she sang just one line.

"*Solace shall sweetly sing for evermore.*"

"Moira." Kit's voice made Moira break off. "Forgive me, but … I know that tune. What is it?"

"An old Scottish ditty. I sang it when I was a child myself." She turned her head and looked at the door, in expectation of her sons' arrivals. "Nay, I am not sure what brought it to mind today. Perhaps the hot weather."

"Perhaps." Yet Kit's curiosity was roused. She was certain she had heard that tune somewhere before. "There's something familiar about it."

"I am surprised, for I have not heard it myself for many years." Moira gave Kit a curious look. "Aye, I think the last time I heard it was twenty years or more ago."

"Where was that?"

"It's a day I look back on with sadness." Moira looked down at the ground. "I heard a father sing it to his daughter. I have nay wish to look back on that day."

"Why is it a sad memory?"

"They were both lost to this world soon after. The father and the daughter." Moira raised her chin. "I should not sing the song. Despite its merriness, it makes me sad."

Voices were heard beyond the door.

"Ye are growing even more demanding, Abigail, now ye are grown."

"Ye move too slowly for my liking, that is all."

On the other side, the Earl of Ross and Niall appeared with an excited Abigail and a grinning Iomhar. The brothers both looked tired, and there was dirt smeared across their fine clothes.

"What happened to ye two?" Iomhar asked, gesturing to the dirt. His older brother Duncan, the Earl of Ross, shook his arms and the dry sods fell to the floor around him. Niall chuckled and wiped some of the mud from his cheeks.

"Ye two been rolling around in soil?" Rhona asked, walking through the hall toward them.

"We fell off our horses, running from a man in the tavern. It seems our brother was dressed so finely, they thought him a target." Niall gestured to Duncan, who frowned. "They tried to pick his pocket."

"That is hardly the news we should be imparting, is it?" said the earl.

"Aye, aye, I ken." Niall held up his dirtied palms in surrender before he went on. "The drunkard we met had some information for us. It seems Lord Ruskin has been seen in London."

CHAPTER 11

"Say it again," Iomhar breathed.

"Can we not sit down and eat? Look at the three of ye." Moira gestured between the three brothers. "Ye are all so busy pacing ye cannot rest. Ye can talk as ye eat, can ye not?"

Niall sat, but neither the Earl of Ross nor Iomhar managed it. The earl was too busy picking at the dirt on his doublet, and Iomhar was gripping his high-backed chair, leaning over it.

"He's in London, Mother," Iomhar said in a low voice.

"He *may* be in London," Kit corrected him.

She was sitting between Moira and Rhona at the candlelit table, aware that Moira was piling her plate high with the turnip and rabbit stew that Elspeth had made them. Rhona kept filling up her glass of wine and Kit thanked her for it with a smile.

"Ye doubt what we have learned?" the Earl of Ross asked.

"How much can the word of a drunk be relied upon?" Kit's words took the wind out of the earl's sails, and he sat down heavily. Iomhar did the same, sitting opposite Kit.

"Ye do not believe we should put faith in this information?" he asked.

"No." Kit began to eat, with Moira already adding more to her trencher. "I have plenty, thank you, Moira."

"Ye need more," Moira replied, smiling. Since she had come to London, she had developed a habit of taking care of Kit, in the same way she did her own children. She now reached across the table and added more stew to Iomhar's trencher as well.

"Niall, these past few months you have spread the word that you are looking for information on Lord Ruskin's whereabouts. Yes?"

"Aye," the youngest of the three brothers answered, spooning turnips into his mouth.

"Then almost every man in every tavern has by now heard that a wealthy earl and his brother are looking for information and are willing to drop a few coins just to hear something of him."

"She is right." Rhona nudged Kit good-naturedly.

The two of them had grown closer these last few months and it was not unusual for them to spend evenings playing cards together, games that were frequently disturbed by Iomhar, who would then conveniently win most of the time. When she had been at Chartley, Kit had missed those quiet, playful evenings. Laughter had seemed easy.

"How poor did this man look?" Rhona added.

"He wore rags." Duncan sighed heavily.

"Aye, he was looking for a hearty meal, and ye gave him the money to pay for one." Rhona gestured to her bowl as she spoke. "I agree with Kit. It sounds to me like ye have been deceived."

A silence overtook the room. It was only disturbed by Moira adding more stew to everyone's bowls but her own. In the end, Iomhar took the ladle off her, and added some more to her trencher.

"Ye are certain of this, Kit?" he asked.

"You know Lord Ruskin better than I," she said simply. "Tell me this. A man who is so loyal to his cause, where would he be when he discovered from one of his spies that Mary Stuart was due to be arrested by Walsingham's men?"

"Ah." Iomhar dropped the ladle into the stew pot in the middle of the table. "He'd stay close to his queen."

"I believe so. The chances of him being in London are slim."

Another silence descended on the room. The hope that had rippled through the family after Duncan and Niall's return now faded. Abigail prodded her food but ate little. Opposite her, Rhona sighed audibly. The three men all slumped forward, their elbows on the table. From their matching stances, Kit guessed it must have been a position their father had adopted during times of stress.

Moira was the only one who held herself tall. She said little, and her lips were pressed together. She was hiding her thoughts, as she had so often done over these last few months. Then she spoke.

"Perhaps it is a good thing that man is not here." She broke the silence and pulled one of the candles a little closer to her trencher, so she could see her food. The warm glow landed on her face, making the shadows under her eyes seem deeper than before. "I would not wish to see any of ye chasing after him again."

"Mother," Iomhar said quietly, "ye ken we cannot let the matter go."

"We cannot," Niall seconded. "Not until he faces a court for what he has done."

Kit's eyes found Iomhar. He looked briefly at her before glancing down at his food. She wondered if Iomhar would let Lord Ruskin see a court, or if he would take justice into his own hands.

"And what would be the price, I ask ye? Hmm?" Moira sat forward. "Another of ye lost from this family?" Her breath hitched and her voice shook.

"Ma, that is not what they are saying," Rhona pleaded.

"It is not something they can vow will not happen, is it?" Moira asked sharply. When she received no answer, she looked at Kit.

"No one can promise that." Kit would not lie to her.

Moira stood abruptly.

"Mother?" Niall tried to stop her from going, but it was too late. Moira was already hurrying to the door.

"I will not lose anyone else from this family. One death before his time was enough. Nay more!" Moira's voice broke and she walked out of the room, with a hand to her mouth.

"Kit!" Niall hissed.

"What did I say?"

"Ye could have said nothing. We will not die in the pursuit of our father's murderer."

"It is not a vow you can keep for certain. You know that as well as I do." Kit looked at Iomhar. He didn't argue with her but nodded. "I will go after her."

"Let me." Rhona was already on her feet, but Kit stood too and took her shoulder, urging her to sit down again.

"I am the one who upset her with my bluntness. I should apologise. Eat, Rhona, please."

Rhona sat down again, but her eyes stayed on the door, looking at the place where her mother had disappeared. Kit took a candle from the table and left the room, following the path Moira had taken.

Eventually, Kit heard a sound in the darkness that drew her toward Lady Ross. She was humming that same tune again, yet this time it sounded mournful.

"Moira?" Kit called as she entered the corridor. Moira was sitting halfway up the staircase, as if she had lost the energy to continue all the way up, her head resting on the banister beside her. As Kit crossed to the bottom step, Moira lifted her head. Tears glistened on her cheeks in the candlelight.

"Moira, I'm so sorry," Kit whispered.

"Why should ye be?" Moira asked, her voice husky. "Ye were right, Katherine. It is not a promise my boys can make, as much as they may wish to." Kit could not help but smile at Moira calling the three grown men that sat in the dining room boys. They had all left childhood long ago, but it was a testament to her love for them that they would always be her precious children. "They may not be as honest as ye always are."

"Honest, or blunt, I am not sure." Kit walked up the stairs and sat a few steps down from Moira. She placed the candle between them. "I am sorry all the same for what I said."

"Do not be," Moira said again. "Aye, it is a fear I've had for some time." She stared into the candle flame. "Ever since I lost my husband, I have feared what one of them, if not all of them, would do. Each day I see the hunger in their eyes. Do I wish for justice? Of course I do. Yet I know that it is not always possible." She smiled sadly. "My husband would not have wanted them to forfeit their own lives in return for justice for his death."

"A good man," Kit said softly.

"Aye, the best of men." Moira began to hum the tune again. Kit didn't disturb her.

An image flickered in Kit's mind. She was a child again, walking with someone, her small hand clutched in their larger one. A male voice was singing the same song in a tone so deep it seemed to echo through her bones.

"You mentioned a father singing that song to his daughter," said Kit. She felt a curiosity burning within her. "That was the last time you heard it. Who was that? The man?"

"Someone I knew long ago." Moira stared into the distance. "He was singing it to his daughter after his wife had passed." She frowned. "It was shortly before they were both lost to this world. That is why the song makes me sad — it conjures thoughts of death." She sighed. "I suppose that is why I'm singing it today. Hearing of my boys and their quest to find Lord Ruskin, how that man himself may be searching for us…" She trailed off and swallowed. "Death seems nearer than before."

"Who were the father and daughter?"

"The father was John Stuart, Commendator of Coldingham." Moira smiled sadly. "He was the illegitimate son of James V, King of Scotland. He married a good friend of mine. Well, they eloped." Her smile grew a little. "She was the daughter of the Countess of Lennox. They married in secret and they had a daughter. But my friend lost her life giving birth to the girl." Moira rested her elbows on her knees, fidgeting with the skirt of her gown. "John was a devoted father — loving and kind. And despite his responsibilities, he always found time for his daughter."

"What became of him?" Kit whispered, entranced by the story. She had known little about the Scottish royal family, apart from James VI, Mary Stuart's son, who now sat on the throne. The existence of an illegitimate line was news to her.

"He remarried. A woman by the surname Hepburn, I think." Moira wrinkled her brow, trying to recall what had happened. "The marriage lasted just a year. He died of a sickness in the winter of sixty-three. A sad day it was. I remember writing to the family, to ask for news of the daughter. They told me she'd drowned."

Kit sat forward, nearly knocking over the candle. "Drowned? How?"

"No one knew. A maid claimed to have seen the child in the river by the house, but they never saw the child again." Moira sniffed and wiped her cheeks with the back of her wrist. "Whenever I hear that song, it makes me think of poor John Stuart and his daughter. She was barely three years old."

"She drowned..." Kit repeated the words, feeling a strange darkness settle over her. "What was the girl's name?"

"Did I not say?" Moira met her gaze. "It was the same as her mother's. Katherine." She raised a hand and gestured at Kit. "Ye asked me once whom ye reminded me of the day that ye arrived at our home in Scotland. It was Katherine Douglas's face I saw in your own. The Countess of Lennox's daughter, and the wife of John Stuart, Commendator of Coldingham. But that is impossible, is it not? They had nay other children, and that poor girl died."

"When? When did she die?" This time Kit leaned so far forward that she succeeded in knocking the candle over. They both scrambled to put the flame out as it fell against Moira's wide skirts. They flattened their palms to the silks and the candle wick, casting themselves into darkness. "I'm sorry," Kit whispered.

"Ye are full of energy, Kit. One could almost say ye are excited."

"No, I am not that." Kit couldn't describe what she felt. The news that she resembled this woman, Katherine Douglas, was unsettling. It had shaken her to her core and left her with trembling fingers that she lifted from the spent candle. "Please, tell me. When did she die? The daughter, Katherine?"

"Not long after her father — in the winter of sixty-three. Twenty-three years ago."

"Excuse me, Moira. There is somewhere I need to be." Kit scrambled to her feet in the moonlight.

"Katherine, where are ye going?" Hearing Moira address her by her full name only unsettled her all the more. "Katherine?" Moira said again, standing.

"I ... I have to go." Kit hurried to the door at the front of the house, Moira following her. Kit grabbed her hat from a nearby hook and pulled it onto her head. The night air was still so warm that she didn't bother with a cloak or a thicker jerkin as she stepped out into the darkness.

"Where are ye going?" Moira called from the doorway behind her. "Katherine, the nightwatchmen will be out — if they see ye, they'll arrest ye for breaking the curfew."

"Then so be it. I have to be somewhere. Goodnight, Moira." Kit turned and nodded at Lady Ross, then left. She headed to the stable around the back of the house to look for a horse. Inside the house she could hear raised voices. No doubt Moira was speaking to the family of the strangeness that had just passed between them and Kit's hasty exit.

Once the horse was prepared, Kit pulled herself up into the saddle and made her way around the house, glancing up and down the street to ensure the watchmen weren't about. The moon lit her path with a silvery glow, making it easy for her to see how empty it was. There were no watchmen, no neighbours pressing their noses to the glass windows, curious at the sound of the horse's hooves. It meant Kit could move freely around the streets.

The front door opened and before Kit could leave, a face appeared in front of her.

"Iomhar!" she hissed. "Return to the house."

"Where are ye going at this time of night?" Iomhar stood in her path, his feet planted wide on the cobblestoned road. "Ye wish to be caught by the watchmen?"

"Walsingham would get me out of gaol soon enough." She tugged on the reins, preparing to ride around him.

"What is it? What's wrong?" Iomhar took a step forward.

She had told him her secrets before now. She wanted to tell him of her suspicion. Yet if what Moira had said was true, if Kit did look like this Katherine Douglas, then there could be a greater secret in her past than even she had ever suspected.

"I'm sorry, I cannot talk now." Kit pulled on the reins and circled Iomhar with the horse.

"Kit? Kit!" Iomhar tried to race after her, but she galloped off, and after a few strides he gave up. She glanced back once, watching him stand there in the moonlight in the green jerkin he wore. Then he was gone as she turned a corner.

CHAPTER 12

"Barn Elms." The words escaped Kit in a breathy whisper as she stared at the manor house. She had ridden a long way that night, despite the darkness and the watchmen prowling the roads. She'd come all the way to Richmond with the intention of seeing Walsingham.

Clicking her tongue, she urged the horse on and they trotted down the gravel driveway, toward the grand manor. At this time of night, the red brick walls looked brown, and the windows were speckled with an even deeper shade of black. Only a few of the windows glowed with candlelight to show that someone was still awake in the house.

Kit left her horse tied to the railings at the front of the house and approached the entrance, jumping up the front stoop. Knocking relentlessly on the door, she didn't let up until it was answered. Rather than it being answered by the steward, Withers, who had so often looked at Kit with narrowed eyes and distaste, it was another face that Kit knew all too well.

Frances, Lady Sidney, stood in the doorway.

"Good Lord, who knocks so much at this time of — oh…" Sir Francis Walsingham's daughter broke off when she saw Kit. "You are disturbing us. Go home." She tried to close the door, but Kit slammed her foot in the gap. The heavy oak door nearly squashed her. Kit cursed at the pain and thrust her shoulder into the wood, heaving it open. Lady Sidney leapt back, startled by her forceful entrance. "It is late," she said bluntly, with a hand on her chest. "Most have retired for the night already."

"Has your father retired?" Kit asked. When Lady Sidney didn't answer, she knew the truth. Kit closed the door behind her and picked up a candle from a ledge nearby, carrying it with her as she marched down the corridor. "Where is he?"

"We have talked of this much." Lady Sidney followed her, clearly displeased. "You are not welcome in this house."

"You have said it much, but I do not have time for your petty jealousies tonight. I have something graver to speak of with your father."

"Leave this house!" Lady Sidney demanded, cutting in front of Kit. "Be gone, Kit Redcap."

The childhood insult no longer cut through Kit. She simply smiled into the vexed face of Lady Sidney, which was turning red. "As I said, this does not concern you. The sooner you let me see him, the sooner I'll be gone from this house." Kit walked around her. Lady Sidney pulled on her arm, but Kit tugged it away so fast that Lady Sidney staggered back.

"Do not touch me again." The deathly quietness of Kit's voice made Lady Sidney shrink back. "As I said, I have no time for you tonight. You can curse me all you like when I am gone, but for now, you will tell me where your father is."

Lady Sidney raised a hand and pointed down the corridor. At the end of the hall was a closed door. Kit hurried toward it, leaving Lady Sidney in the darkness without a candle.

When she reached the door, she knocked just once and opened it, not waiting to be admitted.

"Franny? If that is you, it really is time we retired for the night," Walsingham said from where he was hunched over in a settle bench. He looked distinctly uncomfortable. Despite his grand house and the number of candles that were available around him, some even made out of beeswax rather than the cheaper tallow Kit was so used to, he had lit just one candle. It sat beside him on a small table, where a glass of red wine kept him company. The scent of the wine mixed with the cloves and cinnamon that had been brewed in it hovered in the air.

"I am not your daughter," Kit corrected him. "She is currently trembling in the corridor. I think I may have scared her."

Walsingham's head shot up. "Kit? Well, it would not be the first time you have scared her." He smiled a little. "The first time she hid from you was when you were both just girls. She hid behind my legs and pointed at you, as if you were some sort of devil."

"I remember it all too clearly." Kit closed the door, Walsingham eyeing her curiously. "I must speak to you."

"It's an odd time of night to have a conversation."

"Yet it must be done." Kit took a deep breath. "Tell me this. Who are John Stuart, Commendator of Coldingham, and Katherine Douglas?" Her words were simply said, and Walsingham's reaction was immediate.

He sat back on the bench, knocking the arms with his elbows and planting his feet on the floorboards beneath him. He blinked rapidly as he stared at Kit.

"You know the names." Kit broke the silence when he said nothing. She stepped forward, depositing the candle on the nearest table, and moved around the furniture to stand in front of Walsingham. "You know them, do you not?"

"It would be hard not to. Anyone who took an interest in the Scottish royal family would know of the late King James V's children, even his illegitimate ones. John Stuart was one such illegitimate son."

"You speak so casually, and yet your face betrays you…" Kit motioned toward him. Walsingham had paled and his thin lips trembled. "There is something more to this. Who are they, exactly? John Stuart and Katherine Douglas?"

"They married. Well, they eloped," Walsingham said hurriedly. "She was scarcely more than a child herself. They both died a short while later."

"What became of their child?"

"Enough of this." Walsingham picked up his glass, downed the contents, then slammed it back down on the table. "No more. We are not speaking of them."

"Why not?" Kit asked, stepping forward. "If these two names mean nothing to you, if they are simply two people who lived in Scotland long ago, and have been dead for over twenty years, then why are you shaking? Why are you so pale?"

"I am tired. That is all. I do not have my pills to comfort me, for someone took them from me." He raised an eyebrow in her direction.

Kit shook her head. "Someone told me this evening that I look like this Katherine Douglas."

Walsingham's eyebrows shot up. He reached for a carafe and poured some more wine into his glass. His arm shook and he managed to slosh half the red liquid over the rim.

"Do I?"

"I would not know. I never met her." Walsingham shook his head sharply. "What is the meaning of all of this? As you say, these people died long ago. You'd be better off forgetting that you had ever heard the names at all."

"Why? Why would I be better?"

"I am not talking of this." Walsingham drank the wine and banged the glass down on the table again. "Forget the names, Kit. That is an order." He moved to his feet.

"And I must follow your order, must I?"

"Yes!"

Kit stared at him, appalled.

"I will hear no more of this. Go home, Kit. Never say these words to me again."

The door behind her opened. Kit looked around to see Lady Sidney standing in the doorway. She had evidently been listening to their conversation, and now she held the door wide, ready for Kit to take her leave.

"You should go," Lady Sidney ordered. "Neither of us wish you to be here."

Kit looked to her mentor. "You deny me even now?"

"Those names mean nothing, Kit," Walsingham replied.

"And I should believe that the way I believe all of your lies," she said, heading for the door. Lady Sidney skulked back. "You fear me," Kit whispered to her as she passed. "I wonder if you fear the right person in this room."

"What does that mean?" Lady Sidney asked.

"It means I wonder —" Kit paused and glanced back at Walsingham — "how well you know your father." With these parting words she marched down the hallway.

"As Iomhar said," Kit muttered to herself as she left the house and hurried to her horse, "spymasters always have their secrets."

CHAPTER 13

The door creaked as Kit pushed it open. The sitting room of Iomhar's house was not as empty as she thought it would be. Despite the early hours of the morning, and the lack of candlelight suggesting everyone was in bed, one person had not retired for the night. Iomhar lay on a settle bench. His soft snores filled the air.

Kit slowly shut the door behind her, wincing as it creaked a second time. Creeping across the room, she tried not to wake Iomhar. His green jerkin was untied at the neck, showing a glimpse of his white shirt beneath, and his boots were kicked to the side of the room. His head was propped on a cushion filled with wool, and his chin lolled forward. He slept deeply, not stirring even as the floorboards creaked beneath Kit's feet.

Kit fetched herself a tankard from the sideboard and proceeded to pour herself some mead from a jug. She drank thirstily, for she had not taken a break on her ride back to the London house. She had repeatedly turned the meeting with Walsingham over in her mind, but she felt no more settled than she had done when she'd first left the manor house. She was more convinced than ever that he was keeping secrets from her.

Sitting beside the papers she had laid out on the hearth to decode, she tipped back the tankard and downed the mead, raising her eyes to Iomhar. He snored a little louder in his sleep, but did not wake. Part of her wanted to prod him, to ask why he had not retired for the night, and tell him where she had been. In the end, she resisted the temptation, deciding some secrets could stay secret. "For now," she murmured.

Placing the tankard down on the hearth beside her, she fetched the jug and poured herself a little more, then lit a candle with a tinderbox and placed the flame near to the papers. Leaning forward, she resumed her attempt to decode the letters.

The ink shapes blurred before her tired eyes. Whenever she yawned, the words morphed together. She pressed her fingers to her eyes, trying to keep herself awake. She didn't have time to sleep, not now. Mary Stuart was on the run and with no sign of where she had gone, these few fragments that had been left behind by Joan could hint at something.

Kit turned the pages and saw something familiar on the paper. She had seen the unicorn many times, but now she saw an emblem within the text, some sort of shape upon a shield. Reaching into her doublet, she retrieved the letters from Mary Stuart's chambers that she had hidden there. Unfurling the papers, she scattered them across the hearth. Some had only one or two coded words written on them. Others were covered with writing. She sifted through the papers, picking one up before tossing it aside, until she found the one she had remembered from Chartley Castle.

Amongst the coded words there was a small symbol that matched the emblem on Joan's coded letter. A tiny shield had been drawn and in that shield there was a writhing snake. Its tail was coiled on the left-hand side and to the right it reared its head with its forked tongue stuck out. The body of the snake was wrapped around a basilard that pointed downward.

"It's the same shield. They speak of the same thing." Kit had no notion of what the shield referred to, but it was plain that something in the two letters was aligned.

She turned to tell Iomhar of what she had found, but in the flickering candlelight, she saw his eyes were still closed. He was fast asleep, and she had no wish to destroy that peace.

"It can wait until morning." Stifling a yawn, Kit pushed the letters away and raised her body from the hearth. Blowing out the candle, she crossed the room to a second settle bench and lay down on it. It didn't matter how hard the wood was or how uncomfortably the arm of the seat pressed into her neck. She was too tired to register the discomfort; her eyelids closed within a few seconds.

Kit was in the water. Her small hands reached for the surface, as if she could use it to pull herself upward, but nothing happened. She simply sank deeper into the water.

Looking down, she saw the pink gown with the pearls that beaded her neck. One of her stockings was falling from her foot, floating limply in the water. Beneath her feet, she could see nothing but endless blue and green murkiness. Kit's legs moved, kicking madly as she looked up.

The silhouetted woman in the French hood stepped away and was replaced with bright sunlight streaming through the water.

Kit tried to scream for help. Her lips parted, but her mouth filled and no sound came out.

A bony hand reached through the water. It was there, as it always was these days whenever Kit had the dream. The hand took her wrist, and she was pulled upward, the grip strong as she was tugged from the depths. Her head broke the surface, and she saw Walsingham's face.

He was younger, though that illusion only lasted for a split second. It wasn't long before the dark hair became grey and his face turned gaunt, as she knew him now.

"Kit?" he said.

"Kit?"

She sat bolt upright and clutched the covers beneath her, finding she was no longer on the settle bench where she had fallen asleep, but on a bed. Flicking her head back and forth, she looked around.

It was morning and the sun shone brightly through the windows, making her squint. She was still dressed and had been sleeping on top of the covers of the bed, with only her boots missing — they had been tossed on the floor nearby.

"Kit?" The voice said her name again.

Iomhar was standing in the doorway to the chamber, leaning on the doorframe. He had some papers in his hand and was staring at her. "Ye were dreaming. Again," he murmured slowly. "Ye know ye make noises when ye dream?"

"I do?" Kit rubbed her eyes and stretched, trying to stifle a yawn that escaped her regardless.

"Something about water, and Walsingham." Iomhar raised an eyebrow. "The same dream as always, I gather."

"You would be right." Kit drew herself up into a seated position and leaned against the bedhead. "How did I end up here?"

"Some kind friend might have carried ye to a more comfortable bed." Iomhar smiled and returned his focus to the papers in his hand. Kit realised that he was looking at some of the letters she had left on the hearth the night before.

"Thank you," she whispered.

He glanced up long enough for them to share a smile. "Ye going to tell me where ye went last night?"

"No. Why did you not retire for the night to your own chamber?"

"I thought the settle bench looked more comfortable," he said wryly.

"Iomhar, I am being serious."

"Ye cannot expect a confession from me if ye will not tell me where ye went." He held her gaze. "Ye rode away as if the flames of hell were at your horses' hooves."

"Maybe it felt as if they were," Kit murmured. "Last night … it was nothing important. Simply a question I wanted answered by Walsingham."

"I'd place a wager on the fact he did not answer it." When Kit didn't reply, he smiled. "I see I am right."

"You always seem to be," Kit said grudgingly.

"Ah, I think that was a compliment."

"A very small one."

"Ye can praise me with more compliments in a minute, for I think I have found what ye have been looking for."

"What is that?"

He turned the top letter around so she could see it. It was the one they'd found in Mary Stuart's coffer. Unable to see the details this far across the room, Kit clambered off the bed and crossed the space, coming to stand at Iomhar's side.

"Ye left these two letters out," Iomhar said, showing her the two he had in his grasp. "Would it have something to do with this shared symbol?"

"Yes, they both have it." Kit tapped the paper.

"I know this symbol," Iomhar said.

"You do? What is it?"

"What's going on here, then?" Niall's voice made them jerk their heads around. He appeared further down the corridor, a smile on his face as he walked toward them. "Ye spending the night in Kit's chamber now, Iomhar?"

"Niall." Iomhar's voice deepened in warning, but Niall walked on quickly, heading for the stairs. "I will not say anything, but ye'd be wise to run along before our mother catches ye."

"Niall!" Kit matched Iomhar's sharp tone. Niall increased his pace and took the stairs two at a time, disappearing fast. "Your brother…"

"I'll give him another warning later. For now, look at this." Iomhar thrust the letter toward her. "I think we have just found an answer to who the Rose is."

"How?" Kit took the letter, raising it to her face so she could examine the emblem of the snake wrapped around a basilard again.

"It is a family crest. The Drakes bear this symbol. Robert Drake, Lord Buckingham, sits on the privy council. He's a lesser councillor, but he's there. I've seen this symbol in Walsingham's own papers."

"The Rose," Kit said, running her finger over the symbol. "Perhaps we have found him at last."

CHAPTER 14

"This is it?" Kit asked the driver as she and Iomhar pulled up in a cart outside a grand house in Drury Lane.

"It is." The driver held out his palm and Iomhar dropped a few coins into his hand. The driver nodded and urged them off the cart with an impatient wave.

"Privy councillors have fine homes, do they not?" Kit paused to admire the house. The building was set back from the cobblestoned road, with great timber beams and a lofted rooftop taller than any other house in the street. On one side, the building was bordered with red brick, while on the other the timber beams were painted black. The glass windows were lead-lined.

"Who is to say Lord Buckingham bought this from his work on the privy council?" Iomhar said, jumping down from the cart and standing behind Kit. "If he has been working for Mary Stuart's supporters, then he could have been paid by them too."

"Perhaps." They stepped forward together, staring at the impressive building as the cart disappeared down the road.

They had sent Niall to Seething Lane that morning with a message for Walsingham. Their letter spoke of what they had found in the coded letters, along with a suspicion Kit had after deciphering one of the letters belonging to the missing maid, Joan.

It was clear from the letter that Joan had been conversing with Robert Drake, for he wrote of multiple communications between the two of them, asking for news of Walsingham.

Once the maid had departed Seething Lane, she would have been looking for somewhere to hide.

"She could be here," Kit said quietly to Iomhar. "Where else would Joan go but to Drake, the man paying her for information?"

"Aye, she could be," Iomhar agreed. "Here's what we'll do. I'll arrest Lord Buckingham and whilst the house is in uproar, ye can look for Joan."

"Very well." Kit nodded as Iomhar knocked on the oak door.

The door swung open and a small man with white hair tied at the nape of his neck greeted them, bowing deeply.

"The Earl of Ross's brother to see Lord Buckingham."

As the steward nodded and let them in, Iomhar whispered in Kit's ear, "Sometimes the rank helps to open doors."

Kit followed him, but the steward held out a hand.

"Your servant boy can wait outdoors, sir."

"That's nay servant boy," Iomhar chuckled and beckoned Kit forward. The steward tried to get a better look at Kit's face, but she walked quickly around him, following Iomhar into an adjoining sitting room.

It was reasonably small, despite the grandness of the house, suggesting this was where the privy councillor met those he thought beneath him. In the air, the scent of honey and tallow fat mixed with the smell of that morning's breakfast.

"What's this? The Earl of Ross's brother?" said a voice in the corridor. A man entered the room a moment later, followed by a woman Kit presumed to be his wife. Lord Buckingham was not far off Walsingham's age, with a bulbous round head and small beady eyes. He stepped forward and greeted Iomhar with a deep bow. "I have not been visited by Scottish nobility before."

"Have ye not?" Iomhar said with a hint of sarcasm that only Kit noticed.

"You are most welcome, most welcome indeed. May I present my wife, Lady Roslyn Buckingham."

"How do you do." The lady curtsied and smiled sweetly at Iomhar. Her eyes flicked to Kit. "Your servant can wait outside."

"She is not my servant."

"She?" Lady Roslyn spluttered.

Kit smiled and offered her own curtsy.

"How unnatural," Lady Roslyn muttered, her fingers fidgeting with her pearl necklace. The words caused any humour Kit may have felt to vanish. She looked at Iomhar and nodded, urging him not to dally.

"I am here on business, Lord Buckingham. Ye are under arrest. I am to take ye to the Tower."

"The Tower?" Lady Roslyn cried. She dropped her necklace and reached for her husband's arm, dragging him back across the room.

"Pray, do not make this difficult, my lady. Your husband would be wiser to come with us without protest. Walsingham and Lord Burghley will wish to speak to him."

"What is this all about? This is absurd!" Despite Lady Roslyn's protests, Lord Buckingham had fallen silent. He did not have his wife's anger, nor her confusion. He stared at Iomhar levelly, then nodded once.

"Good. If ye will, my lord, this way." Iomhar took Lord Buckingham's arm, steering him out of the room.

"No, no! You cannot take him." Lady Roslyn's voice rose as she followed them toward the front door. Kit took advantage of her turned back to dive down the corridor and deeper into the house.

"Where are you?" Kit whispered, opening doors and glancing inside, looking for any sign of the missing maid.

Above stairs, she found the master's and mistress's chambers, easily identifiable by their fine furnishings, stained-glass panels in the window and the heavy curtains that were draped around the four-poster beds. A coffer in one of the chambers no doubt contained clothes that were fine and well made. A third chamber in the guest wing was not nearly as fine, but was clearly occupied. Maid's clothing was slung across a coffer and the familiar white coifs were hung over the bottom of the bed on small wooden hooks.

"She's here," Kit murmured to herself.

There was a creak of floorboards and Kit spun on her heel, leaving the bedchamber and hurrying across the landing. On the stairs, a maid scurried down. Her face was turned away and her hair was hidden in a coif.

"Joan!" Kit snapped at her. The maid halted and raised her head. The same blue eyes Kit had seen at Seething Lane stared up at her. "You cannot run."

The maid hastened away, jumping the last few steps to the floor. Kit cursed and raced after her, copying the action and leaping down the last three steps in an effort to catch up with the maid.

She sprinted through the house, darting into a parlour where she upturned a settle bench. It fell against the open door, closing it fast so Kit had to snatch her fingers away to stop them being trapped. She drove her shoulder into the wood, but it didn't budge. Gritting her teeth, Kit threw her entire weight against the door. The settle bench slid loudly, the wood scraping across the floorboards. The gap was now big enough for Kit to slip through, and she ran on, jumping over the fallen bench and reaching for a door on the other side of the room.

"Joan!" Kit called.

Raised voices reached her ears. It was a heated exchange between Iomhar, Lady Roslyn and the steward, who was appealing for help in the street, calling for someone to send for a constable.

"Joan?" Kit barked the maid's name again. Another sound reached her ears — the heavy thud of something falling over.

Kit pushed through the nearest door. She entered a dining room. On the opposite side was another door, standing ajar. Through that gap, she could see that a window had been opened.

Joan was trying her best to climb through the window, but the skirt of her gown kept catching on the frame. She had knocked over a small table beside her, smashing a glass vase that had rested on top, the wooden floorboards scattered with glittering shards.

Kit crept through the doorway, trying not to make a sound and alert the maid to her presence. Joan had one foot out of the window when the glass shards crunched beneath Kit's boot. She froze as Joan flicked her head around, and their eyes met.

"No good can come from running further, Joan."

The maid ignored the words and vaulted through the gap, dropping to the earth on the other side. Kit followed her. Without the encumbrance of a gown, she followed with ease and soon caught up with the maid.

"No!" Joan called out, as Kit grabbed her arm. She flung her hand at Kit's face, trying to push her away, but Kit grabbed her wrist and bent it back. "Ow! You'll break my arm, you fool."

"Then stop struggling!"

Joan fell limp in Kit's grasp and capitulated. Kit pushed one of Joan's arms up behind her back, taking such a hold of the maid that she would no longer be able to run away.

"Release me. I pray you, please let me go. They will kill me for this. Have you not seen what they do to traitors? They will hang me!"

"You are a spy." Kit turned to march the maid toward the front of the house. Despite Joan's protests, Kit doubted that she would hang. She was very young, practically still a child. Now they knew her father had known nothing of her spying ways, Walsingham had planned to return her to him. An intelligencer could watch over a spy well, even if that spy was his own daughter. She would be sent home to her father and punished for her crimes with a warning. First, they had to know what Joan had learned of Mary Stuart and her escape from Chartley Castle. "You are under arrest, Joan."

The maid cried. They were no small wails, but great heaving sobs as Kit led her around the house.

"What will my father say when he finds out?"

"This is an unhappy room," Iomhar whispered as he and Kit stood in the doorway of the dungeon in the Tower of London. "I shudder to think how much blood and how many tears have been shed here."

Kit nodded and rubbed her hands over her arms. The summer heat did not penetrate the cold stone walls this deep underground.

A few steps down and inside the room, Lord Buckingham sat on what appeared at first glance to be a table. Closer inspection revealed the straps on the wooden slab, attached to great metal cogs and wheels.

"It's the rack. It breaks men's bones," Iomhar murmured.

So far, it had not been used to torture Lord Buckingham. Walsingham and Lord Burghley stood in front of him. The three men sat on the privy council together. What would have been judged to be a meeting of councillors in any other room, in this dungeon had taken on a dark note.

"The betrayal, Buckingham. The betrayal!" Lord Burghley seethed and struck the flagstone flooring with his cane. The dull thud echoed around them. "You have sat beside me for years, a good councillor, and a loyal one too, I thought. That was clearly my mistake." He released a shuddery breath.

"A mistake shared by us all." Walsingham's voice was quiet compared to Lord Burghley's booming tones. "Your decisions always seemed to be for the good of the country, Buckingham. Always."

"I did what was right for our people." Buckingham lifted his chin with the words. "I never wavered in my duty, and I never will. I could do good from my small part in the council. It wasn't until these last few years that I saw how much good I could do."

"By trying to put Mary Stuart on the throne?" Burghley asked, striking the flagstones again with his cane.

"Queen Mary." Buckingham's voice took on a sharpness. "She is the rightful queen. Did you not read the ballads and the sheets? The queen you worship has been excommunicated by the Pope. She has been damned to hell."

"She is your queen," Walsingham reminded him solemnly.

"No. No, she is not." Buckingham shook his head. The white hair at his temple shuddered with the movement. "She is the pretender queen. The Pope has authorised her assassination. What was I to do?" He held his hands out in a supplicant manner, as if he was a boy that had been taunted by the promise of sweetmeats, rather than a man that was speaking of murder. "I had to do something. The balance of power had to be reset. Elizabeth must be gone, and Mary shall take her place."

"This is madness!" Lord Burghley stepped back, shaking his head. "You honestly believed such schemes would work? Did you give your name to this Babington plot too? Were you one who prayed for its success?"

"Make me a martyr if you will. I will gladly go to my grave as one." Buckingham smiled. "I will not apologise for supporting the rightful path of God."

"He's ready to die for his beliefs," Kit whispered to Iomhar in the doorway.

"It is what zealous men are prepared to do, both Catholic and Protestant."

"Not all men are willing to murder, though," Kit reminded him. He didn't answer her but shifted his weight between his feet. "What is it you are not saying?"

"I think many a person is capable of killing. It's not always a case of cruelty or maliciousness. Some men kill because they think it is the right thing to do." He stared at Buckingham. "I do not like it, nay, but it is the way the world is."

"We are not all killers." Yet a lump formed in Kit's throat with the words. She was a killer. She had become one in the winter when she had fought for her life. She had been haunted by that guard's face in her dreams, a ghost that would not rest. Since then, she had vowed never to take another's life. Come what may, she would do what she could to avoid more death.

Iomhar had told her it was not murder, but self-defence. It would be a hard thing to argue now, faced with their current conversation.

"Enough," Burghley said to Buckingham. "Tell us where she is."

"Queen Mary?"

"Mary Stuart," Walsingham said. "The *former* Queen of Scots."

"Queen Mary is in hiding. Where, I do not know." Buckingham smiled again. "I pray she stays hidden from you. May one of her men rise to put her on the throne yet, where she belongs."

Walsingham shook his head. He and Lord Burghley turned away from Buckingham and climbed the short steps to where Kit and Iomhar stood.

"He will not tell us anything," Walsingham said in a low voice.

"He's lying," Kit said, capturing their attention. "He knows where she is. He just does not want to tell you."

"Then we'll get it from him." Lord Burghley raised his cane and pointed it at the rack.

"With respect, my lord, he has expressed a wish to die a martyr. Nay, I do not believe he would tell ye anything under torture," Iomhar said.

"Perhaps there is another way to find out what he knows," Kit murmured.

"Then find it." Walsingham walked past her. The atmosphere between them had been chilly following her visit to Richmond and did not look to thaw anytime soon.

CHAPTER 15

Iomhar thrust open the door to Lord Buckingham's house. The steward trembled on the other side, leaping back so far that he collided with the mahogany-panelled wall.

"You cannot just demand entry to this house," the steward argued, waving his arms madly. "This is still Lord Buckingham's house."

"Ye believe it to be. Soon enough, it will be seized by the Crown for the master's crimes." Iomhar held the door open and Kit stepped in. "Where are we to begin looking?"

"Anywhere that Lord Buckingham may hide his papers." She strode through the corridor with Iomhar at her heel. The steward's panicked cries were soon turned in another's direction.

"My lady! My lady! They are here again."

Lady Roslyn appeared in front of them. She blocked their entrance to a room Kit could see was full of papers. A table was pushed to one side, almost as black as the ink that peppered those papers. Beside the table there were stacked shelves and stepped buffets, covered with a series of scrolls and books. They were all neatly organised, with one book resting perfectly on top of another.

"Where have you taken my husband?" Lady Roslyn demanded, stepping forward and knocking her farthingale into Kit's legs.

"To the Tower," Kit answered simply. She brushed the lady's farthingale aside in her bid to enter the room.

"You have no manners. None!" Lady Roslyn complained, clinging to the doorframe as Kit hurried into the room and headed for the shelves. Iomhar followed her, though he glanced back at Lady Roslyn.

"Your husband has confessed to being a traitor to our queen." His deep tone made Lady Roslyn freeze. "He gladly admitted it. Any rights he had to privacy are gone, my lady. Aye, even more so when we are hunting a traitor queen, for he had a hand in helping her escape."

Joan had confessed under questioning that she had been feeding information to Lord Buckingham for over a year. In exchange for that information, he had promised her money. Her head had been turned by the promise of gold and it had not been long before she was telling him every word she had managed to overhear in Seething Lane. She had told Lord Buckingham too of their commission to arrest the Queen of Scots. Somehow, Lord Buckingham must have passed that message to a fast rider, some messenger that was able to remove Mary Stuart from Chartley Castle before they could reach her.

"He may not have kept any coded papers here," Iomhar said now, joining Kit by the shelves. "The risk of discovery would be too great."

"We must check." She waved a hand at the desk, and he turned over the papers that resided there, sifting through them.

Kit opened books, searching for codes, familiar names, even the now familiar emblem of the Scottish unicorn, yet she found nothing. In her frustration, she tossed the books aside, some of their pages falling out like leaves.

"How dare you?" Lady Roslyn fumed at the mess.

Ignoring her, Kit turned her attention to the scrolls on another shelf. These were papers that related to the council. Her eyes grew wide at all the private information Lord Buckingham had taken home with him. "Iomhar?"

"Aye?" He moved to her side.

"Do you remember two years ago papers were found on a Jesuit priest we arrested? Papers that should never have left the council's rooms? There are more here." She offered up the scrolls for Iomhar to see. He took them, flicking through them and nodding.

"Aye, ye have your spy. It's the evidence to back up his own confession."

"My husband is no traitor," Lady Roslyn snarled from the doorway. "He would not do such a thing."

Kit looked at Lady Roslyn, uncertain whether the lady truly believed in her husband's innocence and had no knowledge of his crimes, or if she was in collusion with him.

"What do you know, Lady Roslyn? Of all that your husband has done? How did he explain Joan's presence in this house?" Kit waited for an answer.

Lady Roslyn fidgeted with the sleeves of her gown, her tearful eyes never once leaving Kit's face. "She is the daughter of a friend of his. She had nowhere to go after she was dismissed from employment. My husband offered her shelter."

"Why did Joan not go to live with her father?" Kit's question hung in the air, unanswered. "She does not know the truth," Kit whispered to Iomhar, who had collected all the papers together, ready to confiscate them from the house.

"Nothing more is here." Iomhar shook his head. "If Lord Buckingham communicated with Joan by letter, then those letters must be somewhere."

"I know." Kit was no longer searching the room. She was staring at Lady Roslyn as she dabbed her cheeks, drying her tears. "Roslyn."

"You should address me as 'my lady'," Lady Roslyn said sharply.

"It is hardly dissimilar to Lord Buckingham's codename, is it? The Rose? I wonder…"

Kit nodded at Iomhar, and he gathered up the rest of the scrolls as she left the room, moving past Lady Roslyn's shoulder.

"How dare you?" Lady Roslyn cried, following Kit. "Come back here at once!"

Kit took the stairs two at a time, with Lady Roslyn struggling to follow at such a pace with her farthingale and gown.

Remembering where she had seen the two grand chambers in her search for Joan, Kit headed for the lady's chamber and threw open the door, going straight to the coffer.

Lifting the lid, she felt for a secret compartment, but there was none. Next, she reached for the window and felt around the frame, but there was no space for a letter to be pushed away and hidden. She turned her attention to the gowns within the coffer and pulled them out, feeling along the hems for the sounds of wrinkled paper.

"What are you doing?" Lady Roslyn ran into the room and tried to snatch the gowns back. "These are my gowns —"

"My lady, listen to me. If my suspicion is correct and you know nothing of your husband's treason, then you must understand it is possible that he has hidden the greatest evidence of his treason by planting it on *you*." Kit's words took the wind out of Lady Roslyn's sails. She stood very still, a lone tear sliding down her cheek. "He used the codename 'the Rose'. So similar to your own name, is it not?"

Lady Roslyn let go of the gowns. "My husband would not do that to me. He would not."

"We do not always know what goes on in the hearts and minds of those we trust." Kit thought of Walsingham, then pushed the thought away. "If your husband has hidden something in this chamber, my lady, then you must tell me where. Or there is a chance that you could be found guilty of treason as well."

Lady Roslyn raised a hand to her cheek, as if she had been struck by Kit's words.

"I would never..." She trailed off, then raised a shaking hand and pointed across the room at a chest. It was raised high on legs with a glass mirror set at the back between two panels of wood. "I often found him by my chest."

Kit dropped the gowns back into the coffer and walked over to the chest. She opened the cupboard doors. Running her hand along the side of one of the panels, she found a small gap. As she prised it open with her fingers, the wood popped loudly, then swung open, revealing a secret compartment. Inside, there were three letters that slid down onto the wooden top of the chest.

"No," Lady Roslyn murmured through her tears. "He cannot have done this."

Kit took the letters. On one page she caught sight of the Scottish unicorn, and on another, there were a series of coded emblems.

"Thank you, my lady." Kit thrust the letters into her doublet and was about to walk out when she caught sight of Lady Roslyn. She was no longer the formidable and outraged lady she had been, but had collapsed against the wall as though she no longer had the strength to hold herself up. "I am sorry," Kit whispered.

Lady Roslyn nodded and waved her away. "Please, leave me be now."

"As you wish." Kit left as swiftly as she could, saddened that she had turned a woman's life upside down.

"Any news?"

"A little patience would be a great virtue at this moment, Iomhar."

They had returned to Iomhar's house and were now surrounded by paper.

"Aye, but it hardly comes easily, does it? Not when Mary Stuart is on the run." Iomhar smiled and nudged Kit's shoulder. "Or shall we go to Phelippes for help with decoding?"

"I do not need him." Kit returned her focus to the letters in front of her, scattered across the table.

"Aye, I thought ye might say that." Iomhar chuckled and stepped back.

Kit glanced down at the letters on the table. Mary Stuart's, Joan's, and Lord Buckingham's. Amongst the group was the one letter she had begun to decode, but others remained a mystery to her, using a different code altogether. She had started to see a pattern between some of the letters. It was plain they all used the same coded system, but without a key word or a clue as to how to crack the code, she was struggling.

Night was drawing in and Iomhar lit candles to keep them company. He laid them around the table, making the letters glow in the orange candlelight, with the black ink shining up at the two of them. Kit scribbled notes on errant pieces of parchment, trying out different possibilities in her effort to crack the code.

"I know I have seen this before." Kit tapped the symbol at the bottom of one of Lord Buckingham's letters. "I cannot remember where."

"It will come to ye." Iomhar looked up as voices grew louder elsewhere in the house. "I wonder if ye will remember it before my family lose their patience."

"They are tired of being in London, are they not?" Kit asked, scribbling more notes on the parchment.

"They wish to go home." Iomhar sighed and sat on a settle bench on the other side of the table. "Yet without knowing where Lord Ruskin is, they cannot risk going back to Scotland. They fear he will come after us all this time."

Kit paused in her work, raising her eyes to Iomhar. She knew what he really meant. The family were afraid that Lord Ruskin would come after Iomhar again.

"He will not come after you in London. It is too risky," Kit said slowly.

"I know." Iomhar sat forward, his eyes on the codes that were plaguing Kit. "It does not stop my family wanting their lives back. I can hardly blame them for it."

"Lord Ruskin." Kit jerked with the words. She took Lord Buckingham's letter with the symbol at the bottom that felt so familiar to her and isolated the different parts of the emblem. There was an ornate letter K and an even more flamboyant number three. The two were entwined, as if the figures had lovers' arms. "I wonder…"

"What?" Iomhar asked, resting his elbows on the table.

"There is that impatience of yours again."

"Me? I am the most patient man I know."

Kit wrote out the alphabet twice. Above one set of letters, she put in a series of numbers, but shifted the numbers along so that the letter R was represented by the number three. On the second alphabet set, she wrote another alphabet above it, with the letters shifted back one so that the letter L was represented by the letter K.

"What are ye doing?"

"I am taking a guess, but it might just work."

Assuming that each letter of the alphabet was either represented by a number or an alternative letter, Buckingham's letter opened out before her, the words translated into something new. Mary Stuart's letters used the same code, and Lord Ruskin's name appeared everywhere. The letter K and number three wrapped together repeated itself throughout the letters, and other pictorial codes could now be deciphered. It was plain there was a recurring symbol that represented Elizabeth. It was a crown wrapped around the number fourteen.

"It is from Lord Ruskin." Kit was on her feet so fast that she knocked over her chair. It clattered against the floor, making Iomhar jerk his head up. "Look, this is what it says."

"Which one?"

"The letter to Lord Buckingham." She thrust the parchment into Iomhar's hands.

"How did ye do this?"

"Lord Ruskin. By supposing that the letter could be from him, it has been revealed that the code is made up of two different ciphers that have been slotted together. Read it, Iomhar. Read what it says." She waved her quill in the air excitedly.

Iomhar's gaze darted across some of the wording before he read aloud. *"If your information is right, then we must move her. It is imperative our queen is carried away at once. I have already put plans in place for Queen Mary. By the time you receive this letter, the task shall already have been achieved. She will be taken from Chartley and delivered to…"*

"Go on," Kit urged.

"To Longtown Castle." Iomhar lowered the translation down to the table, his brow furrowed. "That castle is as good as ruined, abandoned by its owners, the Nevilles."

"How do you know that?"

"The curse of having an earl for a brother. He knows much about the aristocratic families of both Scotland and England. The castle is in ruins, Kit. Perhaps Lord Ruskin believes he can hide his queen there without her being seen."

"There's more." She nodded at the parchment, and he raised it again, grimacing as he read on.

"*She will be kept at Longtown until I can find a way for her to flee these shores. We may be able to take refuge in Ireland, or even one of the Scottish islands —*" He broke off sharply. "She intends to flee these shores."

"Then we need to get to Longtown before she can escape."

CHAPTER 16

"Ye cannot do this alone."

"I am hardly doing it alone, am I?" Iomhar argued, turning to face Niall as Kit ignored them both. She pulled a bag over her shoulder and pushed open the door, striding out into the dawn light. The sun had only just risen over the distant rooftops, and she had to set off within the next few minutes if she hoped to reach Longtown Castle in Herefordshire by the next morning.

"Aye, and that sounds wise," Niall said with thick sarcasm as he followed Iomhar and Kit outside, to where their horses awaited them. "Iomhar, ye think Lord Ruskin will be there with Mary Stuart, aye?"

"Aye." Iomhar loaded up his saddle, thrusting a sword into his belt and the pistol he carried into a leather loop attached to the saddle.

"Then ye cannot go alone." Niall placed his hand over the saddle.

"Good morrow to you, Niall," Kit called as she pulled herself up into the saddle. "When did I disappear into thin air? He is not going alone."

"Ye know what I mean, Kit. Lord Ruskin wants ye both dead, and ye think it wise to ride up to the castle where he is staying and knock on the door? I can see him rubbing his hands together with glee right now."

As Iomhar tried to step up into his saddle, Niall pulled on the reins, upsetting the horse so it trotted away a few paces and stopped Iomhar from climbing up.

"Ye wish to come?" Iomhar asked sharply. "Ye cannot."

"Why not?"

"It's a commission from Walsingham." Kit pulled on her reins, circling Iomhar's horse to stop it running away any further. "We are not going alone, Niall. I have sent word to Walsingham this morning, and the soldiers he gathered to accompany us last time to Chartley will now follow us to Longtown. We are not alone." She held Niall's gaze, aware that the words seemed to bring him no comfort.

"Ye could end up dead." Niall was blunt, staring at Iomhar. "Our mother grieved ye once for a year because of Lord Ruskin. Ye wish all of that to happen again?"

"Ah, my love to ye too, brother," Iomhar said wryly, then clapped his brother on the shoulder, a serious expression on his face. "I'm going to be surrounded by soldiers."

"And he'll be with me," Kit argued.

"Aye, she's right." Iomhar nodded in her direction. "Kit's saved my life more than once. I will not die on this commission, Niall. Ye know as well as I that this is the best chance we have had of finding Lord Ruskin since we left Scotland."

"I would be happier if I was coming with ye," Niall muttered.

"Look after this house instead," Iomhar pleaded. "Watch our mother, our sisters, and keep an eye on our brother too. If he keeps trailing through taverns looking for information on Lord Ruskin, he will soon find himself a victim of another pickpocketer, perhaps one who is more ruthless in wanting to get hold of his money."

"Aye, I know. I'll watch him." Niall stepped back, out of the path of the horse.

"I'll return, Niall."

The brothers embraced silently, then Iomhar returned to the horse and climbed into the saddle.

"Ride safely," Niall called. "And Kit?"

"Yes?" She turned to face him.

"Keep an eye on my brother and watch over yourself as well. Our mother will not be happy when she rises to see ye two have left again."

"We'll return." Kit flicked the reins of the horse, urging the animal into a gallop. Iomhar followed suit and they rode fast across the cobbles, moving onto nearby track roads and travelling along the embankment beside the Thames as they headed out of the city. They would change horses on the outskirts of Oxford before carrying on toward Herefordshire. With fresh horses, they could ride through the night and be at Longtown by the next morning.

When they reached the edge of town, Laidlaw awaited them. He stood with the soldiers that had been gathered. They hovered by their horses along the Thames. Marlowe and Somers stood with him, whispering between themselves.

"Walsingham says we are to go to Longtown?" Laidlaw called as he pulled himself into the saddle. "You two are certain of this? Or are we on another hunt with the deer already bolted?"

"We're as certain as we can be," Kit said, prompting her horse to move ahead of the others. As they rode on, sometimes slowing their pace to give the horses a break, Kit caught sight of Iomhar's expression.

"Your face will bring us clouds," she said as she moved her horse alongside his own. "What plagues your thoughts now? Lord Ruskin or Mary Stuart?"

"Both," Iomhar said simply. "One killed my father, the other ordered it. How would ye feel?"

Kit could not answer him, for she had never known what it was like to have a father. "We are there to arrest them, Iomhar. Remember that."

Iomhar chose not to answer her.

"This is Longtown Castle?" Kit slowed her horse. It was still dark with the moon bright overhead and stars blinking down, like a thousand eyes peering at what they were doing. Alongside her rode Iomhar and Laidlaw. Behind them were Somers and Marlowe, who led the soldiers, urging them to be quiet.

"No fine castle, is it?" Laidlaw scoffed at the site before them.

Kit had to admit the intelligencer was right. Unlike many castles that she had seen built on high hills and clifftops, with the advantage of far-reaching views, this one was set in mostly flat landscape, with the yellow stone keep of the castle on a small mound. At one time there may have been a moat that surrounded the bailey, but it had long ago dried up. In stretches there were muddy banks and other sections were simply covered in overgrown grass that would reach the knees.

What the castle lacked in location, it did not make up for in structure. The vast and sprawling estate was peppered with trees that were growing through the stonework. Where walls and battlements had once been stacked high, they were now falling down, with holes in the walls large enough for a cart to ride through.

"They can hardly hold their position here for long, can they?" Kit asked, turning to Iomhar. He had barely said a word for the last few hours of their journey. "Iomhar!" Kit hissed, trying to get his attention.

He turned to face her. "Nay. They did not think they would be discovered here, did they? The best place for Mary Stuart to hide would be somewhere nay one would think to look. Think on it, Kit. If we were to search the castles in all of England, would we have come here?"

"No," she conceded. "We would have picked somewhere with better fortifications."

"Aye. Lord Ruskin may be a villain, but he is nay great fool." Iomhar patted his stallion's neck, trying to calm him. "He knew where to hide Mary Stuart."

"We need a plan." Laidlaw beckoned Somers and Marlowe to come forward. The two intelligencers were yawning, and the young Marlowe could barely sit straight in his saddle after riding through the night. "We ride in with the soldiers. We will cause a furore and they'll have to surrender, out of fear."

"Lord Ruskin does not feel fear easily." Kit shook her head. "We are talking of a man who had the audacity to stride into Hampton Court wearing a yeoman's uniform. He planted gunpowder in the late King Henry's chamber. You think a man with that courage will drop to his knees before our soldiers?"

"The man would be an idiot not to surrender."

"Only if you do not give him a chance to escape." Kit shook her head. She could see that Laidlaw resented her interference. His hands were curled tightly around the reins of his horse.

"Enough," Laidlaw muttered. "You expect me to follow the orders of a jade?"

Kit flinched at the insult.

"What did ye call her?" Iomhar's voice was deeper than she could remember hearing it for some time.

Laidlaw gestured to Kit. "Who else would go around wearing such clothes than a horse for hire? What else could she be?"

Somers and Marlowe stayed silent. They looked at one another, then turned away, pretending interest in anything else around them.

"I am an intelligencer for Walsingham," Kit said, holding Laidlaw's gaze. "I am no whore, no flap, no jade, nor any other word you care to insult me with."

Iomhar had stepped down from his horse and walked to Laidlaw's side. "Get down," he ordered, pointing at the ground.

"Iomhar, what are you doing?" Kit asked, but Laidlaw had already moved down from his horse. He puffed out his chest and held his head high.

"You expect me to quake at the sight of you, Scot?" Laidlaw asked.

Iomhar moved so fast that Somers and Marlowe exclaimed in surprise. He struck Laidlaw cleanly in the nose. The man staggered back, clutching at his nose and struggling to stand straight.

"Nay more insults." Iomhar took hold of the back of Laidlaw's doublet and held him up. "Ye insult her again and it will be something worse. Ye are simply angry that she pointed out something ye were too foolish to notice. Ye make the soldiers run at the castle and the inhabitants will scarper, like rats from a flood. They'll have a planned escape route. Lord Ruskin does not put himself in situations he does not know he can get out of. We do what Kit says, aye?"

Laidlaw scowled but said nothing.

"Well?" Iomhar barked at Somers and Marlowe.

"Yes, yes," Somers said quickly.

"We'll do what Kit says," Marlowe added.

"Good." Iomhar released Laidlaw and pushed him toward the horse. He walked away, coming close to Kit's horse.

"You did not need to do that," she whispered. "You think it is the first time I have been insulted because of the clothes I choose to wear?"

"It does not make it right, Kit."

She watched the way he angled his head away from her, his teeth gritted. He went a long way to protect her sometimes, even when she did not ask him for it.

Laidlaw pulled himself back into the saddle, pressing his now heavily bruised nose gingerly as he checked for blood.

"We approach quietly," Kit said, raising her voice for the others to hear. "We set up a circle of soldiers to watch from afar, and the rest come in with us. We do not make a sound and we catch them unawares."

"Sounds wise to me," Somers agreed, with Marlowe nodding hastily at his side.

"Any argument, Laidlaw?" Kit asked. He shook his head silently. "Then we go in."

Kit glanced at Iomhar as he retreated to his horse. Something in Iomhar had changed on their ride to the castle, and she feared what he would do when he saw Lord Ruskin again.

Kit climbed through a gap in the wall, two soldiers close behind her. They each carried a sword in their hand, and one held a pistol, though his fingers shook so much around the handle that Kit was not sure how good his aim would be if he had to shoot.

Staying low to the curtain wall of the castle, Kit pointed soundlessly along the edge, urging the men to follow her. She cast a glance across the estate, but she could not see where the men were breaching the outer walls. She knew Laidlaw and Marlowe led a path on the northern side through the castle.

Iomhar had taken the east wing, and Somers the west. It left Kit on the south side, clambering over notches in the earth where grass had grown around old stones that had once been a set of stairs, leading toward the keep.

Silently, they crept across the earth. The only sound was the occasional thud of their boots on the stones. Kit shot a warning glare at one of the soldiers who was heavy-footed. He proceeded to walk on his toes after that, with his knees bent beneath him.

They passed one of the towers set within the walls, built separately from the body of the castle as standalone buildings. They headed for the keep and the great oak door that was shut.

"It is a ruin," one of the soldiers whispered to the other. "Surely no one would hide here?"

Kit tried the door, but it was firmly locked.

"Who locks a ruined castle door?" the other soldier asked and offered his pistol to Kit, but she shook her head. The pistol would be too loud, and she didn't want those inside to be alerted to their arrival. Taking hold of one of the daggers from her belt, she thrust the blade into the gap between the door and the stone frame and worked it around the lock. The latch popped out of place and the door swung open.

Inside, a wooden chair discarded at the side and topped with an empty flagon showed that the seat had not been empty for long.

"Someone was here." Kit pointed to the spiral staircase, urging the two soldiers to keep up with her. She led the way, climbing the stairs as quietly as she could.

With only arrow slits for windows, patches of moonlight fell on the stairs, but there was nothing more to light their way. Placing her palm to the wall, Kit felt her way up the stairs, holding out one of her daggers in front of her.

Creeping up to an open door, she halted, with a finger to her lips. The two soldiers nodded and raised their swords, showing they were ready. Kit opened the door. It creaked loudly, revealing the glow of candlelight in a chamber beyond.

"Who's there?" a voice called from within.

A man raised his eyes from a trencher in his lap, full of bread and some sort of stew. When his eyes found Kit's he leapt to his feet, dropping the trencher.

"Arrest him," Kit ordered.

The soldiers ran forward. As the guard tried to escape, heading for another door, the soldiers closed in on him from both sides. One took hold of his arms, fixing him to the spot, while the other raised his sword, warning the man not to move again. He breathed deeply, making his chest rise and fall.

"Where is Mary Stuart?" Kit asked, walking forward. The man's pale eyes shot toward her. "We know she is here. Tell me where she is."

The soldier pressed his sword closer to the guard's neck. He jerked back, trying to get as far away from the blade as he could.

"She's…" His voice trembled and he looked upward.

Kit turned her eyes to the ceiling. "She's in the keep?"

"Yes."

A bell rang out. Kit felt her stomach knot, for there could not be a soul within the castle walls that did not hear it. "Damn," she hissed. "They have raised the alarm. There goes our chance of a surprise attack."

CHAPTER 17

Kit raced up the spiral staircase with one of the soldiers behind her. The other had been tasked with getting the guard out of the castle. She tripped on the stairs, but recovered fast and moved on. With the bell ringing out across the castle, it would not be long before Lord Ruskin's men came to find their queen.

At the top of the staircase, Kit found a door firmly shut. Driving her shoulder against the wood, she winced at the pain, for it had been bolted tightly from the inside. Twitching her head at the soldier, she motioned toward the door. He nodded, and together they ran at it.

The wood splintered around the lock, and the door slid open. Kit still had to heave it forward to move it, and when enough of a gap appeared, she poked her head through to see a coffer had been placed against it.

Panicked cries erupted outside of the keep and in the grounds, and metal clashed against metal.

"Where is the queen? Protect the queen!" one voice bellowed above the others.

Kit slid through the gap and pushed the coffer out of the way, allowing the door to open fully so the soldier could follow her in.

At the back of the room, three women stood. Two of them were ladies-in-waiting, judging by their clothes and the way they stood before their mistress. This early in the morning, their hair was undone and loose around their shoulders. Their lips quivered, visible in the light from the candles they had lit, but they said nothing, too petrified to move.

Between the two ladies, Kit saw a face she recognised.

"Good morrow to you, Mary Stuart." Kit stepped toward the former Queen of Scots.

Mary's dark eyes found Kit's and narrowed. "She lives…" she whispered.

Kit could not resist a smile, realising that Mary's favoured supporter, Lord Ruskin, had not admitted to her that he had not succeeded in killing Kit.

"I live, as you can see." Kit gestured for the ladies-in-waiting to move aside. "We have come for Mary Stuart. Step aside."

One lady stepped away, but the other latched on to Mary's arm.

"Unhand me, foolish girl." Mary shook her off. The accent was a mixture of French and Scottish. She stepped forward. "Ye have come for me, but ye will not take me." She smiled victoriously. "I am protected here."

"That is debatable." Kit motioned for the soldier to move to the ladies-in-waiting. He stepped forward, cutting them off before they could run for the door. Kit took a great stride forward, coming closer to Mary Stuart and the candlelight.

There was a hasty blink.

"Katherine." The word escaped Mary so suddenly that Kit held herself still.

"Katherine who?" Kit had not told the Queen of Scots her full name.

"I see a ghost…" Mary's eyes narrowed, then her head jolted to the side as cries went up from outside.

"Get to the keep, before the soldiers can!"

"Protect the queen."

"Ye see?" Mary laughed deeply. "They will not let ye take me. I am safe from ye."

Kit heard footsteps on the stairs behind her. She reached forward, with her dagger outstretched.

The ladies-in-waiting screamed, their cries echoing off the lofted ceiling. Mary leapt back with her hands raised, but she was too slow. Kit took her shoulder and swung the Queen of Scots around, so that she was in Kit's grasp. With her dagger placed to Mary's neck and her other arm braced across Mary's shoulders, the former queen stilled.

"Ye would kill me?" Mary asked breathily.

The door burst open. Men dressed in dark colours hastened into the room, their swords and pistols outstretched. In the middle of the group a man moved. His face was one Kit had seen many times before. The pale features greeted her with a sneer and the shocking blond hair was tousled, as if he had jumped from his bed. He wasn't fully clothed, with a doublet thrown loosely over his shoulders and his shirt not tucked in but hanging loosely around his hose. It was the first time Kit had seen those pale eyes widen in fear.

"Do not move!" Lord Ruskin barked at his men, holding his palms outward. "Miss Scarlett, ye would not kill a queen."

"I see no queen in this room." Kit had no intention of killing Mary. She didn't even intend to draw a drop of blood, but with Lord Ruskin uncertain of her intentions, it gave her power. She had vowed not to take another life from this world, and it was a promise she intended to keep, no matter what the provocation. "Lower your weapons to the floor. Do it now, if you wish her to live."

Mary tugged at the arm Kit had around her shoulders. Kit merely pressed the blade closer to her throat. Mary gasped and held herself still.

"Do as she says," Lord Ruskin ordered. The men dropped their weapons. The clattering of the swords and pistols mixed with the ringing of the warning bell, which still echoed across the castle grounds.

"Kick the weapons away." Kit held Lord Ruskin's gaze. When he did not follow her order, she shifted the blade across Mary's throat. "Do it."

He kicked his sword away. It clattered by Kit's feet. His men followed suit, and soon enough, none of them had a weapon within reach.

"I hear sounds," Kit whispered with a smile growing on her lips. There were heavy footsteps on the spiral staircase, and Iomhar appeared in the doorway, followed by soldiers along with Somers. They strode into the room.

"On your knees," Kit ordered Lord Ruskin and his men.

"Do it now!" Iomhar barked.

The men dropped to their knees, all bar one. They hung their heads and lifted their hands, allowing the soldiers to bind their wrists with ropes, rendering them incapacitated. The one man who had not adhered to the order stood stock still, staring at Kit.

Iomhar moved to Lord Ruskin's side and pulled his sword.

"Iomhar!" Kit called to him. The blade was a mere hair's breadth from Lord Ruskin's heart. "Iomhar, do not do it."

Kit did not take her eyes off Iomhar. Each breath he took was laboured and slow as he stared at Lord Ruskin. It was the first time he'd had Lord Ruskin at his mercy since discovering the truth about his father's death.

"This man is a murderer," Iomhar said, his voice deep.

"Then he should face a court for his crimes," Kit called. Their voices were nearly lost amongst the noise of the soldiers taking out Lord Ruskin's men. "Iomhar!" Kit snapped, trying to get his attention.

A muscle twitched around his eye. It was the only sign that he had heard her at all.

"This will not help," she called to him. "You kill him, and you are the one who will face a court for murder."

Lord Ruskin held himself like a marble statue. Kit was no longer sure if he was afraid, or resigned to the fact he might die.

"Iomhar!" Kit called again. Mary made another bid for freedom, but Kit pushed the former queen down to her knees. "Do not move."

"Ye…" Curses escaped Mary's lips, but Kit didn't pay attention. She was focused on Iomhar's hesitation and his grasp on his sword, so tight that his knuckles were white.

"Think of your mother. She could not bear seeing you in prison." Kit's softer words broke through to Iomhar the way nothing else had done.

He lowered the sword. It was abrupt, and he breathed heavily with the movement. Kit released a breath she hadn't realised she was holding, the relief palpable in the air.

"Take him away," Iomhar ordered, nodding at two of the soldiers. They took Lord Ruskin's arms and bound them behind his back.

"Weak!" Lord Ruskin spat at Iomhar.

Iomhar calmly wiped the spit from his cheek and turned his back. Lord Ruskin was manhandled out as Iomhar walked across the room. He stood in front of Mary, who stared up at him boldly. "I see your face at last," he said in a dark tone. "It surprises me ye are just a woman, when I expected to see a demon."

"Ye traitor! Ye betrayer!" she shouted at him.

"No more," Kit ordered and pulled Mary Stuart back to her feet. "Your prison awaits you."

"Ye cannot put her in a gaol cart. Are ye blasphemers? Ye cannot do it!" Lord Ruskin's bellows pierced the air as Kit pushed Mary Stuart into the gaol cart.

The sun was rising and had bled a red light over the castle and its embankments. On a track that had once led to a drawbridge, gaol carts had been lined up. Lord Ruskin was thrown into one, where he rattled the bars angrily, shouting with spittle hanging from his lips. Iomhar watched this cart more than any other, scarcely taking his eyes off Lord Ruskin.

"Ye are all blasphemers. Ye will be punished for what ye have done. May God smite ye for your sins!" Lord Ruskin's cries abated as the cart was led away.

Mary Stuart sat in her cart with her ladies-in-waiting beside her. Her hands were very still in her lap, but her gaze was animated. It jumped from the soldiers that kept watch over the cart, to her ladies, before finally resting on Kit.

"Katherine," Mary said again.

Kit flinched and held herself by the bars, no longer climbing down from the cart.

"Kit? Are ye coming?" Iomhar called from a distance, but she didn't respond. She waited for Mary to say more.

"Katherine."

"You say the name as if you know me," Kit said in a low voice.

"Nay. I see a ghost." Mary tilted her head to the side. "My cousin died long ago."

"Your cousin?"

"Katherine Douglas, daughter of the Countess of Lennox. My cousin." Her dark auburn brows knitted together, making her long face look more angular than before. "Her daughter died. I am certain of it."

Kit staggered off the cart. It was the same name that Moira had mentioned when she had spoken of the tune she sang. A pair of hands caught Kit under the arms as she stumbled.

"Are ye well?" Iomhar asked, his face appearing over her shoulder as he released her.

"I…" Kit wasn't sure. She closed the barred door, but Mary stood up in the cart. She reached out through the bars. Her fingers brushed Kit's chin.

"She died, I know she did," Mary said again, yet her face had paled. "Perhaps I am wrong…"

The cart lurched forward, and Mary stared at Kit as she was carried away.

"Kit? Who was she speaking of?" Iomhar asked.

"There is something I must tell you."

CHAPTER 18

"We have to stop for the night," Laidlaw's voice boomed across the group as they came to a stop in the forest.

Kit shifted in her saddle, looking around at the group. Soldiers flanked the four gaol carts they escorted. Inside one was Mary Stuart and her ladies. In the other there was Lord Ruskin and the rest of his men.

"We should not stop." Kit lowered her voice and moved to Laidlaw's side. "We need to move on. The privy council wish for Mary Stuart to be held at Fotheringhay."

"Out of fear of being struck again, I'm tempted to agree with you, but look at the men around you. They are exhausted from riding through last night. If we do not rest soon, they will fall down. Best to be on our guard on this journey than fall asleep in our saddles." Laidlaw rode away, issuing orders to the soldiers to set up camp.

Kit watched him go, muttering to herself. She longed to argue with Laidlaw, but looking around at the soldiers she soon saw she was not the only one yawning. Grudgingly, she accepted Laidlaw was justified. If they did not rest, the group's exhaustion could mean they would not make it to Fotheringhay at all.

As the soldiers started fires with the dried wood they found in the Forest of Dean, Kit climbed down from her horse and threaded the reins around the nearest tree branches. They had made little progress on their journey since leaving Longtown, but with the carts, they couldn't travel much faster.

Kit looked between the groups that naturally formed. The soldiers that were alert kept guard over the carts, while some men ate around fires and others slept. Kit sat far away from the others. Perching on a fallen tree she leaned forward, staring at the earth and trying not to think of Mary Stuart, who was a short distance away.

Firewood was dropped by Kit's feet. She jumped, looking up to see Iomhar standing before her.

"Ye never seen wood before?" he teased and lowered himself to his knees, piling the wood into a triangular shape to start a fire. "Are we going to talk of this, or ignore it?"

"Ignore it," Kit said succinctly. As they had left Longtown that morning she had told Iomhar of what his mother had said about John Stuart and his wife, Katherine Douglas. She'd also revealed Walsingham's reaction to her mentioning those names, and what Mary Stuart had said to her in the gaol cart.

"Ye wish for me to ask the question that is bothering ye?"

"No. I wish not to speak of it at all."

"They could be your parents, Kit."

She pulled at her jerkin. It was more of a waistcoat, designed for the hotter weather, and it clung to her far too tightly for comfort.

Iomhar stayed silent as he lit the fire using a small tinderbox he carried in his pocket. The flames grew between them, bathing Iomhar's face in an amber glow.

"They are not my parents." Kit broke the silence. She slid off the fallen log and sat closer to the fire, wanting to be near the light. "Mary described Katherine Douglas as her cousin."

"Aye, if she was the daughter of the Countess of Lennox, she would be."

"Who was the countess?"

"The daughter of Margaret Tudor, King Henry VIII's sister."

Kit stared at Iomhar open-mouthed.

"Royalty, Kit."

"I am not royalty!" Kit hissed. "What would it matter if I looked a little like this Katherine Douglas? That means nothing."

"*Iosa Criosd*, Kit! Ye must see there's something in this."

She had rarely heard Gaelic from him, only back in Scotland, and when his mind seemed most tormented.

"Aye, taking the Lord's name in vain." He shook his head. "Ye said that my mother spoke of a daughter." Iomhar leaned closer to the fire. The flames appeared to dance in his eyes, making the green hue golden. "A daughter that —"

"Died. She died. Your mother said she drowned." Kit spoke with vigour. She reached for the neck of her doublet, delving beneath the shirt to pull out the necklace she always wore these days. It was the chain Iomhar used to wear, with the Celtic shield knot pendant. She clung to it, the metal warm between her fingers. Iomhar had insisted Kit kept it. "It means nothing. Just a resemblance…"

"Not even when both my mother and Mary Stuart say ye look like her?"

"Nothing!" Kit repeated wildly. When Iomhar leaned back, she softened her voice. "I am sorry, it is just…" She shook her head. "Look at me, Iomhar." She held her arms out wide. "I am hardly royalty, am I?"

"Ye look like Kit to me," Iomhar said with a small smile. "Yet that is not to say ye do not have royal blood in ye."

"This is madness." Kit lifted a stick and poked the fire, making the yellow flames dance higher. "Walsingham said he found me in the street. I was a beggar girl, and I pulled on his cloak one day."

"Aye, I see. So suddenly ye are going to reject the certainty ye have had for so long that Walsingham has been lying to ye over how ye met?" Iomhar asked wryly. "Ye are going to ignore the dream that has plagued ye for so long?"

"Iomhar —"

"And what was that again? Oh, aye, I remember," he said. "Ye were drowning in that dream."

Kit swallowed and shifted her position.

"Ye are going to ignore all of that?"

"Perhaps I should," Kit whispered. "I would not wish to jump to the wrong conclusion, just because I have a dream about drowning." She thought back to the pale pink silk gown with the pearl neckline that she had discovered in Walsingham's chamber. A girl born to royal parents could certainly wear such a dress, but so could a well-to-do merchant's daughter. The gown was not proof of her descent. "I do not wish to speak of this anymore."

Iomhar sighed deeply and moved to his feet.

"Where are you going?"

"I will be back shortly." He walked away, leaving Kit by the fire. She raised her head and caught sight of Mary Stuart across the camp. She had fallen asleep in her cart, with her head lolling against the bars behind her.

Iomhar returned and Kit shifted to the side, making room for Iomhar to sit down beside her against the fallen tree. He had some bound muslin cloths in the palm of his hand.

"Eat, Kit."

She took the parcel and unwrapped it. They ate in silence for a minute or two, sharing the manchet bread and the cheese they had brought with them. When Kit grew tired, she leaned against Iomhar's side, resting her head on his shoulder. He didn't say anything but simply passed her a flagon of wine when she yawned.

"Ye may not wish to speak of it, Kit." Iomhar broke the silence between them. "But this is not something ye can ignore."

"I am no royal. I know it to be true."

"Aye, ye feel it in your bones, do ye?"

"Perhaps I do." Kit raised her head from his shoulder.

"Ye think I feel like the son of an earl? Or the brother of one?" he asked with a small smile. "It is not something ye feel, Kit." He offered her some of his bread.

"Do you not want it?"

"Ye eat it."

She took it from him, munching on the few chunks that were left.

Kit swigged from the flagon of claret, then rested her head on Iomhar's shoulder again. It wasn't long before her eyelids grew heavy, and she couldn't fight the exhaustion any longer.

As Kit's eyelids closed, the names drifted into her mind.

John Stuart and Katherine Douglas.

"Fire! Fire!" The shouts erupted from the camp.

Kit's eyes shot open. Iomhar was at her side, taking hold of her elbow and pulling her to her feet.

"What the…?" Kit trailed off.

The forest was alight with flames, leaping from one tree to the next.

"A soldier … must have been careless with his fire," Iomhar muttered and took Kit's hand, dragging her away from their own fire that had long ago burnt out.

The soldiers were trying to pour water on the nearest trees, but their attempts were feeble. One soldier threw a flagon of wine onto a tree. The liquid caught fire and he leapt away, staggering on his heels.

Something caught Kit's eye. Between the men that fought the blaze, there were silhouettes of bodies.

"Someone else is here." Kit tugged on Iomhar's hand.

The shadows moved toward one side of the camp, where Mary Stuart and her supporters were held in the carts.

"They're here for her." Kit ran, releasing Iomhar's hand as she sprinted toward the carts. Iomhar followed behind her, but they couldn't get far.

As they neared the carts, the flames spread. The small trees and bushes that separated them from the carts caught alight, and they were forced to jump back, cowering from the flames with arms raised over their faces.

"Get back!" Iomhar took her arm and pulled her away.

"Men!" Laidlaw bellowed, trying to be heard above the roar of the fire. "Do not let the carts leave. Do not let Mary Stuart escape."

Kit peered around Iomhar's shoulder to see they were too late. What soldiers were still with the carts were being attacked. One man was knocked out by a sword struck across his head. Another soldier that refused to relinquish his place was shot. Men tried to make it through the flames, but they couldn't without risking burning to death. Their own friends held them back, saving them from the burns.

"Get the queen. Let us part!" a familiar voice called. Kit jerked her head back and forth, searching for a face she knew.

Before she could find it, she spotted Lord Ruskin being released from his gaol cart, along with his men. Mary Stuart was let out too and she stepped down regally, taking the hand of the man who offered her help. She smiled in triumph.

Two soldiers moved before her, swords outstretched ready to force Mary back into the cart. The man beside her offered her a weapon and stepped forward, taking one of the soldiers away with a blade at his throat. The second soldier advanced toward Mary, but the blade was forced from his hand as Lord Ruskin knocked it to the ground. Mary advanced on the soldier with the basilard in her grasp.

Kit held her breath, certain for a moment that Mary was going to cut the man's throat.

"No," Kit whispered. "She would not."

Lord Ruskin said something to Mary. Her hand shook but she stepped back reluctantly. The soldier was forced to the ground by Lord Ruskin, then Mary walked away, heading toward the horses that awaited her. The others followed.

At last, Kit found the face she had been looking for, the face that belonged to the voice she'd heard. Graham Fraser stood amongst the group. He said something in a low tone to Lord Ruskin and they both turned to gaze at Kit and Iomhar. His hand was bound with bandages and what appeared to be leather, reminding her of the injury she'd left him with in Seething Lane. He bore no weapon in the hand, showing it was weak.

"I should have killed Lord Ruskin when I had the chance," Iomhar muttered.

"You wish to be a murderer?"

"Nay. Do I wish to stop what more death that man could cause? Aye!"

Graham Fraser and Lord Ruskin turned to follow the others to the horses.

"The fire is spreading. If we don't want to be burned alive, we retreat to the road. Now!" Laidlaw called to the soldiers.

Kit searched the trees, looking for any way through in order to follow Mary Stuart, but there was no path.

"Laidlaw is right." Iomhar took Kit's hand. "If we want to live, we have to retreat."

"What of Mary? What of Lord Ruskin and Fraser?"

"We live to catch them another day, Kit." He pulled her away before she could argue anymore. The heat followed them, the fire engulfing each oak at their side, as if it raced against them. They ran so far that Kit's lungs burned.

When they escaped the trees, they staggered to a stop. Marlowe was shaking, his thin body trembling so much that it was a wonder he was not sick. Somers was arguing with Laidlaw, each one asserting that it had been the other's duty to stay awake and keep watch for an ambush.

Kit stood beside Iomhar, her hand still in his as she stared at the flaming trees. Within hours, this part of the forest would be reduced to ash and burnt wood.

"They will take her somewhere else to hide now," Kit said through heavy breaths. "Lord only knows where that will be."

CHAPTER 19

The sun was strong as Kit leaned forward in the saddle, guiding her horse along the Thames as she rode into London. Her cheeks were burnt, but she did not know if they were burnt from the sun or from being so near to the fire the night before.

"Shall we go to Walsingham?" Iomhar asked as they turned their horses away from the river.

Behind them, the soldiers followed, riding up a path toward the barracks stationed by the river. Laidlaw, Somers and Marlowe were amongst them, though they had barely paused their argument since they had left the Forest of Dean. Each intelligencer blamed the other, though Kit feared it had been everyone's responsibility. If they had continued on their journey, then Fraser and his friends would have had little chance of catching up with them.

"Kit?"

"Fraser must have gone to Longtown Castle and seen Mary Stuart was gone. He could have tracked us easily to the Forest of Dean."

"Aye, I agree. Kit, ye did not answer my question. Shall we go to Walsingham? He will need to hear of what has happened."

The mere thought of seeing Walsingham made Kit feel sick. She was not sure what reason was greater for not wanting to see him — the fact they had let Mary Stuart escape once more or that he had lied to her again about her past.

"I have no wish to see him." She turned her horse and crossed in front of the arguing intelligencers. "No more." Her quiet words were enough to silence them, though Laidlaw puffed out his chest, irked that she was taking command again. "We are all to blame for what has passed. It does not rest on any one man's shoulders. We should have been alert and watching for men like Fraser, not thinking of our tiredness."

"Walsingham will want blood for this," Laidlaw hissed.

"Then tell him of it," Kit ordered, holding Laidlaw's gaze. "You go to him and reveal what has happened."

"I will." Laidlaw jerked his head at Somers and Marlowe. He clearly had no qualms about revealing a failed task to Walsingham. She rather wondered if he intended to blame her in some way for it. "You two, come with me. We'll see him this morning."

They turned and left, but Kit did not follow.

"There was a time when ye would not have held back if a message had to be delivered to Walsingham," Iomhar said, pulling his horse up beside Kit's own.

"I have no wish to see him." She glanced at Iomhar to find he was smiling. "How can you smile on a day like today? Lord Ruskin is free, as is Mary Stuart. Everything we have been working for is like dust through our fingers."

"Do not mistake me, Kit. Ye saw my rage last night at their escape." The smile faded a little, but it was still there. "Let us just say I am glad to see the hold Walsingham once had on ye is loosening. Shall we head home?" He flicked the reins of his horse and rode down the path, heading toward the city.

Kit followed him, thinking on the fact that Iomhar had referred to the house as their home.

They pulled the horses up outside of the house as a sound from inside made them both still. Someone was wailing, crying with great heaving gasps, and another was shouting, raging.

Iomhar didn't even bother to put his horse in the stable but strode into the house, opening the door wide. Kit hastened to follow him, barely taking the time to throw the reins of the mare around the nearest wooden post before hurrying into the house and closing the door behind her.

They both stood in the hall, listening as the argument continued.

"We have to go back, we have to," Duncan was insisting.

"How can we?" Niall argued. "After this, none of us are safe."

"Would ye two lower your voices a little? Abigail is already crying in her room. Ye wish for the entire road to hear your argument as well as her?" Rhona demanded, her voice almost as loud as her brothers' despite her words.

"I pray all of ye would keep your heads. It will not do to lose our minds now," Moira's voice broke in. It sounded as though she was holding back her own tears.

Iomhar marched through the hall. He thrust the door to the front room open, revealing his family. "What has happened?"

"Thank God ye are back." Moira moved toward him and embraced him tightly. Iomhar held onto his mother, looking over her shoulder at the rest of his family. Kit hurried in behind him and closed the door, her gaze darting from one face to the next.

Rhona was standing by the window, fanning herself in the heat. Her brothers were in the middle of the room, turned toward one another in their argument, both of them sweating and red in the face.

"Why do ye smell like smoke?" Moira asked, leaning back from Iomhar.

"We had to run from a fire."

"Another fire?" Moira released Iomhar and covered her face with her hands.

"Another?" Kit looked at Rhona, who grimaced.

"Aye, another," she confirmed.

"What has happened?" Iomhar peeled his mother's hands away from her face, pleading with her to look at him. She could no longer hold back the tears that streaked down her cheeks.

"I have received a message this morning from our steward back home," Duncan said swiftly. He took a letter from his pocket and held it in the air. "Our home ... it is gone."

"Gone?" Iomhar repeated, releasing his mother and moving toward his brother. He took the letter from the earl's hand.

Niall explained what was in the letter without waiting for Iomhar to read it. "Someone has burned it down. I say someone, when in fact the steward saw a group of men. They burnt the entire house to the ground. The staff fled for their lives, for they feared being murdered. Aye, that is why we left Scotland. Someone is vying for our blood."

"It's gone," Iomhar whispered, his eyes darting across the letter in his grasp.

"All of it?" Kit asked, stepping forward. "The entire house burned down?"

"Yes, the entire house." Moira wiped her tears and reached for the nearest chair. She sat down heavily. Rhona found a handkerchief and offered it to her mother. "It is all gone. The life we have known has gone with it." Moira held a hand in the air and splayed her fingers. "It's vicious, brutal, as if someone wishes to destroy any evidence we exist at all."

"Someone," Kit repeated and looked at Iomhar.

"I know what ye are going to say." Iomhar looked up from the letter. "Ye think Lord Ruskin ordered this."

"He already wished to silence you, to stop your interference. You said yourself men were watching this house, probably on his orders. With us going after Mary Stuart at Chartley, he would have been alarmed, wanting to stop the people chasing her. He could have easily sent a message to his men watching your house and given the order. Who else would have burnt your home down other than Mary Stuart's supporters?" Kit asked, holding her arms wide and waiting for another explanation. No one had anything to give.

Duncan sat down on a settle bench and hung his head. Rhona took her mother's hand, and Niall paced at Iomhar's side.

"Aye, she's right," Niall said hurriedly. "Who else but Mary's supporters would do this?"

"What factions do we live in now?" Moira suddenly asked, her tone firm. "Mary has torn our lives apart repeatedly. She took your father, she threw the whole of Scotland into despair with her actions. Now look at what she has done. I shudder to think how far she is willing to see others fall, just so she can find a throne to rest her weary bones on." Moira stood suddenly. "I pray this will all be over someday. Yet I can no longer dream of returning home, can I? That home is gone!"

"A house can be rebuilt," Iomhar murmured.

"It is not the same. Our home is gone." Moira's breath hitched, and she ran from the room. Rhona ran after her, trying to calm her.

The three brothers and Kit stared after them.

"Our mother's fears are well founded," Duncan said eventually. "Yes, a house can be rebuilt, but the home we had, the one we have known, is gone. We cannot return or even consider rebuilding until Mary Stuart and her supporters are gone. They would simply burn it down again. Once the threat of her return is over, those that run around Scotland following Ruskin's orders will desist too. We must wait, it seems."

"Then we wait," Iomhar replied, his voice grave. "When Mary Stuart faces a court, we'll return home. We'll build a new house for the family, and we'll begin again."

Kit's breathing quickened, and she reached for a settle bench, holding onto the back of it. It was a harsh reminder of what Iomhar had vowed to her when they had returned from Scotland in the winter.

If Mary Stuart faced court, Iomhar intended to go home to Scotland with his family. He would not come back to London again.

CHAPTER 20

Kit crumpled Walsingham's message between her hands as she approached Seething Lane, Iomhar at her shoulder. The message had arrived at Iomhar's house earlier that afternoon and she had ignored it for as long as possible, but as the sun dropped, she could ignore it no longer. She had to see him, for he had demanded her presence before sundown.

Kit knocked at the door. It was quickly opened by Doris, who wore a grave expression. The smallest of smiles overtook her lips when she saw Kit and Iomhar, but it faltered.

"He is most upset, Kitty. Most upset. I cannot remember the last time I saw him in such a state. He paces and yells, then he paces and yells some more." She heaved a great sigh and ushered them into the house, closing the door behind them. "Go up, go, he is waiting for you." Doris fidgeted, wringing her hands as they walked down the corridor.

Kit stuffed Walsingham's message into her doublet, having no wish to look at the words that had been written with such anger and haste that the handwriting was almost impossible to read. As they reached the door, Walsingham's voice called from within before Kit had a chance to knock.

"Enter!" he barked.

Kit opened the door and walked in.

"Well?" Walsingham stood before them as Iomhar closed the door. "I had Laidlaw come to see me this morning."

"Then ye know what has happened," Iomhar answered him. "Ye do not need to hear it from our lips as well as his."

"You think not?" Walsingham turned his pointed chin in Iomhar's direction, scratched his beard, then flicked his head back to Kit. "You let her go."

"Let her go? You speak as if I released her from my grasp and waved as she took her leave of me. Did Laidlaw not speak of all that happened? Did he not tell you of the fire and the soldiers that lost their lives trying to keep hold of her?"

"This is badly done indeed. When I send you two after a prisoner, I expect that prisoner to be caught."

"Yes, and a once queen is just like any other prisoner, is she not?" Kit sat down in the nearest chair, flicking her boots onto the stool in front of her. Iomhar stood beside her, placing his elbow on the back rest. "Most prisoners we fetch are not guarded by battalions, or even by men like Lord Ruskin. It was no easy task you set for us."

"So that's it? You abandon the endeavour?" Walsingham held his arms out wide.

"We did not abandon it. We raced after them as soon as we could work out a way around the fire, but we could not follow their tracks. I am sure Laidlaw has told you all this." Kit levelled a glare at him. She felt distant from him now, as if an abyss sat between them. She wondered if the man she had believed him to be all her life was truly who he was, or if he was another. Just because he was not the Rose, as Iomhar feared he could be, it did not mean the secrets he kept were any less dangerous. "We returned to let you know of her escape. Without knowing where she went, it would have been a stab in the dark to follow a path out of the forest in the hope of finding her."

"And you? You say nothing?" Walsingham turned his focus on Iomhar.

"My family's home was burnt down today by Mary Stuart's supporters. I do not doubt they hoped to make a point, to say that my family and I were not welcome anymore, for we supported James as King of Scotland. Do you believe I would not race after Mary Stuart if I had any idea of where she had gone?" Iomhar's question was sombre.

Walsingham turned away. He cursed, moved restlessly, then faced them again. "Of all the intelligencers I have, I thought that you, Kit, *you*, I could trust with bringing Mary Stuart to me."

"We barely survived the fire, though I thank you for asking after our welfare," Kit said. "If you wish to talk of trust, then may I remind you of the secrets you keep from me?" He stepped back, as if she had struck him. "I have done everything you have ever asked of me, my whole life. I fail you and you question your trust in me?" Kit moved to her feet and turned her head to Iomhar, indicating that they were leaving.

"Where are you going? Kit, we are not done with this conversation." Walsingham braced his arm across the door, refusing to let her pass. "I wish to know everything that happened. Everything! Right down to every leaf that caught fire last night and led to Mary Stuart's escape."

"There is nothing more I can tell you. Step away."

"I will not."

Kit reached into her doublet, knowing what would make him move away. She took hold of the box of pills she had hidden there, then tossed them through the air. Walsingham scrambled to catch them. He missed them and they fell to the floor. The box broke open and the pills scattered away, some falling through the gaps in the boards. Walsingham dropped to his knees and tried to gather them together, scooping them up in the palms of his hands.

"Kit? Kit!" he called as she walked out of the door. She didn't have to look back to know that Iomhar followed her down the stairs, toward the entrance of the house.

"Ye have shaken off the shackles at last," he murmured as they reached the door.

Doris appeared in the doorway of the kitchen, her blue eyes wide as she glanced up at the ceiling, listening to Walsingham's voice boom and his feet thud against the boards. "What has happened now?" she asked, her voice tremulous.

"Best to leave him alone for a while until his mood has calmed, Doris." Kit touched the housekeeper's arm softly and then stepped out of the house, hurrying through the cobbled square. Iomhar raced to catch up with her.

"What does this mean, then?" Iomhar asked, trying to get her attention.

"I am tired of listening to Walsingham demanding trust from me when he offers nothing in return. That is all."

"Kit?" Iomhar said as they walked down the road. "Ye know this is not the life that always has to be yours."

"What do you mean?" Kit stopped, prompting Iomhar to do the same. They stood facing each other.

"Ye do not have to do as Walsingham asks. Ye do not even have to be here anymore."

"In Seething Lane?"

"In London."

Kit swallowed and looked away from Iomhar, staring at the busy streets she had known all her life. There were maids hurrying to their business, some arm in arm, others carrying great baskets full of laundry that they were bringing back from the rivers. There were coachmen and cartmen driving down the street, whistling at their horses. The cobbled road was a flurry of activity. These were the roads Kit had grown up in, the only ones she knew.

"It is my home," she whispered, tearing her gaze away from the people as she looked back at Iomhar.

"It does not mean it always has to be. Remember what I said to ye last winter?" He stepped toward her, lowering his voice. "Ye could make another place your home."

"Scotland?"

"Aye."

A horse rode too close to them, the rider calling out to apologise for the close brush. Kit took Iomhar's hand and pulled him out of harm's way.

"Think on it," he pleaded. "That is all I ask."

As they walked down the street together, Kit tried to think of the people around her. The maids, the cartmen, the errand boys who held out their hands in the hope of earning loose change from passers-by. Yet in the end, she couldn't focus on any of it. She thought of the pressure of Iomhar's hand in her own instead.

"Ye have barely eaten, Kit." Moira slid the trencher toward Kit.

"My apologies. My thoughts are elsewhere." Kit toyed with her knife over the trencher, but she made no effort to eat.

"She's melancholic," Abigail said on the other side of the table. "Would the physicians bleed her?"

"Abigail." Rhona nudged her sister's arm, trying to stop her from talking.

"It's what they do, is it not? For the melancholic." Abigail shrugged innocently.

"Talk of something else, Abigail, I beg ye," Iomhar said from beside Kit. He slid another trencher toward her. It was filled with marchpane.

"Thank you." She snatched up the marchpane, thankful for his kindness and relieved to have the sweet taste on her tongue.

Conversation soon moved on. Around Kit, the family spoke of the Blackwood house that had been burnt down. They spoke too of how they would rebuild it, if they ever returned to Scotland. The discussion of another life simply left Kit feeling more lost than before.

She picked up more marchpane and fiddled with it in the palm of her hand, morphing it into a new shape. Images flicked through her mind. She saw herself leaving Walsingham's house, walking out hand in hand with Iomhar, then she was back in the Forest of Dean. She saw the moment Mary Stuart escaped from her cart and thrust a dagger at one of the soldier's throats.

"She's a killer," Kit whispered to herself.

"What was that?" Iomhar asked, leaning close.

"Excuse me." Kit dropped the marchpane and stood. The family fell silent, watching as she left the room.

Stumbling into the front room, Kit thrust her hands into her hair, pulling at the short locks. She was not alone for long. A candle appeared in the room and Iomhar came with it, shutting the adjoining door behind him.

"What is wrong?" he asked, placing the candle down on the mantelpiece.

"Mary Stuart. She is a killer, yes?" Kit asked, facing him. "You told me as much once."

"Aye, they say she helped arrange the murder of her second husband. Either she conspired with her lover to have it done or suggested it was done. Either way, Lord Darnley was murdered." Iomhar's expression darkened. "Ye heard from Lord Ruskin's own lips how she ordered the murder of my father too. Ye do not need to be in any doubt of what that woman is capable of, Kit."

"I know. She handed me to Lord Ruskin to kill, though she pleaded with him not to do it at Chartley."

"Aye, so ye know her nature. Why does this have ye in such a fluster?"

"What if she has done it before?"

"What?"

"What if she has killed before?" Kit asked. "Do you remember when I went to Lady Ruskin's house, back when you and I first knew each other?"

"I remember ye pretending to be a Scottish aristocrat to gain entry, aye."

"There was a painting on the wall. The picture was of Mary Stuart, and she wore a French hood."

"What of it?"

Kit blinked a few times, recalling the memory that stirred in the recesses of her mind. She was the child in the water again, reaching for the surface in a desperate attempt to escape from drowning. She saw the silhouette of the woman above the water, and the shape of the French hood on her head.

"Kit, ye are making little sense," Iomhar said. "Why is a French hood important?"

"Whoever left me in the water wore a French hood," Kit whispered.

"Many women wore such a thing. Nay, that is not evidence of anything."

Iomhar was right. Many women used to wear French hoods. Many in Scotland would have worn them too, as the queen had spent years in France and what the queen did, many ladies copied.

"Perhaps not." The woman had been silhouetted with the sun behind her, the features impossible to make out. "But Mary Stuart is capable of murder, yes?"

"Aye," Iomhar said, without hesitation.

"Knock, knock," Niall's voice called from behind the closed door. "Sorry to interrupt your moment alone, but there's something ye must see, Kit."

"Another time, Niall?" Iomhar called.

"It cannot wait."

The door opened.

"This has just arrived for ye, Kit." Niall proffered a letter at her side, and she took it, recognising the handwriting at once to be Walsingham's.

She tore open the blank red seal and read his words with haste.

We are to see Queen Elizabeth tomorrow. She will want answers for why Mary Stuart is not at Fotheringhay.

"What is it?" Iomhar asked, Niall hovering at his side.

"Walsingham wants me to see the queen with him tomorrow." She smiled sadly. "Maybe he hopes to blame me for Mary's continued escape, so that the queen does not turn her anger on him." Kit folded up the letter and put it in her doublet.

"Will ye go?"

"I have to." She had no choice. She still worked for Walsingham. Even if what Iomhar said was true, that she could have a life somewhere else someday, a life in which she was no longer an intelligencer for the spymaster, it was irrelevant in that moment.

Mary Stuart needed to be caught, and Queen Elizabeth wanted answers. She feared her cousin's plots could one day succeed. One queen warred against another.

"I will go first thing tomorrow." Kit moved to a writing bureau in the corner of the room and took out some parchment to reply to Walsingham, to inform him she would meet him at Richmond Palace.

CHAPTER 21

Walsingham fidgeted in the heat. He pulled at the high white collar around his throat, flattened what little hair he had left on his balding head, then returned his hat to his temple and dabbed his forehead with a white handkerchief. At all times, he avoided Kit's gaze, no matter how intently she stared at him.

"Walsingham?" she muttered his name, trying to get his attention. He took a few steps away from her, his court-style shoes tapping on the black and white tiled floor. She followed him, ignoring the fact that he was walking toward Lord Burghley, who awaited their queen on the other side of the great hall.

"Where is she?" Walsingham called impatiently to Lord Burghley.

"Hunting. It's a wonder there are any deer left in this park." Lord Burghley huffed and struck his cane against the tiled floor. He kept his focus on the door that had been opened to let in some air. The light summer breeze whistled in through that vast gap, but it did little to ease the heat in the room.

"Walsingham?" Kit reached Walsingham's side again. "You will not talk to me?"

"You are here to talk to the queen, not I," he said and stepped around her.

"What of those names we talked of?" She followed him. "Do they mean something to you?"

He stiffened, then angled his head away and reached Lord Burghley's side. "She hunts too much these days," he said conversationally, still ignoring Kit.

Kit walked across the great hall of Richmond Palace. The tiled floor stretched wide, the view only interrupted by a long, thin mahogany table that extended across the middle of the room. The walls were panelled with an equally dark wood, and were adorned with paintings. Kit knew none of the painters, but she thought they all had a similar tendency to make the sitter look weary. A painting of Queen Elizabeth hung at the far end of the room. Her dark eyes stared out from the lacquered surface, her face austere, the skin lacking the wrinkles that it bore today.

There was something in the painting that reminded Kit of the one of Mary Stuart she had seen hanging at Lady Ruskin's house. The face shape was not dissimilar, and there was something in those eyes that was very familiar.

The sounds of horses' hooves clomped past the window. Lord Burghley and Walsingham each stood a little taller and moved back from the door, ready to greet their queen. Kit moved to stand a little distance from them, her back to the row of paintings on the walls. The hair rose on the back of her neck, as if the eyes in those paintings stared at her, waiting for her to move again.

"You are here? Already? You startle me." Queen Elizabeth's voice was louder than the last time Kit had been in the royal presence. She spoke even before she entered the great hall. Striding into the room, she took off her riding gloves and passed them to a lady-in-waiting behind her.

Walsingham and Lord Burghley bowed low, and Kit quickly followed with a curtsy. Unusually, the queen did not wave her hand to urge them to stand again, but let them stay there with their backs bent and their heads at awkward angles.

"I would have thought you would be content to hide from me, seeing as you have lost the person who threatens my life." Her voice boomed across the hall with the words.

Kit kept her eyes on the black and white tiles, scuffed after years of ladies' and gentlemen's court shoes striding back and forth across it. She didn't lift her eyes to the queen, but could tell from the heavy breathing and the firm clicks of her boots that she was nearing Walsingham and Lord Burghley.

"You have lost her," she said in a much quieter voice. "Lost her!" The words echoed loudly. The sudden changes in volume made her ladies-in-waiting whisper, disturbing the silence that followed. "Away. All of you. I do not need you here for this conversation."

Kit angled her head enough to see the retreating ladies. They passed through the hall, heading to the nearest door and into another part of the house.

Kit, Walsingham and Burghley silently remained in their uncomfortable positions as they waited for the ladies to leave. A door was closed heavily behind them.

"Rise, all of you," the queen muttered.

Walsingham's back clicked audibly as he stood straight. Kit's eyes flicked to the queen. She was red in the face, almost as red as the wig that topped her head.

"Your Majesty," Lord Burghley began, his voice meeker than Kit could ever remember hearing it before. "It is a regrettable situation, I will confess —"

"Do not speak to me as if I am one of your councillors, another lawyer, or maybe even one of your clerks. We do not speak of matters of state, but of murder, Burghley." The queen's words rang around the room, making a glass sconce in the wall shudder.

When Burghley said nothing more, she moved her hands to her hips and stepped away, turning her back on the men.

"You come to explain to me that my cousin has fled, yes? What more can you have to say in person than what Walsingham sent in his message last night? She has fled. For all we know, my cousin could have left England's shores by now."

"We do not believe that to be the case, Your Majesty. Not yet, at least." Walsingham stepped forward.

The queen flicked her head toward him. Kit half expected Walsingham to step back, cowed by the strength of her glare, but he held his ground.

"You need not be afraid, Your Majesty. We will protect you, as we have always vowed to do."

"Enough!" the queen barked. "We are not here to talk about fear, but of action. Of my cousin." Her hands fidgeted restlessly, smoothing her skirt and bodice. Eventually, she snatched them from her hips and clasped them in front of her. "What happened? What precisely happened?"

Walsingham and Lord Burghley turned to look at Kit. Kit glared back at Walsingham. Her suspicion was correct. Walsingham and Lord Burghley were taking the chance to blame another for the failure to arrest Mary Stuart.

Kit rather thought the other intelligencers should have joined her. Laidlaw, Somers, Marlowe, and even Iomhar should have been with her. Gritting her teeth, she jerked her chin in the queen's direction, to find those dark eyes flashing with anger.

"Well? They are looking at you and waiting for you to speak. So speak!" the queen ordered.

"We arrested Mary Stuart and her men where she was hiding at Longtown Castle, Your Majesty. It was no easy journey from there to Fotheringhay, and the progress was slow," Kit explained carefully. "We were ambushed in the Forest of Dean by more of her supporters. The trees were set on fire. They killed some of our soldiers and escaped with Mary Stuart and her men." An image flashed in her mind of Lord Ruskin running away from the camp. "We were unable to follow them after the fire, Your Majesty." Kit bowed her head as she fell silent.

"This is madness," the queen muttered, more to herself than any of them. She hung her head and pulled at some loose wisps of her wig. When the wig shifted, she stopped, stood tall and flicked her gaze around them all. "You must find her." With these words, her eyes settled on Kit.

"Your Majesty," Walsingham began, "we will..." He trailed off as the queen waved a hand at him, urging him to be silent. She walked past Walsingham and Lord Burghley, closing the distance between herself and Kit.

"You have seen her, more than once," Elizabeth murmured. "Tell me, what is my cousin like?"

"Your Majesty?" Kit frowned.

"Is she as bloodthirsty as my council claim?" She cast a glance at Walsingham and Lord Burghley, then turned back to Kit. "That letter..." She swallowed, the sound loud enough for Kit to hear it. "She had no care for it, did she?"

"She cared for it as little as she does for you, Your Majesty."

Kit's words shook the queen. She clasped and released her hands in front of her, her long fingers curling like a cat's claws.

"Come with me!" she barked and walked out of the hall, through the door and into the sunlight. The two men went to follow. "Not you two! Kit Scarlett, follow me."

Kit hurried after the queen. Walsingham paled, his lips pressed together in an uneven line, and Lord Burghley protested in a low voice to Walsingham.

"This is absurd. She now wishes to speak to your pet alone?"

"She is not a pet," Walsingham said darkly.

"A pale imitation of an intelligencer, Walsingham."

"Enough."

Kit listened to no more of their argument. She followed the queen out to see the train of horses that had pulled up alongside the house. Groomsmen came to collect the animals, but Queen Elizabeth strode away from them. Yeomen started from a distance, hurrying forward when they saw the queen alone, but a sharp wave of her hand soon made them fall still.

The two women stepped down the driveway of the house and toward the Thames. The queen moved her feet to the edge of the riverbank and stared into the grey waters. Kit stood back, ensuring there was a distance between them. When the queen realised that Kit had not followed, she nodded pointedly at the space beside her.

"Men keep their distance. They always do. It is something I have encouraged. A queen cannot be seen to be on the same level as the men around her, or they would try to take advantage of that power." She huffed. "I see no such danger in this moment. Stand beside me."

Kit moved to stand at the edge of the riverbank. Elizabeth shifted her hands, moving them back to her hips. Tilting her chin high, she stared out over the river.

"Kings and queens never have a day where they sit easy on the throne. Judging by my own troubled path to take it, you'd think I would have known that on coronation day. Yet I was young, naïve, perhaps even foolish." She smiled a little. "I believed that when they gave me that crown, I would be safe at last, as I had never been before. How wrong I was indeed. During her reign, my sister was once charged by her council to sign my death warrant."

Kit blinked. She had known of the past Queen Mary's reign and the troubles that had come with it, but no one truly knew what had passed between the late Queen Mary and the current Queen Elizabeth.

"She refused to give that warrant her signature." The queen's voice deepened. "We never discussed why. Sometimes I indulge myself by believing that my sister could not kill her own blood. She may have denied that we were kin at times, angered by the manner of my birth and my mother. Yet she could not kill her own blood in the end. She could not do it.

"If you find Mary Stuart again, they will give me a death warrant to sign." She flicked her head back in the direction of Richmond Palace. "They will tell me that she must be stopped. That I must be the one to sign for her death." The queen's head turned slowly toward Kit. "What queen should kill her blood?" she asked, her voice just a whisper.

Kit's mind returned to the moment Mary Stuart had cast her out of Chartley Castle. She had been prepared for Lord Ruskin to kill her, as long as it was somewhere far away from the castle. There were the tales too of the murder of her former husband, and, of course, the fact she had ordered the last Earl of Ross's death.

"When that once queen is a murderer herself, it is not a question of familial blood, Your Majesty," Kit said eventually, breaking the silence that had fallen between them. "We are not talking of a queen that sat humbly in a castle. We are talking of one who has conspired in death."

Queen Elizabeth nodded slowly, turning her head toward the river once again. "You would agree with Walsingham and Burghley, would you not, Kit?" She laughed, though there was no humour in the sound. "You believe I should send her to her death."

"I would never presume to tell you what to do, Your Majesty." Kit lowered her voice. "Yet if I may speak from experience, having met this woman more than once and having seen the very words that she wrote to her conspirer, Babington, I can say with confidence that if the balance of the world was altered, had she been the one standing by this river talking of your own head —" at the words, the queen flinched — "she would not hesitate for a moment in signing your death warrant."

The queen said nothing. For a minute there was just the lapping of water against the riverbank. A fish darted, breaking the surface and then diving back down again. The movement shook the queen out of her stillness.

"Return to your master," she whispered.

Kit curtsied and turned to leave.

"Kit?"

She froze, turning on her heel to face the queen again.

"You will find her, will you not?" A muscle twitched in the queen's face and for a moment, Kit saw the same fear she had seen once before at Hampton Court, when Elizabeth had been poisoned.

"I will." Kit made the vow and curtsied again.

She left swiftly, hurrying back toward the palace. Lord Burghley walked past Kit and strode toward the queen, clearly intent on continuing their conversation, but Walsingham waited by the door.

"What did she have to say?" Walsingham asked as Kit stopped in front of him.

"She is afraid, even if she does not wish to show it."

"That is the prerogative of a queen." Walsingham smiled sadly. "I have watched over her for many years. She hides her fears better than most men, but she is made of flesh, blood, and humours too."

"I have promised to find Mary Stuart."

"Then you must."

"Something else must pass first." Kit waited as one of the groomsmen collected the last of the horses from Elizabeth's hunting party. As the groomsman retreated, she stepped toward Walsingham. "If you wish me to find Mary Stuart for you, then there is something I need in return."

"What is that?" Walsingham's brow furrowed.

"Tell me the truth about my past." Kit held her breath, waiting for an answer.

"I told you. No more of this, Kit. It is not for the best." Walsingham turned his back on her and walked away, heading for his own horse.

Kit followed him, her hands clammy as she balled them into fists. She was tired of chasing after Walsingham, of bothering him the way a fly buzzed around the ears of a horse in the sweltering heat. This had to end.

"You will tell me the truth about my past or I will leave your service at once." Kit's threat startled him so much that he missed the stirrup and nearly fell over on the gravel drive. "I will be gone by tomorrow morning. No more commissions, no more visits. You will not see me again." She stood taller. "If you wish for my help to find Mary Stuart, then you will tell me the truth today."

He nodded. It was the slightest of movements, but it let Kit breathe again.

CHAPTER 22

"Why are we here?" Kit asked as they stopped the horses outside Barn Elms. In the daylight, the manor house looked larger than she remembered it. The red-brick frontage stretched left and right and was bordered by fine flowers that had been cultivated by Walsingham's gardeners. The windows gleamed and maids carrying fresh laundry dabbed at their necks and chests in the heat. "Why not tell me what you have to say at Seething Lane?"

"Here, Kit. Let us talk here." Walsingham climbed down off his horse, uneasily. His old bones had struggled with the ride, and he stumbled on his feet. Kit jumped down with ease in comparison and took the reins of his steed, so the horse would not move and pull him off his feet. "Thank you."

Kit passed the reins to the groomsman and followed Walsingham into the house.

"Is your daughter here?" Kit asked, aware of the glower the steward, Withers, gave her as they moved indoors.

"No. She is with her husband today." Walsingham's voice was small as he waved away the steward with an order. "A flagon of mead. Once you have delivered it, we are not to be interrupted."

Kit followed Walsingham into a back room of the house. She'd seen him sit here many times with his wife and daughter over the years, but never her. Not once had she been welcome in this room.

He hastened to close all the windows, locking them tight. He ushered Kit toward a chair, but she stayed standing, shaking her head as she folded her arms across her dark red doublet.

Walsingham sighed and took the settle bench, leaning forward. They said nothing at first but waited for the steward. Once the mead was delivered the steward left, and Walsingham downed half of one tankard. The golden liquid dripped into his beard as he topped up the cup.

"No more delays," Kit said, her voice sharp.

Slowly, he lowered the pewter jug to the table beside his tankard and sat back on the settle bench. "As you wish." He lifted his eyes to meet hers. His expression was one she could not decipher. Leaning back, he rested his hands on the arms of the chair. "We spoke before of John Stuart, Commendator of Coldingham."

"Yes, you spoke of him a little, but who is he really?" Kit asked impatiently.

Walsingham arched an eyebrow at her interruption but said nothing in reprimand. "He was one of James V's illegitimate sons. I cannot remember his mother's name. A lady of the Scottish court." Walsingham was dismissive, waving a hand in the air. "John Stuart was raised in the court, protected by his father. He was given lands, education, and position. After James V's death, he was much in Mary, Queen of Scots' favour, despite the fact he was Protestant and she a Catholic." Walsingham reached for his tankard of mead and took a sip. Slowly, he gestured to the bench opposite him. "You truly should sit down."

"I do not wish to." Kit remained standing, her arms folded.

"Who knows how easy the friendship was at times? Undoubtedly there were disagreements." Walsingham winced. "What knowledge I had of the Scottish court at this time depended on my intelligencers' information. From what I could gather, as half-brother and sister, they tried to make an easy path between them."

Kit felt her mouth turn dry. She had been told by Moira that John Stuart was an illegitimate son of James V, but she hadn't made the connection that Mary Stuart was his half-sister.

"He married." Walsingham sat forward suddenly. "Against his sister's wishes and without permission. He eloped."

"With Katherine Douglas."

Walsingham nodded slowly, looking down into the tankard. "She was the daughter of Margaret Douglas, Countess of Lennox. Margaret Douglas was granddaughter to King Henry VII."

"A royal family," Kit observed uneasily, remembering the words Iomhar had said to her in the forest.

"It was a royal match that should have been sanctioned, but it wasn't." Walsingham shook his head then raised his eyes to Kit. "An illegitimate father, but still blue-blooded, and a legitimate mother would have given any child of theirs a claim to the throne of Scotland."

The words hovered in the air for a moment.

Walsingham sat forward, resting his elbows on his knees. He didn't blink as he held Kit's gaze. "They had a daughter. Her name was Katherine Stuart. Katherine Douglas died giving birth to the child."

Kit felt her heart racing. Moving to the window, she looked out of the glass, trying to absorb what he was telling her.

"I am told John Stuart was a devoted father," Walsingham continued. "I would not know myself. I never met him." The settle bench creaked as he leaned back again, but Kit didn't turn to look at him. "He remarried, a woman by the name of Jean Hepburn. She had little care for the child. Her focus was on her own children and court life. When John Stuart died in November sixty-three, it's said that his last words were that he wished his sister, Mary Stuart, would become a Protestant."

"He said that?" Kit flicked her head back toward Walsingham.

He shrugged. "That is said in whispers only. If it is true, then it shows what divide truly existed between the two of them. More whispers followed. My intelligencers heard information I had to act on." Walsingham topped up his tankard again, taking such hefty gulps that the mead dribbled down his chin and he wiped it away with a handkerchief. "The daughter, Katherine Stuart, was left alone and isolated at Coldingham. Her stepmother left her behind with the staff, having no care for her.

"Mary Stuart had no child at this moment, no issue. She was Catholic in a Protestant country. She had divided her council since her return from France, upset many men that should have been her supporters, and alienated her nobles. The clans had no fealty to her either."

"Why tell me this?" Kit said.

"I am telling you what happened." Walsingham's voice was sharp. "Mary Stuart feared losing her crown. Without an heir, the nobles would look for another to put on the throne. One with royal connections, one from the Stuart family." Walsingham jerked his chin toward Kit. "Whispers abounded that the newly orphaned Katherine Stuart would be the one they chose."

"This child you speak of, what happened to her?"

"An intelligencer of mine overheard a whisper in Mary's court. They heard of Mary's fear, her intention for the child to be gone, so that there could be no other contender for the Scottish throne. She was told that Katherine Stuart was at Coldingham. When I heard this news, I had to act." Walsingham moved to his feet, leaning on the settle bench for support. "That intelligencer knew as well as I that Mary Stuart could have that child killed. It was imperative to work fast."

"What did you do?" Kit asked. He didn't answer her for a minute, and she stepped away from the window. "Walsingham? What did you do?"

"I went to Coldingham. Never have I travelled so fast in my life. No intelligencer could get there in time, so it was up to me to see what would happen next. I arrived at Coldingham and searched the house, desperate to find the child, Katherine Stuart, only to be told by the staff that her aunt, the Queen of Scotland herself, had taken the child for a walk. I raced through the grounds, searching for them. I was younger then and could ride a horse as well as you can now. I saw what she did. I saw with my own eyes what Mary Stuart did to that child."

Kit stared at Walsingham, holding her breath as she waited for him to go on.

"She dropped the child in the river," Walsingham said darkly. "Pff! Gone. As if the child were a trinket she threw away." He downed what was left in his tankard and slammed it on the table. "She watched the child struggle, then walked away."

"I don't believe it," Kit whispered. Walsingham's tale matched the dream she had had so many times before.

"The Queen of Scotland left, turning her back on the child. I raced forward and pulled you out of the water. Yes, you, Kit. I pulled *you* out of the water."

Kit backed up, colliding with the windowsill.

"I was not about to watch a child die. I could not do it." Walsingham shook his head. His eyes were watery, but no tears fell. "I pulled you out, watched you choke and cough up the water. You were small, weak, and the one person you were connected to by blood had tried to kill you. I was faced with a choice. I held you in my arms and carried you back to Coldingham, but by the time I got there, tales had surrounded the priory house. Mary Stuart had told the staff there had been a terrible accident. Poor little Katherine Stuart had tripped and fallen in the water. She begged for staff to come and help find you. I hid with you in the woods. They rode past us, and Mary took them back to the water, but it was half an hour after she had left you there to drown. She must have thought your body had been washed away by the current."

He gripped the back of the settle bench, leaning firmly over it, as if his spine no longer had the strength to stay straight. "I had a choice, Kit. I either returned you to that house, and ... and…"

"And what?" she whispered.

"And waited until Mary tried to hurt you again." He looked up, his eyes finding hers. "Or I saved you. You had no family there. No one to protect you. You needed protecting. You were just a child."

"You took me from Scotland, and you brought me here to London." She clasped her trembling hands together. "What for? What did you hope to achieve?"

"Nothing." Walsingham's voice was small. "If I had left you there, you would have died, Kit. Sooner or later, Mary Stuart would have found a way. Having seen what she had done with my own eyes, I did not doubt my decision. I couldn't leave you there. So, I offered you a new life. It was not the life you had known, no." He walked around the settle bench, holding out an arm and appealing to her. "It was not the life you could have had, had your parents survived, but at least this way, you were alive. Better that, breathing and living another's life, than to be dead."

The words were said quietly, but hearing the truth at last left Kit overwhelmed.

She knew the names of her parents. Yet the tale was sadder than she had been prepared for. She wished to argue, wished to deny it at every turn, but too much made sense. The dreams — the memory of a true event. The way Mary Stuart looked at her, certain she had seen Kit's face before — it all made sense.

"You took me," Kit whispered eventually. She lifted her gaze to Walsingham.

"I gave you life."

Silence stretched between them.

Walsingham sank down onto his settle bench. "You must not blame me. I was a man trying to save a child. I saved you from death, Kit."

"You did," Kit whispered. Her hands shook as she lowered them to her sides. "Yet you took the life I had too, and you never told me." Her words made him flinch. "Why wouldn't you tell me?"

"Your previous life is as dead as if you truly did die that day." Walsingham's voice was firm. "Katherine Stuart died. Kit Scarlett lived." He sighed deeply. "What more could I have done?"

She turned away, looking out of the window again.

"Kit, please, say something."

"I cannot." She marched from the room.

"Kit?" he called after her. "Kit?"

She sprinted to the front door, where Withers was pacing. In his eagerness to see her leave, he opened the door for her.

She ran out of the house to the stables, taking the reins of her horse out of the groomsman's hands, who hadn't finished putting it away. Pulling herself into the saddle, she urged her horse to a gallop down the driveway. She briefly caught sight of Walsingham standing by the open front door as she passed by.

"Kit!" he shouted, his face red as he stumbled down the step. She said nothing as she left him there, calling her name.

CHAPTER 23

Kit leapt from her horse and tossed the reins around a post outside Iomhar's house, hurrying inside with such haste that she nearly knocked Abigail from her feet on the other side of the front door.

"In the name of the wee man!" Abigail clutched her chest and tottered.

"I'm sorry, Abigail. Where's…?" Kit trailed off as she heard voices elsewhere in the house.

Niall and Iomhar were talking loudly, their voices audible from the back of the house.

"That way." Abigail pointed down the hall. "What happened to ye?"

"Nothing," Kit lied, aware that the young woman's eyes followed her as she ran down the corridor.

Kit pushed through two doors before she found Iomhar. He was standing in a back room, the windows overlooking the garden and the river that he had once taught her to swim in. Iomhar was talking loudly to Niall.

"We cannot go back now, ye know that," Iomhar said, waving a hand in Niall's direction.

"I know that we cannot go home, but that does not mean I cannot go to Scotland." Niall shook his head. "For all we know, one of my informants in the battalion may have heard something by now. It could help us to find out where Lord Ruskin has gone, and Mary Stuart too. They will have some men loyal to them in Scotland. That is surely where I need to be."

"The road is nay safe place at the moment, I fear." Iomhar shook his head.

"Ye may have walked into a forest fire, but it does not mean the rest of us would."

"Niall!" Iomhar hissed.

"Aye, just pointing out the truth."

"Iomhar?" Kit tried to get his attention.

"Ah, at last, she returns," Niall cut in. "Maybe ye can talk some sense to us, Kit. We need to know where Lord Ruskin is, and I think the truth lies in Scotland —"

"Not now, Niall." She shook her head firmly. "Iomhar, I need to talk to you." She strode toward the back door and stepped out into the garden.

"Wait," Niall called. "Iomhar and I —"

"Now!" Kit said sharply, well aware she was being rude, but she was unable to calm her temper enough to be reasonable. She walked far across the garden, heading to the river at the very bottom of the lawn that had turned brown in the excessively hot summer. Iomhar followed her, closing the back door behind him and traipsing across the garden.

"Ye going to tell me what is wrong?" he asked, stopping at her side.

"I have something to tell you, but I hardly know how to talk of it." She turned in a frantic circle. "What we spoke of before. John Stuart and Katherine Douglas. They ... they —"

"They are your parents." Iomhar's voice was calm as he stared at her.

Kit breathed heavily. Unable to say the words, she nodded once.

Iomhar exhaled sharply and leaned against a tree. "Then ye are a royal, Kit."

"No. No, I am not." She shook her head frantically. "I do not feel royal. I do not feel a part of that family, for I am not. As Walsingham pointed out to me, that life is a dead one. The person I was born to be, I no longer am."

"Ye have not taken this well."

"Pray, Iomhar, do not call me royal again."

"As ye wish. Shall I not bow, then, every time I see ye?"

She looked sharply at him.

"Thank goodness for that. It would feel strange to bow to ye after so long." He smiled, showing he was in jest. She smiled too, glad he had somehow managed to lighten the mood when she felt as if her shoulders were weighed down by rocks. "What more did Walsingham tell ye, Kit?"

"Much." Kit repeated what the spymaster had said, including John Stuart's plea for his half-sister, Mary Stuart, to become a Protestant. When she revealed that Mary was the one who tried to take her life, Iomhar cursed loudly.

"She tried to murder ye? Ye were a child! A bairn!"

"Iomhar, shh, I beg of you." She waved a hand in the air, desperate for him to be calm. "No one in this world knows of this but us, Walsingham and Mary Stuart, and I wish to keep it that way. Lord knows Walsingham would be furious at me for telling you."

"Who cares what he thinks anymore? Aye, he saved your life, Kit. I can hardly be angry with him for that."

"He gave me a life," she murmured.

"He refused to tell ye of the life ye had." Iomhar's voice was deep. "He moulded ye, carved ye into the intelligencer ye are. He could have raised ye in his own house, as a second daughter to him, but he chose not to. He made ye his … his…"

"His what?"

"I do not know the right word for it. But ye belonged to him."

She nodded and Iomhar breathed heavily, pushing his hands through his hair.

"This is unbelievable," he muttered.

"That is how I feel." She shifted her weight between her feet, still uncertain what to say. "It is hard to accept that I am this child he speaks of. Katherine Stuart. It is not the world I know, not the life I know. Yet I am her."

"Aye, ye are." Iomhar lowered his hands from his hair. "Ye are still that woman. Ye are still technically a royal."

"Iomhar! I asked you not to say that."

"Well, I have to," he pointed out. "Would Mary Stuart not wish to see ye dead again?"

"No." Kit was certain of it. "She has a son who has been happily placed on the throne. James VI of Scotland is the country's king. I am no longer a threat to Mary Stuart in that regard. If she realised who I am, it would mean little to her. She would only wish to see me dead for what I am to her now, her chaser."

"God's blood." Iomhar tipped his head back.

Kit did not know what to think. She knew she should be thankful to Walsingham. He had rescued her, and yet… She felt a kernel of anger growing in her stomach. It flickered like a spark, then grew into a great flame.

She could not talk of it anymore. She turned in a circle, her body restless.

"Are ye well, Kit?"

"I…" She trailed off, uncertain what to say.

"Kit?" Iomhar placed a hand on her shoulder.

"I cannot do this. I can scarcely comprehend it!"

"Come here." Iomhar drew her toward him.

She buried herself in his chest as his arms came up around her and held him tightly. In that moment of silence, she tried not to think of what had passed. She pushed away the thought of her birth and thought of this embrace instead.

"Worry not," he whispered in her ear.

"How can you say that?"

"Someone has to say it." He chuckled and held her tighter. "Ye are still ye. What ye have learned does not change who ye are."

Kit was uncertain how long she stood there in Iomhar's arms, but the sun had dropped when she eventually released him. It cast a burnt orange light across the garden, the amber tinge glistening on the river's surface.

"For now, please, do not tell anyone," Kit whispered.

"If my mother knew your parents, she could tell ye something of them."

"I cannot hear of them. Not yet." It was a curiosity she would satisfy another day. For now, she still burned with anger, and that anger was directed at one person in particular. "Mary Stuart tried to kill me."

Iomhar cursed loudly. "We have to find her," he muttered. "It is high time she paid for all the crimes she has committed. Against my family, against the Queen of England, against Scotland, and against ye."

"I agree." Kit nodded firmly. "There has to be a way to find her, some path we have not yet seen."

"Kit? Iomhar? Are ye two out here?" Moira's voice called across the garden.

"Aye, we're here." Iomhar called back to his mother. He stepped away. Acting on instinct, Kit reached out and took his hand.

"Elspeth has made a fine feast for tonight," Moira continued loudly from the house. "Pray, come in soon."

"We will," Iomhar assured her, then turned back to face Kit, their hands still locked together. "Ye wish to stay out here much longer?"

"I do not know." The only thing she felt like doing was staying with Iomhar, holding his hand. "I suppose I'm wondering how many people I can truly trust in this world. Walsingham ... he lied to me for so long."

"Aye, I know someone ye can trust." Iomhar stepped toward her and lifted her hand. They were hidden from the house by the cover of the trees, though Kit glanced toward it still, nervous that they would be seen. No one appeared.

Iomhar brought her hand up to his lips and kissed the back.

"You did this once before," Kit whispered.

"Aye, and I'll do it more if ye ever ask it of me." He winked at her. "Come, let's get some food."

Iomhar drew her back toward the house, their hands still entwined. When they stepped in through the back door and came face to face with Moira and Niall, neither of them pulled away. Moira smiled as she looked at them, and Niall chuckled.

"I wondered what ye two were doing in the garden," he said mischievously.

"Be quiet, Niall." Moira tapped her son on the arm in reprimand.

CHAPTER 24

"It will work," Kit said confidently, leaning forward on the settle bench. Iomhar sat opposite her, shaking his head, and Niall stood beside them, as unsettled as his brother.

"It would be a risk, Kit," Iomhar said seriously.

"One I am willing to take." She'd been quiet over dinner as a plan formed in her head, a way to track down where Mary Stuart was now. "There is a person in London who we know is loyal to her. We know that he has helped her escape Chartley, and he has been feeding information from the privy council to her people for years. If there is anyone who will have an idea of where she is now, it is surely the Rose."

Niall nodded in agreement as Iomhar rubbed his hands together, deep in thought.

"Would he believe ye are a double agent, though?" Niall asked, his brow wrinkling. "Ye would have to be convincing in your act."

"I can be," Kit said confidently. "I could tell him I am a Scottish agent, and only pretend to be English to deceive Walsingham."

"That means ye will have to do your Scottish accent again." Iomhar smiled a little. "I had to train ye the first time when ye were deceiving Lady Ruskin."

"Aye, ye did, but fortunately, I have had a lot of time to listen to your accent ever since." Kit adopted a Scottish accent. "I can persuade him to believe me. Och, I could do it if I merely had five minutes alone with him."

"Not bad," Niall chuckled with an approving nod. "Ye have improved."

Kit held her arms open, as if presenting herself on a stage. "Then it is settled," she said, returning to her normal accent. "I shall go to the Tower, visit the Rose, and see what he knows."

"Buckingham is a man of position. If ye go dressed as ye are, I am not convinced he will trust ye enough to tell ye anything."

"Then I shall have to wear a dress again." Kit sighed heavily. The gowns Walsingham had once given her were tucked away in her attic rooms across the city, though she had not returned there for some time. "I will need a gown."

"We can sort that." Niall turned away. "Rhona? Ye are closest to Kit's height, aren't ye?"

"Aye." Rhona walked toward them from the other side of the room. She had been playing cards with the earl, her sister, and her mother. "Why do ye ask?"

"We need to borrow a gown." Niall gestured toward Kit.

"I'm sure I can find one that will fit ye." Rhona urged Kit to follow her.

"When will ye go to the Tower?" Iomhar asked as Kit moved to her feet.

"Tonight. It's best this is done under the cover of shadows and not in the daylight. I do not want Walsingham being told by his men that I'm there either."

"Wait." Iomhar stiffened on the settle bench. "Ye do not intend to tell him?"

"Not yet." She followed Rhona out of the room. "I will talk to him when I have something to say, but not before."

"Stop fidgeting."

"I cannot help it, Iomhar. These gowns are so uncomfortable."

"If ye wish to persuade Lord Buckingham ye are a Scottish lady, then ye need to look at ease, Kit."

She huffed as Iomhar took her hand and helped her down from the carriage. The dark green gown was cinched in at the waist with a tight-fitting corset. From the bottom of the bodice, the skirt flowed down to the ground, pleated at the front to reveal a mantle of patterned green and white cloth. The white ruff Rhona had placed above her collarbone itched.

"I am glad we did this at night," Kit muttered. "It would be too hot to wear such a thing in the day."

"Remember who ye are now," Iomhar whispered and stepped back, hiding his face with his hat. He'd taken the guise of her driver to lead her to the Tower. He stood back by the horses, waiting for her to approach the palace. "Ye are a Scottish lady."

His words had two meanings, one of which left her uncomfortable. She pulled at the collar, trying to loosen it around her throat, then approached the gatehouse. Flaming torches were attached to the wall, either side of a portcullis, and a lantern hovered within the gatehouse. A man stood with the lantern, raising it high so he could see her face as she approached. The light bounced off his jaw, showing the grime on his cheeks and the yeoman's uniform that was somewhat dirtied from the prison.

"I am here to see a prisoner of yours." Kit gave no name but stretched a hand between the bars of the portcullis. She opened her fingers, revealing her palm was full of gold coins. The man's eyes widened before he nodded, took the coins and opened a barred door within the portcullis.

Kit stepped inside, being careful to pull the farthingale through the gap. It was ungainly and the hoop bounced off the sides of the bars, but she recovered quickly and stood tall, adopting the haughty look she had so often seen Queen Elizabeth's ladies wear.

"This way," the guard grunted in a low voice. Taking the glowing lantern, he led a path across the courtyard of the Tower.

Kit's eyes flicked to the White Tower, standing tall in the centre of the complex. In the moonlight it had a pearlescent sheen. The myriad of windows were darkened, so she could not see what was beyond them. There could have been prisoners inside, an armoury, or even the royal mint that was placed somewhere in this palace.

She followed the guard around the tower to one of the turrets in the outer wall.

"Who is it you wish to see?" he asked, pushing a key into a large wooden door.

"Lord Buckingham."

He glanced at her briefly, his brows knitting in suspicion.

"I offered many coins for your silence as well as my entrance," she warned him. He nodded and opened the door, not questioning her again.

They passed a sleeping guard who sat in a spindly wooden chair, his head lolling against the wall beside him and spittle hanging from his lips as he snored loudly. They walked up a spiral staircase, so narrow that Kit had to grab her farthingale and turn it at an angle to get through the space. More than once did she nearly trip on the hem of her chemise. She cursed inwardly, not wanting to draw the guard's attention to how ill she wore the gown.

They passed two doors before they found a third. The guard knocked loudly on the wood, making the door rattle in its frame.

"Lord Buckingham. You have a visitor," the guard called through the door. He chose a key from his belt and unlocked the door, gesturing for her to step inside. "I'll be three steps down." He pointed past her down the staircase. She nodded and stepped inside.

The scent of excrement reached her nose and she winced. There was another smell that mixed with the first, one not often found in a prison. It was the scent of bergamot from a man's washed clothes.

On a small straw bed, a man raised his head. It was Buckingham, his face just visible in the light of one burning torch that was attached to the cell wall. He still wore his fine clothes. His face was reddened, as if he suffered in the heat, and his shoes had been placed neatly at the bottom of the bed. The sweet scent wafted off his clothes as he hurried to his feet.

"A lady!" He gasped and bowed to her. Kit stepped forward, allowing him to see her face, just as the door closed behind her. It thudded loudly. "Oh..." Lord Buckingham hesitated, his head tilting to the side as her features were illuminated by the torchlight. "It is you. You are one of Walsingham's ... men."

Kit stepped toward the door and pressed her ear to the wood, listening to the guard taking a few steps down. "At least he has departed a little. It gives us a short time for conversation. Nay, I still fear we do not have long." She took on a Scottish accent and returned to his side.

Lord Buckingham stared at her, wide-eyed. "Scottish?" he murmured, his voice breathy. "You are Scottish?"

"Aye, though few know it." She offered a sad smile. "I am sorry ye have ended up here. We had to arrest ye. It was the only way to distract Walsingham and his men from Mary Stuart's escape."

"I do not understand." Lord Buckingham shook his head, his wide jowls trembling with the movement. "You do not work for Walsingham after all?"

"He only believes I do, my lord." She smiled fully this time. "I have pulled the wool over his eyes for a long time and hidden my identity well, but my time runs short. I must leave London. I intend to help my queen."

"Who knows if she can be helped now?" Lord Buckingham walked away from her, striding across his prison cell. The walls were circular, marred by years of scratches left there by other prisoners. Lord Buckingham laid a hand on the stone to keep himself standing. "They pursue her, relentlessly. The man you have served pursues her. Yet you come here to me now, like this." He gestured to her. "You tell me you intend to go to her? To Queen Mary?"

"I must," Kit said with passion. "I can be of no more use to her here. Aye, I have found out what I could from Walsingham. I know where they are to search for her, where they will patrol. They fear she intends to take a boat and flee the shores. I know what docks they will be watching, but I am not able to get a message to our queen. The last I knew of her whereabouts, she was at Longtown. They have not told me where she is now. Nay, I cannot warn her. I am in anguish, my lord." She walked the other way around the room, coming to face him again. "I must do something to warn her, which is why I come to ye now."

"Me? Why would you come to me? What good can I do for you from in here? I can hardly arrange for your message to be sent." He shook his head.

"I know ye cannot. I intend to be the messenger myself, so the words will not be lost, but I need to know where to find our queen. I pray ye, my lord. Tell me where to find her, so I can warn her." Kit waited, holding her breath. "Ye have been instrumental in moving our queen, of warning her before of what was to come. Ye must know something of her whereabouts now."

Buckingham turned away from her. He shifted his gaze to the arrow slit in the wall and pressed his face to the gap, breathing in the night air. "The world seems full of deceivers. One no longer knows who to trust," he murmured, more to himself than to Kit. After a short silence, he raised his head. "Yet I see more and more we must take a gamble on those around us. As I am, death awaits me." He hung his head.

"My lord, I beg of ye," Kit said, stepping toward him. "Tell me something, please."

"Very well." Buckingham jerked his chin, his mind made up. "You will find her in Cumbria. I have a house near the borderlands — Raven Hall. I offered it once to Her Majesty and her men. I believe they have hidden her there."

"Thank ye, my lord. Thank ye. I shall go to them at once to warn of what is to come." Kit curtsied deeply. "I wish ye well, my lord."

"A kind wish, but a hopeless one." He smiled sadly. "God speed."

Kit backed out of the room and hurried down the steps. Any guilt she might have had at deceiving a zealous man soon faded when she remembered what he had done. He had fed information to Mary Stuart's supporters. Thanks to the spy he had placed in Walsingham's own house, Kit had nearly lost her life more than once.

"I am done. Thank you," Kit said to the guard on the staircase and waited for him to lock the cell door again. He led her back across the Tower courtyard and let her out through the door in the portcullis.

Stepping out, Kit walked with patience toward the carriage that awaited her, never once hurrying, in case it alerted the guard that watched her and made him suspicious of her eagerness.

Iomhar bowed as she approached, completing the illusion of being her servant, then opened the carriage door. "Well? Did he believe ye?"

"He did." Kit smiled. "Raven Hall in Cumbria."

"I hate sitting in these things." Kit slumped down onto the settle bench, but nearly bounced out of it again for her farthingale prohibited her comfort.

The family stood around her. Duncan raised a candle, with his sister, Abigail, holding onto his arm. Abigail, Rhona, and Moira had clearly all been in bed, for they now wore robes around their nightgowns, and their hair was loose around their shoulders.

"She looks so different," Abigail murmured. "Almost pretty."

"Abigail, be quiet," Rhona snapped in her sister's ear. Kit glanced at Abigail, curious at the strange compliment, and happily kicked off the court shoes, her feet aching after being in them for so long. No matter how she looked, she had little liking for such clothes.

"Ye have heard something, then?" Niall asked, hurrying forward with a second candle. "He told ye where she is?"

"He did." Kit smiled as Iomhar passed her a tankard with a tot of whisky in it. She gulped thirstily. "We have a location. Now, we must merely find it. Raven House in Cumbria."

"Aye, I've heard of it," Duncan murmured, stepping forward. "It belongs to the House of Buckingham. It used to be associated with the Howards, long ago, but was passed through marriage to Lord Buckingham."

"He has now offered it to Mary Stuart, so that she and her men may make use of it." Kit's eyes settled on Iomhar. He stood a short distance away from her, his expression grave. He tossed away the low-lying servant's cap he had been wearing and lifted a second tankard to his lips, taking a small sip. "If we were to approach with an army, I do not doubt Lord Ruskin would somehow hear of it. With soldiers we would have to move slowly, too, across the country." Her words caught Iomhar's attention, and he turned toward her.

"Do not tell me ye wish to go alone, Kit. That may be the most foolish thing ye have ever suggested doing." He downed what was left in his tankard. "Think it through."

"Not alone, Iomhar." She looked between him and Niall. "You two have wanted to do this, have you not? You have wished to catch Mary Stuart and Lord Ruskin. I am suggesting that the three of us go. The three of us can cross the country quickly, without causing a stir or whispers wherever we go. We can move hidden in the shadows. You wish to surprise Mary Stuart this time? To have the chance to catch her when she is unprepared? I believe this is our opportunity."

"Well, ye can guess what my answer will be." Niall stepped forward. Moira reached for his arm to hold him back, but he was already shaking his head, his brown hair dancing around his ears. "Ye know I must go, Mother." She swallowed slowly, then nodded. "Iomhar?"

"Ye wish to do this without Walsingham's knowledge, Kit?"

"I will send him a letter to tell him I am hunting for Mary Stuart, but I do not think it wise to tell him. I fear he would not let us go alone. He'd send soldiers. As I said, soldiers crossing that sort of distance would be certain to alert their faction to the fact we are on our way. This must be done without him, for his own sake, though he may not see it in the same light as I do."

"Then ye have my vow as ye have my brother's." Iomhar smiled. "I am with ye."

Kit placed her tankard down on the table and stood, looking at Moira.

"I wish ye luck, the three of ye," Moira said quietly. "I will pray every minute of the day until the three of ye return."

"We will," Kit promised, then took hold of the skirt of her gown and raised it above her ankles, aiding her progress toward the door. "We can depart as soon as I am back in my hose and doublet."

CHAPTER 25

"There it is." Iomhar's deep voice sounded from ahead.

Kit urged the tired mare beneath her to gallop faster. They'd swapped horses on the journey more than once in order to cover the ground so fast, yet still, Kit's current horse was exhausted. Eventually, she drew to a stop at Iomhar's side, with Niall pulling up beside her. They reached the crest of a hill, flanked by heather and low grey stones that sat in the earth like crouching hares.

"Look there," Iomhar urged, "between the trees."

The sun was beginning to rise over the hills. They'd ridden for two days and through the nights too, stopping only to have the occasional nap at inns en route. As the sun appeared, Kit yawned and rubbed her eyes. The morning light fell upon a grey- and red-brick house, turreted as if it was some medieval castle. It sat between two clumps of forest on a mounded hill, with a moat around the edge of the embankment.

"It's isolated," Niall muttered. "That will hardly make the task an easy one."

"We need to get closer," Kit said, flicking the reins and leading the way down the hill toward the castle-style house.

When they reached the edge of the forest, Kit stopped. She left the horse behind, hidden between the trees, then crept toward the treeline with Iomhar and Niall at her shoulders. When the house came into view, she stopped, pressing her body to the side of a tree trunk.

Movement by the castle wall prompted all three of them to hide, choosing different trees to press their bodies behind.

"It's a guard," Niall hissed. Kit bent her head around the other side of the tree to look at the guard. He marched past the castle walls, high on the hill. He hadn't seen them but was walking over a path he had already trodden in the long straw-like grass. He yawned, clearly tired after a night of keeping watch.

"There are more — look again," Iomhar called from a tree further along.

Kit's eyes flicked between the windows and the ramparts of the roof. There were many guards, some wearing a uniform with tartan thrown over their shoulders. Others merely wore blackened doublets that would have hidden them well in the darkness.

"So many guards," Kit murmured, a smile beginning to grow. "They do not want to be caught unawares, as they were at Longtown." It was the confirmation she had been looking for, the certainty that Mary Stuart was there. Why else would they guard the house?

"It's too heavily guarded," Niall hissed and retreated through the trees, beckoning to the two of them. Iomhar followed swiftly, but Kit hesitated, her eyes still flicking between the windows. She could see no one but guards. Some were armed with swords at their hips, others with pistols.

"Kit?" Iomhar called.

She cast one last look at the rooftop and the guards standing there before retreating through the trees after them. They stopped a short distance away, completely hidden from the house.

"I know I can be arrogant, but even I do not think we can break our way into a house so fortified and live to tell the tale," Niall muttered, looking between Iomhar and Kit.

"What happened to your courage, brother?" Iomhar teased.

"It's hiding in my bed right now, like a frightened boy. I am happy to admit it, aren't ye?"

A muscle around Iomhar's eye twitched and he relented, nodding once. "Nay, we cannot break into a house like that particularly easily."

"What do ye mean, *particularly*?" his brother asked sharply. "Not at all!"

"Perhaps there is another way," Kit said, interrupting their argument. "If we cannot get into a house that is so well guarded, then let us find a way to draw Mary Stuart out."

"Ye think she would leave?" Iomhar asked with a short laugh. "Aye, let's just knock on the door and ask if she wishes to take a turn in the grounds. That is likely to see success."

"You are as wry as your brother, sometimes," said Kit.

"I do not want to end up dead."

"We will not." Kit held his gaze, certain of her plan. He shifted on his feet and folded his arms, evidently waiting for her to go on. "We draw her out of the house, to somewhere where we can set up an ambush. She would no longer be on her territory, but on a land of our choosing."

"There's a monument not far from here, a famous curiosity," Iomhar said hurriedly. "I heard talk of it once. Castlerigg. It's a circle of standing stones." He raised an eyebrow at Kit. "If it offered enough hiding places, it could suit us well for an ambush."

"Aye, perfectly well," Niall cut in. "Ye still have not solved how ye intend to get a queen out of hiding and make her walk into open land. Och, she would not do such a thing easily, and ye two know it. Ye will need something special to draw her out."

"Then we offer her the one thing she currently needs." Kit looked back toward the gap in the trees and the house beyond.

When she had met Mary Stuart at Chartley, the former queen had compared her house arrest to the worst of prisons, showing her ignorance of the real horrors of the world. Yet it had revealed something of her character.

"She has no liking for feeling trapped," Kit said slowly, thinking of the guards that had stood at every window. "She will feel it here. She will be longing for her escape."

"So we offer her that escape?" Iomhar asked.

"Yes. We offer it to her under the guise of one of her own, someone she believes she can trust. We use a name we know is loyal to Mary and write a letter from them, offering her safe passage to an island in Scotland. We let her believe we are offering her freedom. She would come to meet us then."

"Kit?" Iomhar's voice was deep as he stretched out a hand toward her. "Think this through a little more before ye hurry to fetch a parchment and a quill from your bag. *Who* would send such a letter that they would believe?"

"Ye cannot send it from the Rose." Niall shook his head. "They will have heard by now that he is in the Tower of London. Any communication from him would not be believed."

"What of the Lily?" Kit asked, remembering the lady-in-waiting who had tried to poison Queen Elizabeth at Hampton Court Palace.

"We do not know where Lady Gifford is. Nay, that would not work. She ran and for all we know could have fled to the Continent," Iomhar said. "They may know her true whereabouts and realise we are lying."

"There must be another." Kit marched away, her hands on her hips. Her boots scuffed the soil, arid and suffering in the summer heat.

"Who else is there?" Niall asked.

"I know another." Iomhar said. "One whom Lord Ruskin might believe, but ye would have to address the letter to him, not to Mary Stuart."

"Who?" Kit asked, turning to face him.

"Who abandoned Walsingham in Northumberland for Lord Ruskin? Who drew me into a trap on Lord Ruskin's orders?" Iomhar's smile grew. "Lord Ruskin believes he is loyal, and we know he is in Scotland. Aye, it's believable that he would be able to reach Cumbria."

"Oswyn Ingleby." Kit matched his smile. "It might just work."

The quill tickled Kit's nose as she finished the letter with a flourish at a small lodging house they'd found. Being careful to replicate the signature she had seen before, she wrote Oswyn's codename: *God's Friend*. More than once she had seen it on letters sent both to Lord Ruskin and to Walsingham. She had to pray now that Lord Ruskin would remember it when the letter landed at the house.

"Are ye sure it will be believed?" Niall hovered at her shoulder, peering down at the letter.

"I am no master forger." Kit wrinkled her nose, thinking of Phelippes, who could have probably accomplished this task much better than her. "Yet it is all we have for the moment." She sat back and stared at the letter.

"It will work." Iomhar appeared at her other shoulder. Resting a hand on the table, he gazed at the lettering. "It is much like the letter Oswyn sent to Walsingham, the one that sent me to Scotland to meet him."

Kit shifted, not liking being reminded of how long Iomhar had spent in a dungeon because of Oswyn's interference. "If I ever see that man again…" she muttered to herself.

"Ye'll have to hold me back if we do." Iomhar smiled, but his expression quickly faltered. "My bet is Oswyn is in hiding these days. He never changed sides out of religious zeal; it was always for the money. When he hears of Mary Stuart's arrest, he will not want to be one of her conspirators brought in."

"Aye, I reckon ye are right." Niall reached down and took the letter, folding it up quickly and melting wax from the candle that sat beside Kit. "I'll deliver it."

"Ye?" Iomhar stood straight. "I should go."

"Nay." Niall was firm. "Lord Ruskin knows your face well, aye?"

"Aye." Kit mimicked his accent.

"And he knows yours too?" Niall looked at her.

"Aye," she said again, with less enthusiasm this time.

"If he happens to be looking out of a window, then he will know some plot is afoot. He has only seen my face once in a fight as he tussled with ye, Kit." Niall held up a finger. "I still have less chance of being recognised. I will disguise myself and deliver it to the door on horseback. Ye two ride to the stone circle. I will meet ye there before sunset, in time for their arrival."

"That is if they choose to come." Kit folded her arms. "We could be waiting at that stone circle all night, and they may not come."

"They'll come," Iomhar said confidently. "If you are correct, then Mary Stuart will be desperate to escape these shores by now."

When the wax had dried, Niall held the letter to his forehead in a salute and hurried to the door of the lodging house.

"Hurry to Castlerigg. I'll meet ye there." He turned and left, leaving the door to thud behind him.

"Should we follow him? We could watch the house, ensure they do not suspect him." Kit looked up at Iomhar, who stood behind her. He leaned on the back of her chair, sighing deeply. "You wish to."

"Aye, he is my little brother."

"He's not so little, Iomhar."

"He is to me." He shook his head. "No. It will draw attention to him if we are seen hiding in the trees, watching him. He is right. We should go to Castlerigg, prepare for their arrival."

"I wish I had your confidence they will come."

"They'll come." Iomhar turned his eyes down on her. There was tension in his jaw, a muscle that twitched. "It was your idea. Now you doubt it?"

"Maybe I'm doing as you wish of me at last and thinking things through."

"Mary Stuart will come."

Kit said nothing, still unconvinced as she stared up at Iomhar.

"We should get going."

They readied themselves in silence. Kit dressed in a black doublet, hoping it would help her hide when night fell. Her white collar was almost grey, and stiff around her neck. Her hose were just as dark, and her boots reached up to her knees. With her belt fastened tightly around her waist, she placed her two daggers in it.

Iomhar was outside before her, preparing the horses in the gathering dusk. They grunted softly, dismayed to be moving again so soon after the long journey north. Before Kit could pull herself into the saddle, Iomhar turned to her and withdrew a sword from his belt.

"Take this."

"You need your sword."

"I have two." He turned to show her there was a second one in his belt. He thrust the first blade through her belt before she could object again. "Take it."

"I have my own weapons."

"It does not hurt to have another." He flicked his head toward the horses. "Night is coming in fast. Let us depart."

Kit pulled herself up into the saddle, glancing down at the sword in her belt. She was unused to the long weapon. She'd been given lessons years ago when she was a child, but Walsingham had urged her not to continue. Swords should only be carried by soldiers and gentlemen of rank. It would have made her stand out in a crowd when he wished for her to blend in. Yet tonight that hardly mattered.

They rode away from the lodging house. As the sun dropped in the sky, a greyness crept in. It bathed the landscape in a silverish light. By the time they reached Castlerigg, the sun was just a crown of gold on the horizon, peeking out from behind one of the nearest mountains. The temperature had dropped, and the wind buffeted Kit so much that her hat repeatedly flew off her head. She snatched it from the air and stuffed it inside her black doublet.

The standing stones appeared on a platform of land, nestled between a bank of hills. No matter where Kit looked, she saw no flat land on the horizon, only more cresting mountains. Some glistened in the last light of the day, others were grey, almost a dusky purple, with the peaks of those hills melding with mist and cloud. To one side of the stones, the land met a sharp drop and the cliff face crumbled. Kit steered the horse far away from the edge, not wishing to tempt fate.

Iomhar led them toward a bank of earth, a distance from the stones, and dismounted from his horse. Kit was slow to follow, for her eyes lingered on the stone circle. It covered a vast space on the flat land. Some of the stones were merely small rocks, no taller than her hip. Others were much taller and towered over her head, glowing silver in the fading light. The grass was uneven beneath the stones, as if the ground was reaching up to reclaim the rocks and pull them back into the earth.

"We'll leave the horses here, out of sight." Iomhar pulled his steed behind a bank of pine trees and Kit followed, tearing her gaze away from the stones. With the horses tucked away behind the pines, they strode out in silence until they stood between the rocks once more.

Wind whistled past the mountain tops and between the stones, hitting Kit so strongly that she had to dig her toes into the ground so she did not fall over. Iomhar did the same, planting a hand on one of the standing stones.

"We'll be knocked from our feet in battle if the wind continues in this vein."

"She will not escape again." Kit spoke with fervour, thinking of Mary Stuart's face when she had escaped in the Forest of Dean. "She will be arrested for all that she has done. Her freedom ends tonight."

"Ye speak with a passion I have not heard from ye before, Kit." Iomhar released the stone and stepped past her. "I am surprised ye do not wish for something more than her arrest."

"What do you mean?"

"This woman tried to kill ye." Iomhar's eyes darted to the horizon.

"She will face the punishment of a court for other matters. What she did to me, no one knows of it. Only Walsingham." Kit closed her eyes and tried to picture Mary Stuart standing above her as she drowned, but still, she could not recall that face. It had happened too long ago.

"One death ... it deserves another." Iomhar's voice deepened.

Kit walked around the nearest stone and reached his side. "That is what you truly think, is it not?" she asked, thinking of the moment he'd held a sword to Lord Ruskin's breast. "You nearly killed Lord Ruskin, that day at Longtown. You wished to do it. There was hunger in your eyes."

"Aye, I cannot deny that." He shook his head and turned to her.

"You fought that wish last time. If he comes tonight, will you fight it again?"

"I hear something." Iomhar looked around.

"Iomhar?"

"Not now, Kit." He nodded at the horizon. Between two cresting hills was a horse, galloping madly. It was Niall. When he appeared at their side, breathless, his horse was snorting restlessly. "Well?" Iomhar asked.

"They read the letter," Niall said, jumping down from the horse and panting to catch his breath. "I lingered, to see what they would do next. A group left the house mere minutes after the letter arrived. They are coming this way."

"Then we need to hide," Kit exclaimed and looked around, searching for the perfect spot to conceal their presence. In the distance, the sun had dropped completely, and the moon had risen overhead.

CHAPTER 26

"Ye are certain of this?" Iomhar asked, holding up the gunpowder flask as they hid behind the bank of pine trees.

"It will work, trust me. Let us play them at their own game." The flask was barely visible in the darkness, but Kit could just see moonlight glinting off its brass edges.

"They are here." Niall appeared from behind a vast Douglas fir and pointed through the trees. Kit pressed her shoulder to the nearest tree trunk and peered around the bark, looking out to the stone circle.

A party of riders was nearing the stones, riding slowly. There were just five. A lady rode amongst them, in the very middle of the group.

"What exactly did ye say in that letter?" Niall asked Kit with a smile. "It has sent her running."

"I told her that I, Oswyn, had a way to get her out of Cumbria and to an island in Scotland. I told her an entourage of Walsingham's men were heading this way, and she had to move tonight if she wished to stay safe. She had to bring few men, for the boat would not carry more."

"Aye, clever," Iomhar murmured on her other side. "She has ridden here without delay."

Kit smiled and watched the group that fell still in the middle of the circle. The moon hid itself behind the clouds, causing the silhouettes of the riders to merge with those of the stones.

"Now, Iomhar, go," Kit urged and he stepped out from the trees, creeping forward and bending low to the ground. He didn't make a sound as he moved.

"I hope ye are right about this," Niall muttered behind her.

"Have a little faith, Niall."

"Aye, that's a lot to ask with what we are about to do." He reached into his doublet and pulled out a small tinderbox. She took it from his grasp and together they crept out from behind the trees, following Iomhar and the path he had taken toward the stones.

They crept up the bank, practically on their knees. The wind was so great, rustling the grass, that their own footsteps were not heard. As they approached the circle, Kit could hear voices, though she could not separate one face from another in the shadows.

"Where is he?" a woman's voice asked, her accent a mixture of French and Scottish. It was Mary Stuart's voice.

"He will be here. Oswyn may be a bumbling fool, but he has proved useful, aye, many times," Lord Ruskin's voice answered fast.

Keeping her head low, Kit strained to watch what Iomhar was doing. He completed the circle of gunpowder he had begun to lay around the stones earlier, connecting another circle that surrounded the stones and those that stood within. When he reached her side again, tapping her shoulder to show it was done, she and Niall stepped back and dropped their stomachs to the ground, hiding in the long grass. Niall looked warily toward the cliff drop close to the stones, just a few feet from them.

Kit laid the tinderbox on the earth, pulled out a scrap of flint and struck it against the iron wool. It lit in seconds.

"What was that?" someone in the circle barked at the scratchy sound.

Kit pressed the flaming wool down to the gunpowder circle. A line of fire shot out on either side of her, and grew around the stones.

"It's a trap. A trap!" a voice bellowed, one Kit recognised. It was Graham Fraser's voice. "Get out of the circle before the fire…" His voice trailed off as the ring of fire formed around them, caging them in.

The horses were visible now, all trying to move toward a gap in the stones, but the ring of fire completed itself and lit the grass on either side of it, growing wider. The horses neighed in panic, and some tried to drop their riders from their backs. Kit felt two firm hands on her shoulders. Iomhar and Niall were dragging her back from the flames, further down the embankment and away from the heat.

"What is going on? Ruskin!" Mary Stuart howled his name, her face suddenly visible as a hood dropped from her head. She rode a grey that was now rearing up, doing its best to tip her off its back.

"Stay back!" Lord Ruskin ordered, no longer on his own horse, but on the ground with a sword in his hand. He moved toward the flames, his face lit by the orange glow. Kit met his gaze. She could feel him glaring at her and Iomhar. "Someone dampen the flames. Fraser, get your cloak."

Fraser shed a large cloak and tossed it over the flames between the stones. It dampened some of the flames down, enough for people to walk across.

"They're escaping. Go," Iomhar said, but Kit was already running, heading in the direction of the cloak on the other side of the stones. Fraser was the first to run across the cloak.

"Come, Your Majesty." He held out a hand to Mary behind him. She was no longer on her horse and hesitated for just a moment. She took his fingers then bolted across the cloak, screaming when the flames came too near her arms.

Kit halted in front of the two of them, pulling out the sword that Iomhar had given her. Fraser moved forward and drove his own weapon against Kit's, forcing her to back up.

"Run! Run!" Fraser bellowed.

Mary took off, sprinting down the embankment and between the hills, with her skirt grasped in her hands.

With their swords still pressed together, Kit tried to haul Fraser away from her, so she could chase after Mary, but he was too strong. She was pushed back, the heels of her boots sliding deeper into the mud so that ridges formed behind her.

"Run, all of you! Get away now!" Lord Ruskin called, his voice barely audible above the roar of the fire.

Kit's eyes darted to the gap in the flames. Two other men fled, but they did not follow the former queen. They chose a different direction entirely. They came near the ledge of such a sharp drop that one of the men nearly fell. His friend grabbed his arm and hauled him back.

"What are you doing? Get after the queen!" Ruskin roared, escaping the flames and wailing in pain when his arm was burned. Niall was in front of him, blocking his path with a drawn sword.

The men chose not to listen to their master. They sprinted in another direction, leaving Mary quite alone.

Kit pushed against Fraser another time, their faces so close on either side of their blades that she could see the whites of his eyes. He grunted under his breath and forced her back again, with such suddenness that Kit staggered. She barely stayed standing, pushing the sword wide to keep her balance. Fraser advanced on her with his sword outstretched.

Before Kit could block the blow he was about to deliver, another stepped in the way. Iomhar's rapier clattered against Fraser's with quick blows, pushing him back repeatedly. He knocked Fraser's sword so far out that it gave him the chance to strike the hilt of his weapon into Fraser's nose. Fraser toppled, nearly falling over as he clutched his bleeding nose.

"Kit!" Iomhar whipped around. "Get after her."

Kit nodded and ran. She only managed a short distance when more panicked calls reached her ears. Niall was calling to his brother.

"Iomhar, the ledge. Ye fool, the cliff drop!"

Kit skidded to a stop. She looked back in time to see Fraser pushing Iomhar closer and closer toward the ledge of the sharp cliff drop. Somehow, Fraser had gained the advantage in the fight. Iomhar was backing up, with both hands on the hilt of his sword. Quick parries followed, so fast that a spark flew between the metal. The heels of Iomhar's boots hovered over the edge of the cliff and he stood precariously, on the balls of his feet.

Fraser muttered something to him, but Kit was too far away to hear. She only saw what happened next, with the wind whistling in her ears.

Fraser knocked Iomhar's hand with his sword. The cut sliced open his skin and blood spurted. Iomhar tried to recover, but he had lowered his sword so far that his body was left exposed. Fraser returned the blow Iomhar had struck him with earlier, knocking the hilt of his weapon once into Iomhar's nose. His arms waved outward, keeping him on the edge of the clifftop.

Fraser thrust out with his blade this time. A cry escaped Kit's lips as the sword found Iomhar's abdomen. He froze, his arms hovering in the air, then his own sword dropped from his fingers, falling from the cliff and spinning through the air. Iomhar's face stilled, his eyes on Fraser as blood seeped around the blade.

Fraser pulled the sword out from Iomhar and struck again, this time kicking him in the chest. Iomhar tipped back through the air, dropping like a stone from the clifftop. Then he disappeared.

CHAPTER 27

"No!" Niall's roar pierced the air. He shouted the word again and again. More than once he tried to push past Lord Ruskin, to get to his brother, but Iomhar was gone.

"He can't be gone." Kit staggered toward the stones. She didn't think of Mary Stuart, of the traitor queen that was running for her life across the Cumbrian hills. She thought only of Graham Fraser. The man had backed up from the cliff edge with a grin, his lips dappled with the blood from his broken nose. "Murderer! Murderer!" Kit bellowed and she sprinted toward him.

She had once had Graham Fraser's life in her grasp. He had chased her through York, trying to kill her, but she had managed to turn the tide on her opponent. She'd had power over his life. If she had taken that chance, if she had done what she had been so afraid to do at the time and ended Fraser's pursuit for good, Iomhar would be here now. He would not have fallen from that cliff.

"He can't be dead, he can't be," Kit muttered, though she'd seen how deadly the cliff was, with the rocks jutting out at odd angles.

She barely looked at Niall, who fought tirelessly against Lord Ruskin, both red in the face from the exertion and the fire. Her eyes focused on Fraser alone as she closed the distance between them, running with her sword outstretched.

Fraser saw her coming. He laughed. "Miss Scarlett?" he called to her. "Would you like to join him?" He pushed his sword toward her.

She brushed it away violently with such strength that it took him by surprise. He stumbled back, struggling to bring the sword in front of him again. She lunged forward with repeated blows, but despite her fury, he was still the stronger sword fighter.

One hard blow to her knuckles was all he needed. The cut was superficial, but the impact was enough to make her drop the sword. He advanced on her, striding through the long grass. Kit reached for the daggers in her belt, but she was too slow. He reached her first, striking out at her temple with the hilt of his sword.

It was a dull thud that reverberated through her skull. She dropped to the ground, her body weak as she landed on her knees.

She blinked rapidly, trying to keep Fraser in focus. He was there one second, sharp in the firelight, then blurry the next. Her head fell as she fought unconsciousness.

Her hands reached weakly through the grass as she tried to stand, but she saw stars and her vision blurred. In the darkness, she saw Fraser in her grasp at York. If she'd taken his life then, Iomhar would be alive now. She had taken a life once, and had vowed never to do so again. That guilt had haunted her ever since ... and yet...

"I should ... I should have done it," Kit muttered, blinking hard. She saw the grass and the fire, glowing at the edge of her vision. Pressing her hands into the earth, she thrust herself up onto her knees. Her head was heavy, her vision not quite focused.

She saw three figures. Two were forcing the third back, closer and closer to the fire. It was Lord Ruskin and Fraser, backing Niall up until he had a choice, die by their swords, or die in the fire.

Niall managed a blow at Lord Ruskin's face with his own sword. It was enough to make him stagger away, clutching his face in pain, but Fraser was still advancing toward Niall, forcing him closer to the flames.

Fighting the heaviness behind her eyes, Kit pushed herself to her feet and this time, she managed to take the daggers from her belt. Hurrying across the grass, she reached Lord Ruskin first. Before he could recover, she struck him in the back of his head. He hovered for a moment, his pale hair glowing in the firelight, then he dropped to the earth.

"Kit, get back!" Niall ordered her, but she ignored him. He lost his sword as Fraser knocked it from him. The blade landed in the flames, too hot to possibly pick up again. Niall held out both palms to Fraser, a perfect target, defenceless.

"Time to join your brother," Fraser called and stepped forward, the sword outstretched.

Kit ran as fast as she could, her fingers tightening around the dagger in her hand. When she reached Fraser, she didn't hesitate but plunged the blade into his back, to the left of his spine, so it would reach his heart.

An almighty cry pierced the air.

Kit darted around Fraser and knocked the sword from his hand with the other dagger. It thudded to the ground. Kit shielded Niall with her body, the dagger still outstretched, in case Fraser veered forward again, but he could not.

He hovered for a second, his eyes glacial and white, then he fell forward, the thud so loud that Kit and Niall both flinched.

"Kit? Kit!" Niall moved toward her, taking her arm and shaking her. "You ... I could have..."

"Do not say it," Kit barked. She couldn't bear hearing the words. Her eyes shot to the clifftop, and she teared up. It wasn't a feeling she could fight. The tears came fast and streaked her cheeks.

Niall kicked Fraser with his foot, but the man didn't move. He moved toward Lord Ruskin, who was beginning to come round.

"Tie him up," Kit pleaded, her voice breaking.

Niall did as he was told. "Where's Mary Stuart?" he asked.

Kit looked to the horizon, just about visible thanks to the ring of fire behind her. "She has escaped," she whispered. Her heartbeat echoed in her ears. She wished to go after the former queen, but there was a weakness in her now, as if Iomhar was not the only one who had gone over that cliff. She staggered toward the clifftop, nearly dropping the remaining dagger she had in her hands. "He can't be gone, he can't be."

She dropped to her knees on the clifftop, tears still streaking her cheeks. Something caught her eye. From the precipice, she could see a lake between the mountains. A figure ran there, its white skirt gleaming in the moonlight.

"Mary," Kit murmured.

Another voice reached her ears, coupled with a grunt of pain. "Ye going to help me up, Kit?"

CHAPTER 28

Kit's chin jerked downward, and her fingers curled around the stones that lined the cliff edge. Peering down, she saw a figure clutching the rocks with one hand, the other hand pressed to the wound on their stomach.

"Iomhar?" Kit whispered. His head lifted and she saw his eyes in the moonlight, his jaw straining as he gritted his teeth. "Iomhar!" she called, more loudly this time.

"What? What did you say?" Niall called from far behind her, but she didn't answer him.

Kit rushed to lean down over the cliff edge.

"Don't ye fall down here too," Iomhar warned, shifting his grasp on the rocks. He released his wound and reached up.

"Give me your hand, quick," Kit pleaded. She moved with her stomach pressed to the ground and reached down. Iomhar stretched out one hand, but the effort made him slip. "No!" Kit panicked as his legs swung out in the air. He looked down, a strange grunt escaping his lips. Kit caught sight of a few rocks that glinted in the moonlight. The drop would mean certain death. "Try again. Please."

Iomhar clutched the rockface with both hands and thrust his boots against it, then he reached up. "I've always hated climbing," he muttered. "Should have watched ye do it more."

"Just keep reaching up," Kit begged. When Iomhar's fingers eventually found her own, she clutched his hand with both of hers. He was cold, his body having dangled in the wind for so long. "Don't let go," she pleaded, then tugged hard, pulling him up.

Slowly, he emerged over the clifftop.

"*Iosa Criosd!*" Niall cried, his voice growing closer behind Kit.

She didn't turn to look at him but focused on pulling Iomhar to safety. Niall appeared a second later and grabbed Iomhar's other arm. "Ye're not dead yet, brother."

"Not yet, nay," Iomhar agreed, then grunted with pain as they heaved him over the last of the stones. He dropped to his knees on the earth, placing a hand to the wound on his stomach. Kit scrambled to find some cloth, anything that could staunch the flow of blood. She took a handkerchief from her doublet, pressed it to his stomach, then unfastened her belt and wrapped it around him.

"This will hurt."

"What will — ah!" He broke off as she pulled the belt tight. "I could have done with more warning," he muttered and dropped further, with one hand to the ground.

"We have ye, brother, we have ye." Niall clutched his shoulder. "Ye lived through that. How did ye hold on?"

"I do not know." Iomhar lifted his head enough for Kit to find his eyes. "I suppose I've seen ye climb enough times to know something of how to do it." He grimaced and looked down at his stomach.

Kit had no words. Tears escaped down her cheeks as she held onto his arm. "You are alive," she whispered, yet the handkerchief she had placed to his stomach was already bloodstained.

"Only if he sees a physician, fast," Niall said.

Iomhar lifted his head. "Where is he?" he asked, his head jerking back and forth.

"Fraser is dead," Niall hurried to answer. "Kit did that."

Iomhar's head jerked toward her.

"I could not let him hurt Niall. I should have…" Kit broke off, thinking of how different life could have been had she done more to stop Fraser before. "Sometimes, maybe death is necessary."

"And where is Lord Ruskin?" Iomhar asked, trying to stand. As he did, his body grew weak, and he tipped sideways. Niall caught him and lowered him back down to the ground.

"Take a look." Niall nodded at one of the standing stones. Lord Ruskin was bound to the rock. He had come round. Raving shouts erupted from his lips as he demanded to be set free.

"He'll see a court," Iomhar muttered. "Aye, we'll make sure of that."

"Aye, brother, we will."

"Where is she? Where is she?" Lord Ruskin's fury made his legs thrash against the ground as he wriggled in his binds, trying to break free. "Tell me where the queen is!"

Kit looked out from the clifftop. That spectral figure was still running around the lake, desperate for escape. "I'll go," she said and stood straight.

Iomhar took her arm, trying to pull her back down again. "Ye cannot go alone."

"I am not leaving you alone here. Niall, stay with him," Kit pleaded.

Niall nodded. "I will not leave him."

Kit took the one dagger she had left, clutching the hilt tightly.

Iomhar tried to follow her, but he was so weak that he dropped quickly again. Niall held him, urging him to rest.

"The fastest way is down this slope," Niall said, pointing to a gap between the trees. "Ye can catch her up. Go, Kit, go."

"Kit!" Iomhar reached out to hold her back.

Bending down toward him, she flicked open the collar of her doublet and held onto the necklace he had once given her. "I will be fine," she promised him. "I'll come back."

She moved her lips to his cheek, kissing him briefly. His hand reached for her arm, but she was gone already, backing up and sprinting across the land.

"Kit!" Iomhar called, his voice fading on the wind.

She sprinted down the slope that Niall had pointed out, her legs moving so fast that they burned with the effort. As she reached level ground, the figure of Mary Stuart became clearer on the other side of the lake, her cloak billowing in the strong wind. Kit darted around the lake, hurrying after her with the dagger in her hand.

"Mary Stuart!" Kit barked. Mary flicked her head around, her dark hair coming loose and whipping past her ears with the movement. "It is over. Your men are gone. Abandon your escape now."

Mary backed up, shook her head, turned and ran again. Her feet slipped on the rocks on the lake shore, but she stood quickly and sprinted. Kit raced to catch up with her. She was the faster of the two and soon closed the distance between them.

"Mary!" Kit called.

"I am a queen. A queen!" Mary snapped. "Ye should never call me by my name."

The fury pumped through Kit. Mary's pursuit of the throne had resulted in so much death. Had she achieved her aim, even more death would have followed. She would have taken Queen Elizabeth's life, and Kit's own.

"You are not my queen!" Kit called after her.

A panicked shriek escaped Mary as Kit grew near. She darted around the tip of the lake and ran back to her right, cutting through a short valley where the land dipped between the lake and the mountainside. Kit ran after her. Seeing she wasn't going to stop Mary any other way, she tackled her. Her front collided with Mary's back and sent her to the ground.

"Nay!" Mary Stuart roared. Kit took her shoulder and rolled her over. The fine white gown was marred with the silt from the lake and the dark hair that had once been coiffed so elegantly was now in tendrils. "Get off me! Release me at once!" Kit took Mary's arms and tried to bind them together. Mary lashed out, striking Kit's nose.

The impact was enough to leave Kit dazed, and she dropped to her rear on the lake shore. Mary stood again, but not knowing which way to run, she ended up backing toward the lake. Kit recovered and advanced on her.

The former queen stumbled into the shallows, the water coming up around her ankles, then to her knees, soaking the gown. Kit leapt toward her, reaching for her arms and pushing her under the water.

"No more of this, no more," Kit ordered, holding her down.

Mary's face was above the shallows, but her whole gown was wet now. "What have ye done? What have ye done?" she cried, trying to force Kit off her, though she was not as strong. "Release me." When she reached up, attempting to press her fingers to Kit's eyes, Kit acted without thinking, pushing Mary's head beneath the water.

The squeals vanished and were replaced by the sounds of bubbles. When Mary's fighting grew weaker, Kit grasped her shoulders and pulled her to the surface again. Mary took a deep breath, water spurting from her lips as she coughed it up.

"You and I did this once before," Kit murmured, finding she couldn't resist telling the former queen. "Do you not remember? Yet that day, I was the one in the water, and you were the one who left me there to drown."

Mary stilled in her grasp. Those dark eyes looked up at her in the moonlight. "Ye... Ye are she, then," Mary whispered.

"You left a child to die in a river, did you not?" Kit yelled in her face, her hands curling around Mary's shoulders. "You tried to kill a child."

"A bairn they may have put on the throne!" Mary wailed, spitting in Kit's direction. "Ye are she? Ye are that child? I knew ye looked like Katherine. The resemblance was too strong." She reached up with one hand, trying to push Kit's face away. "I should have held ye down in that river. So ye never would have made it out again."

"Damn you." Kit pushed Mary under the water again. The words faded and were followed by bubbles. Kit had the former queen's life in her hands, and she trembled with that knowledge. She had already taken one life tonight; it would be all too easy to take another. Time seemed to stretch out infernally as she listened to Mary struggle.

Yet Kit was no murderer. She heaved Mary above the water and pushed her in the back, urging her toward dry land. Mary coughed and spluttered, falling to her knees in the shallows. She angled her head toward Kit, her eyes wide.

"You are the killer between us," Kit said darkly. Rivulets of water ran from her doublet as she followed the former queen onto the shore.

Mary's chest heaved as she clutched the sandy bank. Intermittently, she looked round at Kit, as if she expected something more. Kit pulled out a length of rope from her doublet.

"You are under arrest, Mary Stuart, once Queen of the Scots," Kit said with a satisfied smile. She took Mary's hand

and forced it forward, binding it to the other. Mary fought against her. "Lie still or I'll throw you back in the water, where you left me."

Mary fell still. "What will ye do now?" she asked as she caught her breath. Her hair was stuck to her face and neck.

"I will take you to Fotheringhay Castle, where you will await trial. Walsingham and Lord Burghley will make the arrangements."

Mary stared at her, as if she expected something more to pass between them.

"Start walking." Kit grabbed her shoulder and marched her forward, back to the clifftops. "It's time you faced a real prison for your crimes, Mary Stuart."

"Your Majesty! I am a queen!"

"I see no crown on that wet head."

CHAPTER 29

Kit jumped down from her horse, her eyes turning on Fotheringhay Castle, which sat ahead of her. It was a well-fortified yellow- and white-stone building, with two turrets guarding the entrance. Guards stood ready on the drawbridge, prepared for their new prisoner's arrival. Over the ramparts the keep could be glimpsed, its crenelations stark in the bright sunlight.

"Your prison awaits you," a guard said with pleasure to their prisoner as he stepped toward the carriage.

Kit still wore the same black doublet and hose she'd been wearing on the night she had captured Mary Stuart. She had not rested on the journey, for fear of someone ambushing the party again to take back the former queen. The guard opened the door of the carriage and Kit stepped forward, folding her arms.

Slowly, Mary climbed down. Her dark hair was in tangles around her shoulders and she held her cloak across her body, as if embarrassed to be seen in such a state with dirt covering her gown. She tilted her chin high as her feet touched the ground, attempting a haughty look that merely made her look proud, rather than regal.

"Take the prisoner to the front gate," the guard said to Kit, "and they'll take her from you. We have prepared well for her arrival."

"Thank you." Kit took the bound wrists of the former queen and led her forward.

"Do not pull me like a naughty child," Mary muttered in her ear, her nose wrinkling as they walked along the track road between the great lawns, toward the two grey turrets of Fotheringhay.

"It amuses me that you still insist on giving orders." Kit raised an eyebrow. "You must know by now that no order you give will be obeyed ever again."

Mary's chin turned down a little.

As they reached the drawbridge, Kit drew Mary to a stop. There was one more conversation to be had before she was shown into the castle.

"Wait," Kit ordered. Mary reddened, ready to argue, but two shadows passed over her face, and Kit turned to greet the men behind her.

Niall stood tall, a hand on his brother's arm to keep him standing. Iomhar stood at an angle, his back bent.

Kit flicked an eye down toward his stomach, thinking of his wound. After they had taken Mary Stuart and Lord Ruskin, Iomhar had been sent to a physician at once. No organs had been damaged, and the wound had been sewn up, yet he would be weak for some time. Iomhar and Niall had taken Lord Ruskin to prison in York Castle, where he awaited trial for his crimes of treason and murder.

For two days they had ridden apart. The brothers had delivered Lord Ruskin and Kit had collected soldiers from Kendal, to aid her in escorting Mary Stuart. This last day, Iomhar and Niall had caught Kit up on the road with the party she led, guarding Mary Stuart with just two men.

"Speak to her," Kit pleaded, her eyes flicking between Iomhar and Niall. "You may not have another chance."

"What is this?" Mary darted her head around. "Who are ye two?"

"My name is Iomhar Blackwood, and this is Niall Blackwood." Iomhar raised a hand and gestured between the two of them. "We are brothers to the Earl of Ross." Mary's frantic movements stilled. "Ye ordered the death of our father."

Niall stepped forward, but Kit blocked his path. "Step aside, Kit."

"You know I cannot." Kit kept her voice quiet. "Just as you two decided Lord Ruskin will face a court for his crimes, so will this woman."

Kit stepped back, her gaze finding Iomhar's own. He nodded, showing he understood.

"We wish to know why." Iomhar's voice was grave. "Our father was one of the men sent to move ye once in Scotland. Lord Ruskin killed him, on your orders. We wish to know why, then we will be done with ye."

"Why?" Mary's eyes narrowed. "How many deaths have been ordered for the greater cause? To enact God's will on earth?"

"Ye see it as God's will that ye should be on the throne?" Iomhar scoffed.

"I know it to be true." Mary's voice didn't shake as she stood tall and pulled at the binds around her wrists. "What passes here today is a travesty of justice." She looked accusingly at Kit. "I should be returned to my throne. I should be Queen of Scotland and England, rather than that whore's bastard child." She said the words with relish. Kit grimaced and looked away, catching the eye of one of the guards who stepped out from the portcullis of the castle. Alongside the guard was a well-dressed man, who was to be Mary Stuart's new host while under house arrest.

"What of our father?" Iomhar asked again, his voice deep.

"He was one sacrifice of many." Mary's eyes widened. "Just another death."

The simplicity of her words made Niall's eyes water. He turned sharply and walked away, unable to bear another second.

Iomhar stared with his lips parted. "A life meant so little to ye," he whispered. "Ye will burn for this, Mary Stuart. For all the lives ye have taken, and those ye wished to take."

"They will not burn me," Mary said with a smile. "Elizabeth would not order it."

"I spoke of hell, not of this world. Ye will burn for it." Iomhar nodded at Kit and retreated, following Niall's path back to the horses.

Kit swallowed uneasily, watching him walk so uncomfortably. It would be some time before he was back to his usual strength, and he still risked infection from his wound. He was not out of the woods yet.

"It is time to meet your host." Kit took Mary's shoulder and turned her around. She marched her across the drawbridge, toward the portcullis that had been raised, and the two men that awaited her.

The guard and the well-dressed gentleman muttered, each shaking their heads gravely.

"Ye still have time to correct this," Mary said. "Release me. Do what God wills. Release me before they can put me in this prison." A muscle twitched around her eye as she looked at the castle. Kit forced her forward again, choosing not to respond. "Katherine? Katherine!" Mary barked in her ear, trying to get her attention.

"That is not my name," Kit growled.

"It is your name, and ye know it. Ye are Scottish, ye were born of royal blood, of my family's blood." Mary's head flicked back and forth as she looked between the castle and Kit.

"Release me from here, before I am shown through that portcullis, Katherine."

Mary tugged, trying to run, but Kit held on tightly, her hands curling around the former queen's thin arm.

"Ye are of my blood," Mary muttered again. "Surely ye would not see your own kin go to her death."

"Then what was it you were doing when you dropped me in that river?" Kit asked, her lips pressed firmly together as she waited for an answer. Mary said nothing as the wind whipped her dark hair around her ears and across her face. "An enemy of your own making, eh?" Kit said, smiling a little at last. "Goodbye, Mary Stuart. Enjoy your prison." Kit marched her forward and delivered her into the hands of the guard. She spoke briefly to the gentleman who was to be her host and then parted with a curtsy.

As Kit walked back across the bridge, returning to her horse, she glanced just once at Mary. The former queen stood beneath the portcullis, staring at the metal spikes. Kit shuddered and turned away, praying she would never have anything to do with Mary Stuart ever again.

Stepping off the drawbridge, she adjusted her doublet, feeling the heat of the day searing her skin. She hurried toward Iomhar, who waited for her by the horses.

"To London?" he asked, his voice soft.

"Home, yes."

CHAPTER 30

"I fear I do not understand." Elizabeth, Queen of England, sat on a throne in the great hall of Richmond Palace. Above her was a painted canopy, richly decorated in purple and red hues, dappled with white stars. At her feet one of her ladies-in-waiting sat on a small stool. It was Lady Hunsdon, the lady that Kit had struggled with so much during her time at Hampton Court Palace. She sat primly, fussing with some embroidery she was working on for the queen. Strangely, Lady Hunsdon had been permitted to stay in the room, while all the other ladies had been sent out.

Elizabeth leaned forward, her hands curling around the arms of her throne. The high white collar of her gown shifted and crinkled audibly with the slow movement. She tilted her head forward, her beady eyes darting between those that stood before her.

Kit stood in the middle. On one side of her was Walsingham, and on the other was Iomhar, who still did not stand completely straight. Their long rides across the country had left him pale and exhausted, struggling to recover from his wound.

"Pray, say it again," said Elizabeth, her eyes on Kit.

Yet Kit couldn't find the words. Her mind was full of what Iomhar had said to her that morning on the journey to Richmond.

"If ye are related to Mary Stuart, Kit, that means ye are also kin to the Queen of England."

She was a distant cousin. The two of them shared some blood and as Kit looked at the queen, she tried to discern some likeness between them, but she could not. When the queen had been poisoned at Hampton Court, Kit had seen her real hair beneath her wig. It had had a reddish tinge to it, and Kit's own hair was dark auburn. Yet that was the only similarity she could draw.

"You say little today." Elizabeth didn't smile as she stared at Kit. "Walsingham, speak. It seems Miss Scarlett cannot."

"Kit and another intelligencer, Mr Blackwood," Walsingham said, gesturing to the two of them, "are the ones who found Mary Stuart, Your Majesty." He spoke slowly. "She was found to be hiding in Cumbria. Her co-conspirators have been arrested. I will shortly bring to you a list of their crimes. Amongst the men is Lord Ruskin."

"How could I forget that name?" Elizabeth wrung her hands. Lady Hunsdon lowered her embroidery and placed a soft hand to the queen's knee. Elizabeth's movements slowed. "How many crimes will be attached to his name?"

"Many, but we wish to add another to the list." Walsingham stepped forward and gestured to Iomhar. "He confessed once to the murder of the late Earl of Ross, Mr Blackwood's father. He will be charged with murder as well as treason."

Kit looked at Iomhar, seeing the surprise in his face. He stared at Walsingham, stunned. After all that had passed between them, Walsingham was making a case for Iomhar to have his justice at last.

"Very well." Elizabeth nodded. She looked briefly at Lady Hunsdon, breathed deeply, then turned to Kit. "I understand from Walsingham that you raced to find my cousin quite alone." She smiled, though it was only a flicker, and then her eyes narrowed. "You took a great risk."

"It was necessary," Kit said quietly, refusing to look at Walsingham. "If a large party had gone to find her, I fear she would have heard of our movements. There are many spies in this land, Your Majesty. The fewer people knew of us coming, the better the outcome."

Elizabeth moved to her feet, stepping past Lady Hunsdon and away from the throne. Not once did she look away from Kit. "I understand I owe you great thanks." She allowed herself a full smile this time. "It seems you have been watching over me again, as you did at Hampton Court."

Unsure of what to say, Kit curtsied, showing her deference. The longer she was with the queen, the stranger it felt to be related to her. Kit could have told her, but what good would come from it? It was a secret better kept close to her chest. As far as the queen knew, Katherine Stuart had died long ago.

"Thank you." Elizabeth's voice softened to a whisper. She reached out and touched Kit's shoulder gently. Kit stood straight and smiled at her. For a brief moment, she saw her as an ordinary woman, rather than a queen, and then Elizabeth lifted her chin high and the illusion vanished. "And thank you too, Mr Blackwood." She turned her smile on Iomhar, who bowed to her. "You have done much in the name of our country."

"In the name of what is right, Your Majesty."

"Well-spoken indeed." She turned away and returned to her throne. As she sat down, she took Lady Hunsdon's hand. "Pray tell, Walsingham, what happens now? My cousin is under house arrest again, but at Fotheringhay. What will become of her?"

"She will face a trial for her treason. The evidence will be presented before you." Walsingham's voice was grave. "There is no doubt about the result, Your Majesty. We know Mary Stuart to be guilty. A death warrant will have to be drawn up."

Elizabeth's lips parted and she grew still. She didn't even blink, despite Lady Hunsdon pulling at her hand, trying to draw a reaction from her.

"Your Majesty?" Walsingham stepped forward.

The queen flinched, as if she was being brought back from some distant dream. She looked around, shook her head, and forced a smile that did not last long. "So much death," she whispered. "Now you ask me to kill my cousin."

"She would have killed you," Kit said. All looked toward her, and Iomhar nudged her arm, urging her to be quiet. "Forgive me, but it must be said."

"I know." The queen did not seem to mind the interruption. She nodded, fidgeting with Lady Hunsdon's hand in her grasp. "I thank you again, Miss Scarlett, and you, Mr Blackwood. Pray, leave me be now." She stood, drawing Lady Hunsdon with her. "Even you, Walsingham." She stopped him from stepping forward with a raised hand. "Leave me be." Her voice was quiet as she left the room, disappearing between two tapestries that flanked a doorway. The door shut hurriedly, and a wail escaped.

That sound was sharp, piercing the quiet air. Kit was startled. Walsingham and Iomhar wore similar expressions of shock as the queen continued to cry out in the next room, as if she had been wounded.

"Nay one wishes to be a killer," Iomhar murmured as he turned to leave the room.

Kit followed him, thinking of the deaths she had caused. She had not wanted to hurt Fraser. "Yet sometimes, it is one life or your own."

"Aye, just so."

They hastened to the door. Walsingham caught up with them and held out a hand to Iomhar, his fingers white and bony.

"Whatever anger I feel toward you for agreeing to Kit's plan to go after Mary Stuart alone, I must admit it was the right decision." He waited with his hand outstretched. "I expect you will return home to Scotland, now you have achieved your aim."

"I will," Iomhar said without hesitation. Kit gulped down a lump in her throat at the thought of Iomhar being gone from London.

"Then let me thank you," Walsingham said in a low voice. "For everything you have done."

Slowly, Iomhar took his hand, and they shook with Kit looking between them. It was a rare thing to see Walsingham shake any man's hand. He preferred bows and slow nods of the head. This was a true mark of respect that he showed to few.

"We may not have always seen eye to eye, on many matters," Walsingham said, "yet I owe you much, Iomhar."

"Thank you, sir. As I do you." Iomhar had never before called Walsingham 'sir' either. "I wish you well."

Walsingham smiled sadly. "As much as I wish I could persuade you to stay in my employment —"

"Ye would not succeed."

"That is what I feared." Walsingham released his hand. "Then I hope I shall hear from you again someday."

"Perhaps." Iomhar bowed to Walsingham and stepped through the door. Kit's eyes lingered on the patch of floor beside her, where his boots had just been.

"Kit?" Walsingham tried to get her attention. "Kit?" Finally, she turned to face him, tearing her eyes away from the floor. "Would you come to see me tomorrow? There is much you and I need to discuss."

"Is there?" Kit wasn't sure what to feel as she stared at Walsingham. That numbness continued. She'd hoped that with time away from him, she would be able to make sense of her gratitude to him, and her resentment of his control, but it had done little good.

"Yes. Come to me tomorrow, Kit. I pray you will." Walsingham departed, leaving her alone in the hallway.

Kit stood in the hall of Iomhar's house, watching the bags and coffers being packed and carried out. The family frequently got into arguments, many of which ended in bickering laughter, as they helped one another pack. Abigail insisted that Rhona had stolen one of her gowns, and pulled open a coffer when it was partway down the stairs. Duncan grumbled that Niall was taking too long and delaying their journey.

The atmosphere was a strangely happy one, with the family excited to be returning to Scotland, yet Kit could not find a reason to smile. She leaned on the wall with folded arms, watching the family pack. She had grown used to being amongst them, not quite one of them, but almost. They laughed with her as they hurried to and from the carriages. Every now and then, Kit caught sight of Iomhar.

They'd had little chance to talk since they had left Fotheringhay. Iomhar was recovering from his injuries and had been constantly surrounded by his family, who feared leaving him alone. Every time Kit had managed to find him on his own, he'd either been asleep, exhausted after recent events, or her courage had failed her. Unable to summon the words she longed to say, she would ask him how his wound was faring instead.

"Ye know this will be no easy task," Niall complained as he walked down the stairs, carrying one end of his mother's coffer. Duncan stood behind him, carrying the other end. "The house was burnt to cinders. The letter ye received said as much."

"Then we will rebuild it from the ground up. Mary Stuart's factions in Scotland are dissolving. Whichever of Lord Ruskin's men did the deed will not dare show their faces now. They will not leave their hiding places," the Earl of Ross said as they reached the bottom floor, dropping the coffer loudly.

"Careful. Do ye wish to break it?" Moira asked as she hurried down the stairs after the two of them.

Kit nodded, in agreement with Duncan's words. Some who supported Mary Stuart had not been caught for their crimes and might never be found. The Lily, Lady Gifford, had been gone for so long that no one had a hint as to her whereabouts. As for Oswald Ingleby, Kit didn't doubt he would be in hiding. He'd only ever sworn allegiance to Ruskin's cause for the money, so he would be doing his best to stay concealed somewhere now.

"Careful with it," Moira pleaded with her sons again as they picked up the coffer and carried it out of the house. "I fear they are used to footmen." She sighed as she moved to Kit's side. "Are ye sure ye will not come with us?" she asked, taking Kit's hand and holding it tightly between her own. Before Kit had time to answer, she continued, "Ye know ye are always welcome, don't ye? Ye can come to see us without notice. I will be there to welcome ye with open arms in the doorway."

"Thank you." Kit smiled at Moira. "It is your home, Moira. My home ... it has always been London."

"Not always," Moira reminded her. Iomhar had been the one to reveal to Moira that Kit was indeed Katherine Stuart, when they had returned from their travels. Moira was both delighted to discover that the child she had once known was alive, and saddened that she had been missing for so long. The night before, Moira had sat for hours at Kit's side, holding her hand and singing the tune that had bothered her so much. "Well," she sighed with a sad smile, "I will miss ye, as I am sure the family will too. One more than any other." She broke off as another's footsteps sounded on the stairs.

Iomhar was walking down the steps with Abigail behind him. He had a much smaller chest in his hands, though it was plainly still heavy.

"Iomhar? What of your wound? Ye must be careful," Moira pleaded.

"I am well enough to manage this small thing," Iomhar assured her.

Abigail kept tapping his shoulder, clearly worried about him. "I can carry it," she said.

"Aye, that will work when ye can barely lift it." Iomhar walked past Kit and out of the house, with Abigail on his tail. As the two left, Moira turned to Kit.

"He will be sorry to part from ye," she whispered.

Kit did not have the words to describe how she would feel when he left. She stared at the open doorway through which he had passed, fighting the lump in her throat and the stinging sensation in her eyes. Iomhar had asked her to come with him when he made this journey back to Scotland. She had thought about it a lot, but not knowing what her answer should be, she had ended up giving no answer at all.

"I do not know if I can leave London," Kit murmured. "It's the life I've known. Walsingham ... he's always been here."

"Aye, but we do not always stay with those that raise us," said Moira. "All I ask is this, Kit." She raised a hand and gently touched Kit's cheek, wiping away a tear that Kit hadn't noticed had escaped. "Make your own decision, not the choice ye think Walsingham would wish to make for ye. From what my son has said, that man has controlled your life enough as it is." She smiled fully this time. "Make it your choice." She kissed Kit on the cheek, grasped her hand tightly and then let go as she stepped past her.

Kit brushed away a second tear and breathed deeply. This was not the time to be weak. The whole Blackwood family were to leave for Scotland within minutes. She had said her goodbyes to Rhona and Abigail, as well as the earl, and Niall had spent much time with her over breakfast, thanking her for her help with finding Lord Ruskin and giving his family peace again. There was still one she had not said goodbye to, and she did not know what she would say to him.

Rhona and Abigail hurried back into the house, brushing past Kit so quickly that they did not notice how she hid her face.

"Are ye sure we have everything?" Rhona asked, pushing her sister up the stairs. "Knowing ye, ye will have left things all over that room."

"I have not," Abigail argued. "Kit helped me check this morning."

"Aye, but ye will still have left something, I am certain of it." Rhona shared a look with Kit, who managed to force a smile. "She is always leaving things behind."

"I had noticed," Kit chuckled, thinking of the number of times Abigail had wandered this house, looking for things she had left in odd places. She'd grown used to this family. Once the sisters had disappeared upstairs, she released a shaky breath. "They are not my own," she muttered.

"Kit?" a familiar voice called. She turned around to see Iomhar standing in the doorway. He wore a dark green jerkin, with black trews and his normal ankle boots, but he bore no weapons around his hips now. His belt was just a plain black strip, buckled at the centre. "Ye and I must speak."

CHAPTER 31

Iomhar stepped into the front room, and Kit followed, closing the door softly behind her. She didn't want to alert any of the family as to where they had gone. Turning back, she found Iomhar standing in the centre of the room.

"How is it?" Kit asked, gesturing to his waist.

"Ye have asked me that many times these last few days. Aye, it is healing slowly. Another scar to add to the few I already bear." He smiled a little. "I will be my old self again in time, but that is all I need, time."

"Time," Kit repeated. Something about that word tightened her gut. She had spent so much time at Iomhar's side.

"It seems we have to say goodbye, Kit."

She moved quickly toward him and wrapped her arms around his waist. He chuckled softly in her ear at the suddenness of the movement, then returned her embrace, his hands resting across her back.

"Ye are holding on tight."

"I am."

"I wish ye'd come with me, then we would not have to say goodbye at all."

"London is my home." Kit breathed slowly as she held her head against his shoulder.

Iomhar didn't argue with her but held her a little tighter. "I know what that means," he whispered. "Ye cannot leave it."

Kit didn't answer. There was a part of her that longed to turn her back on London for good, to be done with fighting for Elizabeth's cause, not because she believed in it any less, but because she was tired of all the secrets that had been kept for so long. She also ached at hearing so much of death. For the last two days, every whisper in the street had been about Mary Stuart. Strangers talked of her impending trial, and the execution thereafter.

"Now, listen to me." Iomhar pulled back an inch, his hands on her shoulders. "This house is yours."

"Pardon?" Kit blinked, uncertain she had heard him right.

"Ye must be mad if ye think I am allowing ye to go back to that loft room. It is not safe."

"I'll be safe enough."

"Nay, ye will not." He was firm. "This house is yours." He released her and reached into his doublet, pulling out the house key and dropping it into her hand. It was a long iron key, cold to the touch. He closed her fingers around it. "It's yours," he repeated.

"It will not be the same." She shook her head, fearing how empty the house would be without him in it.

"Then the offer still stands for ye to come to Scotland, any time." He moved toward her. "And I mean as one of the family, Kit."

"I am not your blood."

"Nay. But ye could be something else." He bent down toward her and found her lips with his own. When he released her, he rested his forehead against hers. "Ye do not need to hear me say the words to know what I feel. That should say it all."

"You never said," she whispered. "Not once."

"Perhaps I was too afraid of your answer." He lifted his head and kissed her again, but on the temple now. She stayed very still. "Now ye know what I feel."

"Iomhar? Iomhar? Where are ye?" The Earl of Ross's voice sounded from outside. "We have to be going soon and ye have disappeared."

"I wonder where he's got to?" Moira's voice followed.

"I can make a good wager," Niall added.

Iomhar chuckled, moving his head back from Kit's. "They are waiting for me."

"I..." The words died in Kit's throat. There was much she wanted to say, but she did not know how. Part of her wished to beg for him to stay, though she already knew what the answer would be. He had to go back; it was time to rebuild the family and the home, after so much had happened to damage the Blackwoods over the last few years.

"Iomhar!" Niall called.

"One more minute!" Iomhar raised his voice enough for Niall to hear him from outside.

"Curious, Kit has disappeared too," they heard Niall say. General laughter sounded from beyond the door.

"Iomhar, I..." Kit's words failed her again. She wished to declare herself, as he had done, but she was all too aware that his family waited for him. She knew, too, that after she said the words, he would leave anyway, and then she would be left here with a wounded heart.

"I know, Kit, I know." Iomhar lifted her hand to his lips and kissed the back. "Ye cannot say it."

"I wish to," she whispered.

"And then we'd say goodbye anyway." He sighed and lowered her hand. "I understand if ye cannot leave this life." He smiled sadly. "Ye still feel too indebted to Walsingham." His words made her head veer back, and she blinked. "He casts a shadow over your life."

"No. No, he doesn't."

"Aye, he does. Why else would ye wish to stay?" He didn't sound angry, more resolved. "As long as it is your choice, Kit. That is what matters."

"Iomhar!" Niall's bark at last drew Iomhar away. He released Kit and stepped back.

"I am coming."

He opened the door, hesitating for long enough to look back at her. "Write to me, aye?"

"I will." Kit nodded and followed him out.

They rushed to the carriages, where the sun greeted them with its strong morning rays. Kit said goodbye to the family again, clutching Rhona and Abigail's hands, and even receiving an embrace from Niall.

"Ye stay safe now, aye?" he said before turning to his horse and climbing up into the saddle. "Iomhar has always said ye do not watch your own back as ye should."

"I do," Kit argued as he chuckled. She waved at the others in the carriage, including Elspeth, who was to return with them. Kit moved toward Moira, who leaned out of the carriage and kissed her on the cheek.

"Take care of yourself, Katherine," Moira whispered, tears in her eyes. "I will miss ye greatly indeed."

"And I you."

Moira wiped another tear away from Kit's cheek, and then they parted as the carriage jolted forward.

"Let us depart!" the Earl of Ross called from his own horse, leading the group. "It will take us a long time to reach Scotland."

Kit stepped back, watching the two carriages and the group of horses. Iomhar was the last to pass her. He reached down and she took his hand, grasping his fingers and walking alongside him for a few minutes, following him all the way down the street. They said nothing; they just held onto each other until they reached the corner at the end of the road.

"Goodbye," Kit whispered.

"Goodbye, *mo chridhe*."

Kit frowned, not understanding the Scottish Gaelic, and then his hand left hers. She stood back, watching him go, until his horse was lost amongst the other riders. He was soon one of many, hurrying about their business.

Kit recalled the moment she had first met Iomhar. She'd been at Edinburgh Castle on a mission for Walsingham. He'd dressed as a Highland soldier and had lifted her hat, realising that she was no guard, and not even a man. Those dark green eyes had bored into her own.

"Kitty? Kitty?" Doris waved a hand in front of her face, then passed her a tankard. "Goodness, your mind is far from here today, isn't it?"

"You could say that. Thank you, Doris." Kit took the tankard and sipped the mead. "This helps, though." She wiped her brow, struggling in the heat of the day, and pulled at her doublet. Sitting back in the window seat, she pressed an arm to the glass, but it was not cool to the touch. She leaned away from it once again.

"We must keep drinking in this weather." Doris topped up her tankard from a jug and then stepped back as Walsingham entered his rooms and took a seat behind his desk. "I will leave you two to your discussions." Briefly, she placed a hand on Kit's shoulder. "I hope to see you smiling again soon."

Kit couldn't even force a smile at that moment. She thanked her for the mead and took the jug, topping up her own cup. As the door closed behind Doris, Walsingham spoke.

"You keep drinking in that vein and you will not be able to walk straight out of this house," he warned, barely looking up from his papers. Kit pointedly took a large gulp, showing she had no intention of following his orders. Slowly, he put down the papers and turned to face her. "You disobeyed me, Kit."

"I did. Which time are we talking of now?"

"How can you ask that?" He shook his head with vigour. "You crossed the country and pursued Mary Stuart, *alone*."

"I was not quite alone." She thought of Iomhar and Niall as she took a sip from her tankard, feeling an ache passing through her.

"You know what I mean." Walsingham's voice was quiet. "You could have been hurt."

"Yet I was not. I did as you asked. I found Mary Stuart and I brought her back to you. Is that not why I have always been here?" Kit asked, raising her eyebrows. Walsingham didn't respond, but merely stared at her. "I've been thinking much of what passed, all those years ago. When you pulled me out of that river, what did you think would happen next?"

"I told you." Walsingham shifted in his chair, his bones clicking. "The house staff spoke of you being dead, so I could not deliver you back into their arms. You were not safe there. I had to give you a new life."

"You did. You saved my life." Kit managed a smile at last. It was a small one, but Walsingham returned it. "I owe you much for that. You gave me life when it could have ended so swiftly."

"I could not watch you die, Kit."

"You saved my life, yet you also stole it." When Walsingham said nothing, she tipped her tankard and downed the rest of the mead. The spicy sweetness tickled the back of her throat as she stood, stepping away from the window. "You stole it, Walsingham."

"Kit, listen." He moved to his feet as well. "What other choice did I have?" he asked. "You could no longer be Katherine Stuart. You had to be someone else to hide you from Mary Stuart. I kept you alive, when there was every chance you could have died."

"And you raised me to be this." Kit gestured down to her weapon belt. She only had one dagger, for she had never recovered the other from Fraser's back.

"Do you dislike who you are now?"

"No." Kit was more capable than she would have been had she been raised as Katherine Stuart. "Yet I had no choice as to who I was. You could have told me about my past at any point. When I reached a good age, you could have given me a choice of what to do with my life, yet you did not." She shook her head. "You kept me here, like I was your pet." She thought of the words that Lord Burghley had used so many times. "Your *pet*."

"You are not a pet." Walsingham moved forward. He clutched the edge of his desk, keeping himself standing. "I kept you alive. Alive!"

"You don't see it, do you?" said Kit. "I have fought for you for years, done what was right, fought for our queen."

"I tried to do what was right," Walsingham insisted, releasing the desk and shakily walking closer to her. The metallic scent of his pills clung to his skin.

"I know." Kit stood taller, her hands loosening from around the mead cup as she placed it down on a table. "Yet I do not have to like it. I cannot stay here."

"What do you mean?" Walsingham reached out pleadingly. "This is your life, Kit. Here, with me. You are a part of this house, a part of this life. You are an intelligencer."

"You made that choice, not I." Kit took one of his hands and held it between her own as she stepped toward him. "You saved me, and I will always be grateful to you for that. You raised me. Not quite my father, but a guardian, certainly." She looked up to see a strange expression on his face. His lips were pursed, and he was blinking rapidly. "Thank you."

"Pray, do not thank me like this is the last we will speak. Don't do that, Kit."

"It is not the last conversation between us, of that I'm certain." She patted his hand comfortingly. "Yet it is the last for now."

"What do you mean?" His grey brows drew together.

"I need a rest from this world." She looked around the room. "This was the life given to me, and now I want to see what else there could be."

"You can't turn your back on this for good, Kit. Please." He grasped her hand between his.

"Maybe I will come back to this world someday, but I need to do something else first." Kit was so certain this was the right decision that she didn't even feel guilty, though she knew she was disappointing Walsingham. "You have to let me go," she said quietly.

He pulled her toward him and embraced her. Kit felt like a child in his arms. So often had she wanted his approval when she was young, but not anymore. Their relationship had changed now.

"I want you to know," he whispered as he patted her back, "I only ever wished for the best for you. I did not know how else to keep you alive, but to teach you how to survive."

Kit stepped back and smiled sadly. "I know, and thank you. I will write to you."

Walsingham nodded and released her hand. "I need not tell you my business will be worse off without you." He chuckled, though there was little humour in the sound. "I shall miss you."

"Goodbye, Walsingham."

"Goodbye, Kit." He reached for her shoulder and held it tight with his bony fingers. Then he released her and returned to his seat, and a shuddering breath escaped him.

"Give my best to your daughter," Kit said as she hovered by the door. "I'm sure she will be relieved to hear I am gone."

"Come back someday," Walsingham said sadly, his body slumped forward in his seat.

"I will."

Walsingham sniffed, sat taller and slid his papers closer toward him. In a moment, he had shifted from being an old man to a privy councillor again, a man of power. Kit closed the door, but found that the staircase was not empty.

Doris was standing on the stairs, her own cheeks streaked with tears. Kit moved toward the housekeeper, who held her tightly.

"You must write," Doris pleaded. "I will make the master read your letters to me, but please write."

"I will, Doris. I promise you that."

"Where will you go?" Doris asked, sniffing as she stepped back from Kit on the stairs.

"I hope to find a new home. I fear London is not that place anymore."

CHAPTER 32

The Douglas firs and pine trees parted. The sun was not so hot here in the Highlands, but as the branches wafted in the wind, Kit felt its warmth on her skin. The cool breeze ruffled her hair, making the short locks dance around her ears as she pulled her horse to a stop.

The last time she had ridden down this drive, it had been snow-covered, and at the end had stood the Earl of Ross's house, made of stone and timber, with great tiled roofs and two turrets on one side. The view was starkly different now.

Where the house had once stood, there was rubble. Blackened stones covered the earth on one side. Workers sifted these rocks, separating those that had been too damaged by the fire from those that could be reused. Where the timber section of the house had been, there was now ash and warped logs.

Jumping down from her horse, Kit left the reins wrapped around a branch and approached the house. The stables were gone too. Some of the workers looked up as she approached, but she didn't recognise any of their faces. As she reached the house, she stood on one low-lying stone, recognising that it had once been the front step.

"Who did this?" Kit murmured, remembering the family's suspicions that Lord Ruskin's supporters had been behind the burning. She longed to know the name of the culprit.

"Ye wish to know who did this?" a voice asked. An older man looked up from where he was sorting rubble. He'd been bent down so far that Kit hadn't noticed him. She flicked her head around, her hand automatically going to her belt.

The dagger she always carried was there, as was the new one she had bought on her journey, to replace the one that had been left in Fraser's back. The handle was inlaid with silver Celtic knots.

"Aye, nasty sight it was." The man screwed up his face, making his nose stand out like a bulbous mushroom. "The flames were almost as tall as the sky."

"You saw it?" Kit asked, stepping over some of the stones toward him.

"Aye, I was called up from the village. Tried to help put it out, but we were too late." He shook his head and tossed one of the blackened stones to the side. It cracked as it landed in the rubble. "We saw the arsonist running away. They sent men after him, but he was too quick. He hid in the forest." The man nodded at the trees.

"I wonder…" Kit murmured. There was one man loyal to Lord Ruskin who had been hiding in Scotland all this time. Oswyn could have been the arsonist, though she had no proof.

The man paused in his task and looked up at her. "What do ye want, lass?"

"I am looking for the family." Kit nodded at the destroyed house. "Where will I find them?"

"They are building a new house beyond those trees." The man waved a thick hand toward the bank of trees. "Aye, slow progress. It may take a while. Good family, they are." He smiled broadly. "Offered us good pay for this task, even though it's tiresome." He picked up another rock and tossed it with the others. "Ye'll find the family at the inn in the village. The Queen's Head. Ye cannot miss it. It has a rather grim sign." The man chuckled deeply.

"Thank you." Kit smiled, despite the ominous words. When she had left London, news had spread that the trial of Mary Stuart had begun. No one doubted how the trial would end.

Kit left the house and rode her horse through the trees, heading to the nearest village. The sun was stronger now, and she unlaced the collar of her jerkin and rolled up her sleeves. The streets were busy and the people looked hot. Maids clutched damp cloths to their necks and farmers used their hats to fan their reddened cheeks.

Kit hesitated when she saw some people walking away from a church. The church was small, built of grey stone. It was so old that the walls were falling down in places, the windows warped at unnatural angles. The door was open, though, showing it welcomed all worshippers. Kit turned and continued down the street.

A sudden wind made the sign attached to an inn thud against the wall. Kit squinted up at it in the sunlight. The Queen's Head. Morbidly, there was an axe painted on the sign. She left the horse with a stable boy and approached the inn, stepping inside.

"We're full up, if ye're looking for somewhere to stay," the innkeeper said, poking his head through a hatch. "All our rooms taken, ye see? The Earl of Ross's family is here."

"That is who I have come to see." Kit approached the man hurriedly. "Are the family here?"

"Aye. They are in the back room, through that door. Just served them a mighty fine feast." The man smiled. "Are they expecting ye, lass?"

"No." Kit breathed deeply. She was suddenly nervous. Iomhar and his family were on the other side of that door.

"Well, go on in." The innkeeper waved at her. "Ye look most anxious to see them, lass."

Kit thanked him. Raising a hand, she knocked on the door.

"Come," the Earl of Ross's voice called.

Kit pushed open the door. Inside, the sun was bright, streaming through a vast lead-lined window. The table was full of food, with golden capons and steaming vegetables. Abigail sat at the table, poking the turnip on her plate with her knife and wrinkling her nose. She ignored both Rhona's and Moira's pleas for her to eat it. The Earl of Ross was at the head of the table, laughing about something, and at the far end was Niall. Elspeth walked into the room through another door, placing another trencher full of food on the table.

Iomhar was not there.

Niall was gulping from a tankard. When his eyes flicked over the rim in Kit's direction, he spluttered and spat his wine back out again.

"Cover your mouth, dear," Moira chastised him and tossed a napkin his way. He snatched it up and waved it in Kit's direction.

"Good day to ye, Kit," he managed through a cough.

The whole family snapped their heads around, looking in her direction. Abigail dropped the chunk of turnip off the knife she had been holding in the air, and Rhona smiled widely. Elspeth nearly knocked a pewter jug off the table.

"Kit!" Rhona leapt to her feet and rounded the table. Moira pushed her chair back so far that it toppled, but Kit managed to hold out a hand and stop it from falling. Rhona embraced her, just as she put the chair back. "Ye are here. Ye have come to Scotland?"

"Katherine." Moira reached for Kit too, taking her hand. "How are ye here? What has happened?"

"I left Walsingham's employment," Kit said slowly. There was a ripple of smiles and murmurs around the room.

"I wonder why," Niall said with a chuckle.

Moira tapped him on the arm. "Ye should learn to be quiet," she said, then turned to Kit. "Why are ye here, Kit?"

"I needed some time away." Kit was not sure what more she could say. London hadn't felt like home anymore. Walsingham had cast a shadow over her life. It was time to see what life would be like without that shadow. "Where is Iomhar?" She looked around, noting an empty chair at the table.

"He's outside," Rhona said in a rush. "Late for dinner, as usual."

"He's talking with a stonemason about the new house," Duncan explained. "Ye'll find him in the courtyard out back."

"At least have some food before ye see him. Ye have had a long journey." Moira gestured to the table. Elspeth set an empty trencher on the table for her.

"I'll see him first." Kit didn't hesitate. "Which way is the courtyard?"

"That way." They all pointed to a large oak door.

"Thank you." Kit smiled and stepped through.

She walked across the courtyard. It was a vast cobbled square, with carts off to one side that held large loose building stones. Kit hastened toward the carts, seeing a balding man talking to a figure she recognised.

"Aye, we'll be there to oversee things tomorrow," Iomhar said to the stonemason, folding his arms across his chest. "We can begin then."

"We'll be there, sir." The stonemason nodded and turned toward one of the carts. Kit stepped behind Iomhar, standing by his shoulder. He didn't notice she was there. "Ye have another brother I have not been introduced to?" The mason offered a nod of greeting, and Kit smiled.

"Ye have met my brothers." Iomhar turned toward her, then jumped back, so startled that he nearly collided with one of the stone carts.

"I'm Kit Scarlett," Kit said to the stonemason with a smile.

"Oh, I … I am sorry, I thought ye were…"

"It would not be the first time."

"Right, well, I should get these carts moving. Good day to ye, sir." The stonemason nodded to Iomhar and stepped into the cart, giving the order to his men to get the horses going. The carts pulled out of the courtyard as Kit faced Iomhar.

He stared at her, his green eyes unblinking. "Ye're here," he managed eventually.

"I am." She smiled. "I could not stay in London."

"Why not?" he asked, stepping toward her.

"Someone said something that turned out to be true. There was a shadow over my life," she murmured. "I want to see what life is like without it."

His smile matched her own. "Ye have left Walsingham?"

"I no longer work for him. At least, for now. I intend to try a different life." She looked at the window of the inn and saw Iomhar's sisters staring through it. The door opened, but it closed quickly again. "I have a feeling Niall is holding your mother back, so I will say this quickly."

"Say what?" Iomhar asked, his own eyes darting to the window.

"I saw a church in the village."

At her words, his eyes flicked toward her again, and he raised one eyebrow. "A church?"

"Aye." She mimicked his accent, making him smile. "I thought I might pay it a visit."

"And why would ye wish to do that?" he asked, folding his arms as he looked at her. "Ye've come all the way to Scotland, to do what, I do not know, and the first thing ye wish to do is go to church? Nay, that does not sound like ye."

"Well, maybe there is a particular reason I wish to go." Kit held out a hand to him. "From what I hear, you have to go to church if you wish to be married." She held her breath, waiting to see what he would say next.

Iomhar stared at her, then blinked, as if he could not believe her words. She lowered her hand, her gut tightening with disappointment, but he abruptly laughed and stepped forward. Raising his hands, he placed them on her cheeks and tilted her head up, kissing her swiftly.

"When do we go to the church?" he asked.

"Are you finished with work? Or perhaps you are wanted at dinner?" She smiled broadly. "I have nothing to do at present."

"Lead the way." He gave her his hand and they walked out of the courtyard, through the archway and out to the road.

Behind them, the door to the inn flung open and Moira ran out.

"Ye cannot hold me back anymore. If they are going to the church, I'm going too."

EPILOGUE

The priory building stood tall, its red-brick towers and slanted roof piercing the blue sky. Kit pulled the horse to a slow stop, with Iomhar on one side of her and Moira on the other. Moira had complained for some distance that her old and weary bones were struggling with the long ride, but now they had reached the building, she made no further protests.

"Aye, it has been many years since I last saw it," she murmured.

Iomhar was the first to jump down from his horse. He helped his mother down as Kit climbed off her own horse and left it behind her, approaching the building with wariness and curiosity, enough to make her hands tremble.

On one side of the priory building was a vast cemetery, with small stones poking up from the earth like hardened molehills. The building was falling into disrepair, with one wall of the tall structure falling down, yet it was plainly still in use. Servants wandered to and fro, carrying baskets of food or fresh linens. On the other side of the building, the fine gardens were being tended to by gardeners.

"It is not what I expected," Kit confessed as Iomhar and Moira approached her.

"What did ye expect?" Iomhar asked and took her hand. She felt the ring on her finger as she grasped his palm.

"Nothing so grand," she murmured.

When Moira had suggested seeing the old priory, the house where Kit had spent her first years on this earth, Kit had initially refused, but eventually her curiosity had beaten her. A few weeks after she had arrived in Scotland, she had agreed to see it, and Moira had insisted on coming too.

"It is so long since I have been here," Moira said, moving forward on the vast yellow-stone driveway. "I walked down this drive with your mother. She was so happy here."

"It's a priory," Kit muttered uneasily as she followed Moira.

"After the dissolution of the monasteries, it was passed into private hands and became a house," Moira explained, approaching the door. "Your father loved it here. He always said it felt as if he was tucked away, hidden from the world of the court."

"He had nay love for court, then," Iomhar observed quietly, as they followed his mother.

"He had a complicated relationship with court life," Moira said honestly, pausing by the front door that was double her height. "He was loyal to the court, devoted, yet he preferred his home life." She smiled softly. "I never saw him as happy as he was here with your mother, and then with you, Kit."

Kit didn't answer, uncertain what to think or feel. Moira turned and knocked on the door.

"Are ye well?" Iomhar asked, leaning down to whisper in Kit's ear.

"I do not remember it, not at all."

The door was answered and the current prior of Coldingham showed them inside. Moira had written to him the week before, asking if they could visit. She'd kept Kit's identity a secret and said that she simply had a curiosity to see the place, since she'd been such good friends with one of the former owners, John Stuart, Commendator of Coldingham. The current prior was such a jovial man that he welcomed them in gladly and showed them around the house himself.

Kit followed slowly, trailing at the back of the group. She felt very little association with the house, but the prior explained that much had changed over the years.

"Do ye remember any of it?" Iomhar asked as they passed through the great hall.

"Nothing." Kit shook her head, rather disappointed.

That morning she had received a letter from Walsingham. He had sent his congratulations to her and Iomhar, adding a section in Doris's words, who was delighted. He had much news to share. Phelippes had recovered from his head injury and had returned to work, surprisingly forlorn about Kit's departure. Joan had been returned to her father and had been shamed for her actions. Her father had put it down to the folly of being so young and having her head turned by the promise of money.

One line brought Kit surprising sadness. Queen Elizabeth had been dismayed at Kit's parting, leaving Walsingham's presence at once at the news, and choosing not to summon him again for a few days. It seemed she placed more trust in Kit's watchful eyes than Kit had ever truly understood. Sometimes she wondered if she'd ever see the queen again, or if they were on different paths from now on. It was understood that she was struggling with news of her cousin's trial, which was delivered to her every day. Kit feared what cries would erupt in Richmond Palace when the execution finally happened. As Walsingham assured her in his letter, there was no doubt about the trial's result, even if Elizabeth was reluctant to sign the death warrant.

Kit intended to reply to Walsingham soon, to tell him that she had come to see the place that had once been her home. She wondered if, in time, she'd hear from him less and less.

"And here we have the gardens." The prior opened a set of double oak doors and led them outside. They passed through a formal knot garden, with Moira leading the way and praising all that she saw.

"It is so like the garden I knew," she said with awe. "I remember these statues, vividly." She hovered by a circle of statues, surrounded by flowers. Amongst the blooms were thistle flowers, their purple petals like threads.

"I wish I knew who they are meant to represent," the prior said, stopping at Kit's side. "Alas, I do not. It was not recorded."

Kit stared at the statues of the three men. They were in various positions of prayer, their heads bowed. There was something familiar about them.

Iomhar moved to her side. "Is something wrong?"

"The first time you came to my attic room, I thought I saw something in your features. You reminded me of something," she whispered. "I did not know where I had seen it before." She nodded at the statue on the left of the group. There was the smallest of likenesses between the two of them.

"Ye remember something?"

Moira and the prior walked on, leaving them alone.

"Something..." Kit turned and walked the other way, her boots crunching on the stones. The garden banked down a hill and she took the main path, until she reached a stretch of grass. "Yes, I have been here before."

A certainty filled her mind as she looked across the garden. It had changed, but the landscape was just the same. She could not recall anything specific, just a feeling that she had been in this garden before. Iomhar followed her, his arm brushing hers as they came to a stop in the centre of the lawn.

His presence at her side stirred something. An image appeared in her mind. She was trailing behind someone across this grass, struggling to keep up and tripping on the hem of her gown. She was reaching out to someone, a tall man who walked in front of her.

"Katherine?" With Moira's call, the image left her. Moira returned to her side, having managed to part from the prior. "So often did I see ye and your father here together in this garden. Do ye remember it at all?"

"Perhaps something," Kit murmured.

"He wanted ye to be happy," Moira said softly, clasping her hands together as she turned to face the priory building. "I do not doubt that if he could see ye now, he would be happy ye had returned. He'd be glad to see ye smiling."

Kit looked out across the garden. She could almost sense the man that had once walked through these gardens, holding out his hand toward her as he hummed a tune.

"Solace shall sweetly sing for evermore."

Gradually, the feeling dissipated. The father she could picture was no longer there.

"I am happy," she said with a contented smile.

Iomhar took her hand, lacing their fingers together. She turned to look at him, finding he returned her smile.

"We can come again, if ye like," he whispered.

"We do not have to. There is something familiar about this place, but it is not home." She looked between the trees and saw that a river glistened in the distance. She knew what had taken place in that river, over two decades ago, but she did not revisit the memory. She pushed it down into the recesses of her mind, finding she did not have to open it again. "I am happy to go home now."

Iomhar smiled and drew her back up the garden. Moira walked ahead, calling to the prior. As they disappeared inside, Kit hesitated. She glanced back at the statues and the lawn.

"Kit?" Iomhar murmured, trying to get her attention.

"I am glad we came," Kit said, before turning back to the house. "I am glad to have seen it."

She was eager to write to Walsingham, to tell him she had been to the house and seen the river. When she wrote, there were two things in particular she wished to say. First, she would thank him again for pulling her from the water. She would also thank him for the life he had given her thus far. Now it was time for her life to be of her own making.

A NOTE TO THE READER

Dear Reader,

Thank you to all those readers out there who have been following Kit's tales. Since the publication of *The Gentlewoman Spy*, the support from readers has been wonderful, and I'm thrilled so many of you are enjoying reading Kit's adventures, as much as I've enjoyed writing them.

This is very much a tale of fiction, written to weave into the facts of the time, but created purely for what I hope is your entertainment. The Babington Plot was the real planned coup through which Walsingham and his men, including a double agent called Gifford, were able to catch Mary Stuart signing off on her cousin's death. The characters around this tale are invented for the story, and I'm sorry to say that Mary did not spring herself from Chartley and dash across the country to escape in such dramatic fashion, but was speedily taken between castles, before landing at Fotheringhay. Yet this story like others in the series was for enjoying, so facts have been changed with a little creative licence.

I wish to thank the whole team at Sapere Books for publishing, including Amy, Caoimhe, and Matilda. If it had not been for their diligent work and their devotion to the written word, I would not have had the opportunity to finally write some stories in my own name.

Thank you to all readers who have enjoyed Kit Scarlett's series or have even joined just for the last step in the journey. Reviews by readers these days are integral to a book's success, so if you enjoyed Kit's tale I would be very grateful if you could spare a minute to post a review on **Amazon** and

Goodreads. I love hearing from readers, and you can talk with me through **my website** or **on Twitter** and follow my author page **on Facebook**.

Adele Jordan

Sapere Books is an exciting new publisher of brilliant fiction and popular history.

To find out more about our latest releases and our monthly bargain books visit our website:
saperebooks.com

Printed in Great Britain
by Amazon